Twinge

Jay Sauls

Acknowledgments:

This book couldn't have been created without the love and support of my wife Sherry. You were patient through all the edits, rewrites, and chapter copies I asked you to read over and over and over.

I also want to thank the members of the Chapin Chapter of the South Carolina Writers Association. You guys ROCK!! And you put up with a ton of bad grammar from yours truly.

And last but definitely not least, to my mom for giving me this wonderful gift of imagination. Also to my brother David for setting the writing bar in the stratosphere. Don't think I'll ever match your wordsmithing ability, but if I can get close, I'll be extremely happy with the results.

Chapter One

Summer, 2001

Andrew Alewine, aka "Copper Top" to his friends because of his bright red hair, lay curled up in bed whimpering. He pulled the bedspread tight over his head. His Star Wars nightlight projected a soft amber glow on the wall but provided no real protection. Once again, he dreamed of the long-abandoned rail line, the tracks wavering and vanishing into the distance after it swept past the depot. The decrepit building sagged, kudzu vines climbing up the sides and over the top and twisting hypnotically in the breeze. And on the abandoned track-side loading dock stood the boy who tortured animals. The shadowy adolescent kicked the puppies and hit them with a stick. One pup lay motionless, its sides no longer rising or falling. The boy laughed and wiped clean a stick covered with blood. Andy never saw the shadowy face, just the silhouette—and the hands. Hands caked with mud, the fingers and nails black.

A knock on his door woke Andy.

"Sweetie, are you okay? Did you have another nightmare?" Soft light spread around the edge of his door as it opened slowly. His mother, eyes tired and graying hair disheveled, peeked into the room.

Barely able to control his fear, Andy pulled the covers off his head and hugged his pillow tightly. He nodded and shivered.

"Is it the same one?" his mother asked, now sitting beside him on the bed and stroking his hair.

Andy nodded again. Tears streamed down his face.

"Sweetheart, they're just dreams." His mother wiped away his tears with a gentle brush of her hand.

Andy burst into new sobs and fell against her.

She cradled his head and rubbed his back. "I know you want a dog, but we just can't have one. Not with your father's health."

Andy tried to sniff back his tears.

His mother pulled loose, kissed him on the forehead, and gently leaned him back on his pillow. "We'll take your bike to the park tomorrow. Maybe your friends will be there, and you guys can go riding." She pulled the covers up to his chin. "Now, let's go back to sleep. Sweet dreams, Andy-man."

Andy managed a weak smile and allowed his mom to kiss him on the cheek. She pulled the door shut and the light from the hallway winked out, taking with it the weak illumination. Sleep had been lurking close by, waiting for him to relax. He felt it pull his eyelids down and slow his breathing. As he surrendered, the other boy approached, dragging another lifeless dog with him. Andy balled his fist and covered his eyes as the dream boy closed on him.

He stood over Andy, glaring down, the sour odor of his skin filling the air. A lifeless dog swung slowly back and forth on its death-leash.

Look at me!

"No!" Andy whispered.

Do it!

"No!" Andy screamed into his pillow.

Hands suddenly grabbed his face and a pair of icy thumbs pulled at his eyes, trying to force his lids apart. His eyes snapped wide and he found himself staring at his bedroom ceiling. The sun now pushed through his blinds, rendering the Star Wars nightlight dormant. Night had passed, taking the shadows with it.

The city park was in full bloom when his mom drove through the entrance. Minivans circled the drop-off zone, stopping quickly and disgorging kids with armloads of sporting equipment. Small sedans parked in the limited shade as young mothers unloaded strollers and toddlers. Andy leaned as far forward as his seatbelt would allow and scanned the acres of baseball and football fields, playgrounds, and walking trails for his friends.

Caleb Saunders rolled past on his bike, weaving through the parking spots, spokes and reflectors glittering in the sun. Caleb waved, swerved suddenly to avoid taking out a handicap parking sign, and circled back, laughing. His white teeth showed easily against his dark skin.

"Mom, stop here," Andy said excitedly and released his seatbelt. "There's Caleb. We're gonna ride the trails." He threw his door open and bolted out of the van the moment it rolled to a stop. He raised the lift-gate to retrieve his mountain bike. After muscling it out, he spun the pedals back once, mounted, and sprinted after his friend.

"You boys be careful!" His mother shouted to him.

Andy weaved between cars and pedestrians.

"Don't leave the park and stay away from the old depot!"

The boys waved as they disappeared around the colonnade of water oaks lining the entrance.

Andy stepped hard on the pedals, his long legs allowing him to out-distance the shorter boy. Within minutes, they had ridden far beyond the ballfields and playgrounds, and now coasted along the winding, lonely bike paths that led further into the park and toward the old-growth forest.

"So whatcha wanna do?" Caleb asked as he tried to bunny-hop his BMX bike over a large root pushing up the cracked asphalt path. He barely caught any air, slipped off the pedals, and almost crashed into a tree.

"Don't know," Andy said, laughing. His friend was always trying to impress him with stunts and generally failed miserably. "I was thinking about riding down the rail lines until they leave the park. Mom says to not go beyond the fence."

"Have you even been to the depot?" Caleb asked as he sprinted ahead of Andy, then circled back. His eyes twinkled. "I've heard it's haunted."

"It's not haunted." Andy said and rolled his eyes. "It's just an old building. Mom says to stay out of it, that it's dangerous."

"Bet you won't go inside." Caleb pulled up beside his friend.

Andy stared ahead, pedaling slowly and not saying anything. The walking path turned to the right, leaving the old rail line and circling back toward the entrance. The park's fence crossed over the tracks, the rails disappearing through a thicket of briars and brush. A break in the fence allowed more adventurous riders to leave the well-maintained trails inside the park and work their way through the dense woods. A rutted trail angled through the gap in the old chain-link barrier. Andy glanced back over his shoulder and slowed. They were a good half-mile from the main parking lot and throngs of people.

Caleb matched his pace, then shot the gap in the fence, splashing through a shallow puddle and spraying the briars with mud. "C'mon, Andy! What's the matter, you scared?" He climbed on the pedals and vanished into the thick summer foliage.

Andy stopped, licked his lips, and glanced over his shoulder once more. Bright late-morning sunshine cast a million shimmers off the windshields in the far distance. He turned back toward the abandoned rails. The woods felt darker, the air uncomfortable.

"Hey, Andy, are you coming or not?" Caleb's voice echoed from deep in the woods.

Screw it, he thought and pushed through the fence gap. The path dropped down beside the old rails, then ran parallel, eventually traveling deeper into the forest. The brush pushed closer to the tracks—briars pulled at his right arm and leg. The hairs on his arms tingled. He glanced over his shoulders. *Who was watching him?* Standing on the pedals, he pushed the cranks harder. Andy broke out into a hard sweat as the wind streamed through his hair. He raced into a clearing, and there sat Caleb astride his bike.

He was smiling, his teeth once again illuminating his face. "Dang, son, thought you chickened out or something!" Caleb climbed from his bike and pushed it around the mounds of debris lining the abandoned depot. "Is this cool, or what?"

Andy coasted up to him, using the toe of his shoe to stop. His heart raced. A cold sweat that had nothing to do with the ride trickled down his back. He slid from the seat and stared at the century-old building. The windows were empty, and the front doors hung from rusted hinges. The loading dock cantered precariously away from the building. A breeze shuffled past, rattling the tin roof. "It's creepy, is what it is," Andy said, not taking his eyes off the dying building.

"C'mon, let's check out the inside." Caleb dropped his bike on the ground and scrambled onto the loading dock.

"I don't know. Mom says we shouldn't be here."

Caleb stood with his hands on his hips. He scowled and made crying motions with his hands over his eyes. "Don't be such a baby! Plus, your mom's not here."

Andy bit his bottom lip. It was just an old building, nothing more, nothing less. And Caleb was right, Mom wasn't here, so a quick look around wouldn't hurt anything. "All right, hang on, I'm coming." He laid his bike beside Caleb's and followed his friend's trail through the scattered debris. Old wooden crates were stacked against the depot. He climbed them, angling toward the deck, the wood cracking and splitting as he ascended. The stack toppled over the moment he jumped onto the platform.

"Caleb, where are you?" Andy called as he carefully walked across the old deck, testing the floor with each step. "Caleb! This isn't funny!" A movement sounded to his right. Andy swung around.

Caleb leapt out a glassless window waving a long, pointed stick. "*En garde!*"

Andy screamed, turned to run, and tripped. He landed hard on the platform, the boards cracking and collapsing under him. He fell through the dock and landed in a tangle of broken, rotting wood, the wind knocked out of him. With no air in his lungs, he couldn't cry or call for help. His panic slowly dissipated when his breath returned and he realized he wasn't seriously hurt, just stunned. He climbed to his knees and staggered across the dirty ground, stirring small gray clouds of power-dry dust. As he neared the edge of the platform, a short rope with a metal tag hung between the planks. He reached up and grabbed the red cord. But it wasn't a rope. It was a collar. A dog collar with tags. When his hands closed around the tags, the light flashed painfully, then the air around him became a vacuum and the illumination under the building turned black.

<h1 style="text-align:center">Chapter Two</h1>

"Andy!" Caleb's voice was sharp, bordering on panic. "Andy, I'm going to get your mom!"

Tall grass and debris broke through his tangled vision. Andy glanced to his right, and the stone pillars under the depot came into view, followed by streaks of yellow sunlight slicing through the wood planks above. He blinked several times, waiting for his head to clear. "Oh, crap, what happened?" he managed to slur.

Caleb laughed and clapped several times. "Man, that was cool!" He knelt beside his friend. "I scared the crap out of you; you hauled ass, tripped, and fell through the floor!" His smile disappeared. "I called to see if you were okay, but you didn't answer. I got kinda worried and jumped down here. You were flat on your back holding that dog collar." He took it from Andy and studied it. "Where did you get it?"

Andy staggered to his feet, brushing dust off his pants. "It was hanging between the boards. How long have I been down here?"

"I dunno, maybe five minutes?" Caleb shrugged.

Andy took the collar from his friend. It held two tags: one was for rabies, and the other one said "Howie."

"That's weird. Think someone's dog got loose and his collar fell off?" Caleb asked.

Andy led Caleb out from under the loading dock and stared at the building, slowly shaking his head. "I think he was chained up under here by someone who likes killing dogs."

"What?" Caleb's eyes went wide as he barked a quick laugh. "That's crazy! Why would you think that?"

Instead of answering, Andy walked around the abandoned depot, kicking at the debris and leaves. "That stick you had—it was used to beat the dogs. The tip is covered with dry blood."

"Ha-ha, not very funny, Andy."

Andy shrugged and continued to circle the building. "I'm serious."

"You ain't got no proof! You're just trying to get back at me for scaring you." Caleb stuffed his hands in his pockets.

Andy stopped and turned to face him. "You don't think so?
"Heck, no, you're just making this crap up."

"Really? What about this—" Andy picked up the corner of a mud-stained canvas tarp and threw it back. Beneath it was the carcasses of several dogs.

The boys gasped and bolted through the brush to their bikes. Caleb mounted his and pedaled hard, not waiting for Andy, and disappeared down the trail toward the park. Andy started to ride his bike, then dropped it. Despite the hair standing up on the nape of his neck, he fought through his fear and walked around the front of the abandoned building, giving it a wide berth. As he moved parallel to the tracks and deeper into the woods, the brush became increasingly dense.

"Howie! Here, boy!" he called in a hushed tone. "C'mon, boy. Let's go home!" Andy paused to listen. The only answer was the sound of the wind through the leaves. "Howie!" He shouted, this time cupping his hands. "You're safe, buddy! That boy's not going to hurt you!"

Andy forced his way through the briars until he reached the tracks. The walking became easier, but rogue thorns tore at his clothing. The rails crossed a small creek. The foliage encroached closer to the rails and the trees grew taller, heavier. The sun struggled to pierce the canopy; shadows filled the space between shafts of light.

"Howie!" Andy shouted again, this time hard enough to hurt. He wanted to turn, run back to his bike, and ride as fast as he could toward the safety of the park. Trickles of fear brought goosebumps to his arms.

"Howie! C'mon boy! I'm starting to freak out and really don't want to walk any farther!"

Caleb would surely be back now, waiting for him at the park—or worse, waiting for him with his mom.

"Oh, crap, I'm going to be grounded forever." Andy reversed his path and jogged back along the tracks, the feeling of being watched intensifying. He ran harder. The sun seemed to be setting faster; the light was dimming. Sensing movement to his left, Andy picked up the pace. He'd walked farther into the woods than he'd thought. The old depot was at least a quarter-mile away and the sun dropped faster.

The brush ahead of him wavered.

Andy's breath came in ragged gulps as the movement in the tall grass became heavier. An undercurrent in the weeds pushed the bramble toward the railbed.

"Mom!" Andy screamed as his pursuer broke free of the undergrowth and knocked him flat on his back. He rolled off the slight rail line incline and into a tangle of briars. Something pounced on his back. Andy rolled into a ball to protect his face.

The pursuer whined and barked, then nuzzled his hair.

"Howie?"

The whine turned to a whimper, then silence. Andy uncovered his eyes and stared into the softest brown eyes he'd ever seen. An expression of pain and gratefulness gleamed from the animal.

Carefully pulling himself from the sticker bushes, Andy climbed to his feet. "Howie?"

The dog—the biggest he'd ever seen—glanced up at him.

"This yours?" Andy took the collar from his pocket and slid it over the head of the big mutt. The dog climbed to its feet, whimpering. His right rear leg was cocked at an unnatural angle, his back and hindquarters were lacerated with welts and cuts, and his fur was matted with blood. One of his ears was split up the middle as if it had been cut with scissors.

Andy crouched down, careful to avoid pressing against any of the dog's wounds, and gently stroked Howie's jawline and head. "Who did this to you?"

Howie stared straight at him as if to say *you know who did this*.

"C'mon, buddy, let's go home." Andy gave the collar a light touch and the big mongrel gingerly followed him along the tracks to his bike.

They traveled slowly, the dog having to stop several times to rest. Each time Andy massaged the beaten dog's neck and shoulders, the only places not injured. When they reached the depot, the sun appeared to be in a full-fledged retreat. Long shadows pushed past the trees and darkened the structure. Tendrils of shadows snaked toward his bike. He kept a soothing hand on Howie's head as they approached.

Andy retrieved his bike and pushed it along the trail as he coaxed the dog to follow with gentle words. The light brightened as they exited the woods, once more becoming noon-time brilliant.

Ahead, Andy's mother frantically paced back and forth, her phone pressed hard to her ear. When she saw him, her face flexed between a mixture of intense relief and hard anger. She stormed over to him. Her sandals slapped hard on the walk-path. Sweat dribbled down her face. "Do you have any idea what you have put me through?"

Andy stopped walking and backed up a few steps.

His mother's eyes were wide, hands clenched to fists. The sleeves of her were shirt pushed up, and her mascara smeared from crying. "There's a dozen people stomping through the woods looking for you! Where have you . . . ." She stopped, her eyes turning towards the beaten animal standing with him. "Where did that dog come from?" Andy let go of Howie and ran to his mom, wrapping his arms around her tightly. He burst into sobs. "I found the dogs, Mom. I found them," he blurted through gasps and tears.

His mother pulled back and dropped down to a knee. She brushed tear-smudged dirt from his face. "What dogs, Andy?"

"The dogs from my dreams. I found them." He wiped his eyes with his arm, reestablishing a touch of composure. "I found their bodies, Mom. They're behind the depot under a tarp. I think Howie was there, too, but escaped."

"Who's Howie?" She brushed the hair out of his eyes.

At the mention of his name, the dog crawled forward, his elbows and belly dragging the ground. He dropped his head at Andy's feet and whimpered.

"He's hurt bad, Mom. We need to take him to a vet."

His mother glanced down at the mixed breed. Welts and scars crisscrossed his body. His fur was matted with blood. One eye struggled to open. The other stared up hopefully. The dog managed to lift his head high enough to lick the back of her hand.

"I think he was tied up under the platform. There's a stick with dried blood all over it. That's what the boy used to beat him with."

"What boy, Andy? Who are you talking about?"

"*The boy*," he said in a whisper. "The one killing the dogs. I think he does other bad things."

"Andy, I don't know if that's blood," Caleb said, walking up. "It's just a dirty old stick."

Andrew flashed his eyes toward his friend, the expression bitter enough to make Caleb stop and withdraw.

His mother pulled him tight against her. "It's just a dream, sweetie. Just a coincidence. The dog probably got hit by a car and ran off into the woods where you found him."

"Yeah, that's what happened," Caleb said quickly. "What your mom said." The boy tried to laugh but quit when he caught Andy glaring at him.

"Mom, we need to get him back to his owner. She's . . . ." Andy's words trailed off.

"Honey, what are you talking about? You couldn't possibly know who the dog's owner is."

But he did—sort of. He visualized a winding trail of flickering smoke coasting through the park and into town. He could sense its travels past the city to a small trailer. A young girl lived there. A very sick girl. A girl who was . . . dying. He tried to follow the contrail-like mist. It vanished when he focused on it. But if he let his mind pinwheel, the iridescent path revealed itself.

"Mom, there's a vet on the way home. Let's take him there. Then we need to let the girl know we found him."

His mom stared down at the dog now lying on its side, eyes closed, barely breathing. "Son, it's just an old stray no one wants— probably doesn't even have a home. I'll call the park office, and they'll take care of him."

"No!" Andy shook his coppery hair. "He's dying, and so is his owner!" He sat beside the dog and lifted its head. "Don't worry, Howie, I'm getting you home," he whispered, then started crying. "Caleb, help me carry him to the van."

"Uh, Andy, I don't think that's such a good idea," Caleb said, dropping to a knee and petting the dog. "I think your mom's right. He's just an old dog. Bet he got hit by a car. Let's just go home."

"Fine, I'll do it myself." Andy grabbed the dog in a bear-hug and tried to lift it. Howie cried in pain but managed to get to his feet. "C'mon, boy." With a finger looped inside the dog's collar, Andy led him down the sidewalk toward their van.

"Sweetheart, wait," his mom said, getting to her feet and following. "I'll pull the van into the park and we'll take him to the vet. But don't be too upset if they put him to sleep."

Andy nodded, settled to his knees, and gently hugged Howie. The dog sagged against him as they waited for Andy's mom to return.

"What did you tell my mom?" Andrew asked Caleb without making eye contact.

"Man, I was scared. I didn't know what happened to you. I waited for you, even rode back down the trail, but you were gone." Caleb turned and watched Andy's mom hurry through the park. "I called and yelled for you, but you never answered. That's when I rode as fast as I could to find your mom. I told her you were missing."

"I guess she was pretty mad?" Andy placed his head against Howie's.

"Oh, yeah, really pissed. When we couldn't find you, she got real scared, started screaming for help. We must've had a dozen people looking for you. Didn't you hear us calling your name?"

Andy shook his head.

"That place is really creepy," Caleb said quietly. "I'm never going back there again."

"Me, neither."

Mary Beth Alewine returned with the van and together they placed Howie on an old blanket they kept for impromptu trips to the park or lake. Despite the law requiring seatbelts, Andy lay on the floor, curled up with Howie, eyes to eyes, nose to nose. When they arrived at the animal hospital, a tech helped carry the dog inside. Caleb, Andy, and his mom waited in the lobby for the doctor's report.

Mary Beth was already considering how many credit cards she was going to have to max out to pay for this fool's errand. Forty minutes after they arrived, the vet stepped through a side door and approached.

"Ms. Alewine?"

Mary Beth stood and met him halfway across the room. "How is he?"

The doctor smiled. "He's going to be fine. Lucky your son found him. He's not out of the woods yet, but should make a full recovery."

"Was he hit by a car?"

The doctor shook his head, took off his glasses, clenched his jaws, and his eyes hardened. "No. I would have to say he was tortured. My guess is someone purposely beat him almost to death. Poor guy has cracked ribs, numerous lacerations, and a broken leg." The doctor pinched the bridge of his nose and wiped his eyes. "The pain would have been excruciating."

"How long does he need to be here?" Mary Beth asked, figuring that besides her credit cards, she would be taking out a small loan on her house.

"We set the leg and stitched up the lacerations, but there's nothing we can do for the ribs. He'll just have to heal on his own. I figure he'll be with us a few days—just depends on how well he does."

Mary Beth put her face in her hands, then glanced up. "I don't mean to sound callous, but how much is this going to cost?"

The doctor shook his head and laughed lightly, more from the tension release than humor. He put an arm on her shoulder. "Nothing. Howie was chipped. We've already talked to the owner. They are on their way over now."

"Oh, thank God!" Mary Beth let out the long, heavy breath she'd been holding. "Money is tight, and I didn't know how in the world we were going to pay." She turned to the boys. "Okay, kiddos, Mr. Howie's going to be fine, and his owners are on their way over to see him. Grab your stuff, and let's go home."

"Ms. Alewine, if you'll wait just a few minutes more, the owners want to thank you. Howie is more than a pet—he's a service animal, a seizure dog for their daughter. Since he's been missing, her condition has worsened. Her parents were worried they were going to lose her. Just word of Howie being found has lifted her spirits."

"I told you, Mom. Didn't I tell you so?"

"Andy, how did you know?"

The boy shrugged. "Don't know, Mom. When I touched his collar, I *just knew*. I felt something deep inside, knew he was nearby, and that I had to find and help him. It was like when you're watching a movie and you know something bad's going to happen and you get all knotted up and tense inside."

"You mean like a twinge of fear?"

"A twinge! Exactly!"

Chapter Three

Spring, 2021

Andrew was typing like mad, the words flowing off his fingers. *Portraits of Pain* was nearly complete—another book in his *Forest Shadows* thriller collection, and this one was good. His other novels, though well written, didn't hold a candle to POP. Another dozen pages, and he could email his agent the rough draft. Then a much-needed break. Later, he'd start the madcap editing. He jumped when long, slender fingers caressed his shoulders and drifted down the collar of his shirt.

"Sorry," his fiancé Vanessa said through muffled giggles. "I thought you heard me come in. Are you at a stopping point?"

Andrew pushed the keyboard back, stood, and cracked his back. He leaned forward and lightly kissed the raven-haired woman, then looked down at the chair.

He'd been writing from that chair for nearly twenty years, starting when he was twelve. Caleb's grandfather had been a semi-successful author, and when he passed, he left it to Andrew—Andy at the time—as an inspiration to continue his own wordsmithing. At first, he found the old high-backed chair creepy. The thought of sitting on a piece of furniture that another writer had died on was unsettling. When he finally settled down and put pen to paper, or thoughts to keyboard, the results were extraordinary. His short story "Light Between the Shadows" got him an A in English. He later polished it and sold it to *Anthology of Horror*. His first check, albeit only twenty-five dollars, made him a pro.

Now the old chair was patched, glued, stapled, and cobbled together. It no longer swiveled, rolled, or reclined. It was just a patchwork chair in its final death throes. But the magic remained.

"This is as good a spot as any. Just wrapping up the last loose ends of *Portraits*. Michelle will be happy to have the rough draft before the deadline."

"And shocked! Try not to kill your agent; they're tough to replace." Vanessa smiled and nodded toward the door. "Most of our friends are here. I've put your books by the table, and Caleb has the grill ready."

"Thanks." Andrew rubbed his eyes and ran a hand through his hair. He was self-conscious of the thin, almost bald spot on the back of his head. His mom always said it was a birth defect, a skin problem when he was born, and hair had never grown there. But many times he wondered about it. He picked up the glass of wine beside his desk and took a deep drink. Wine really wasn't his thing, but it did seem to perk him up after writing. "Okay, let's go entertain the masses." Andrew winked, and his fiancé slipped her arm inside his.

Andrew's house was a rough-hewn log cabin sitting high on a bluff over the Socastee River basin. Centuries-old cypress trees grew along the edge of the river, their limbs heavily laden with Spanish moss that waved in the breeze. A wide deck wrapped the house, providing unopposed views of the forest and river below. His best writing had occurred during the years he'd lived on the bluff.

Andrew inhaled deeply, savoring the scent of steaks on the grill.

The back door swung open, and Caleb marched in with a tray of sizzling meat. "Sorry, man, gotta get." He fist-bumped Andrew as he passed. "Got some shenanigans going on in town, and I'm on-call."

"C'mon back when you're done. I think we're going to be up late tonight. I'll save you some celebratory cake."

"You do that, man."

Vanessa took the platter from Caleb and set it on the kitchen's center island.

"Hey, you going to do any readings?" Caleb asked.

Andrew tensed and shrugged slightly. "I don't know, probably. It just seems to drain me of late. But if I have a beer—"

"Or twelve!" Caleb added with a laugh, his white teeth flashing against his lean face. The fleshy cheeks of his youth were now long gone. His face and five-foot, nine-inch body were chiseled from hours in the gym. He clipped his badge to the edge of his belt and grabbed the service weapon he placed on a shelf above the stove.

"Or twelve," Andrew agreed with a sheepish smile. He took a deep breath. "The twinges have gotten intense lately. Sometimes a twelve-pack is what I need to calm them down."

"I hear ya. Take care, Andy-Man, and I'll try to catch back up with you guys."

"You, too. And, Caleb—" Andrew paused as his childhood friend turned. "Remember to duck."

Caleb flashed a quick thumbs-up and hurried out the door.

"So," Vanessa said as she watched Caleb slide behind the wheel of his county-issued vehicle. "Now that our chef has left the building, who's going to manage the grill?"

"Yours truly! You know my B and B specialty—bloody or burnt. Nothing in between."

"You are a simple man." Vanessa smiled.

"You know it." Andrew exchanged the platter of meat for a clean plate and headed out the door to the deck where hungry friends waited to eat. Despite his professing to have the talent of a poor fast-food cook, the remaining steaks and foil-wrapped ears of corn came off the grill nicely.

Once the beer had started to flow and the steaks were consumed, Andrew stood and tapped the side of his plastic cup with a plastic knife to get everyone's attention. It took a few moments for the conversations to cease, and when it did, he delivered the news he'd been holding.

"I know you guys are all wondering why I've called you here tonight. It's because I'd like to talk to you about a new business venture I'm trying to promote—AMWAY!"

The deck broke into laughter.

Andrew waited for the titters to die down before continuing. "Some of you might be aware that *Nights Pursuit* cracked the *New York Times* top ten list last year. Well, earlier today we agreed in principle to a developmental deal to bring the book to the silver screen."

This time, wild applause erupted.

"Don't know when or how soon or what Hollywood A-lister is going to play me." Andrew struck his favorite pose—Superman— and the deck burst out laughing again.

"This is just the preliminary conversations, might go nowhere. It's just exciting to think about." Andrew raised his cup, once filled with beer and now closing on empty. "And I couldn't have done it without the love and support you guys have given me over the years. Cheers!"

Red and blue Solo cups tapped together around the table as Andrew dropped down, then stood and put a box on the table. "Okay, folks, the *main* reason you are here." He ripped the box open. "These were delivered today!" Andrew held up a fresh, hardback copy of his most recently published novel, *Images between the Shadows*. He was met with a series of *oohs* and *aahs* as he imitated a game-show host. "Twenty advanced copies, all personally autographed to you guys. Once again, thanks for your support."

The signed books were handed out, each with a personal thank you note. And more alcohol was consumed. Music from the high-end shelf system continued to pump pop and dance tunes onto the deck. The floor erupted into a disjointed dance party when "Brick House" by the Commodores jumped from the speakers. The music competed with the crickets and bullfrogs, who were having their own personal jam session. Janson Morris, Andrew's close friend, dropped down on the outdoor couch beside him. "Okay, since everyone is too polite to ask, I thought I would."

Andrew leaned his way, grinning. "What did you do? Wait until I'm all liquored up so I couldn't say no?"

Janson laughed. "Aw, man, it's not that way."

"Bullshit," Andrew said with more than a hint of a slur.

"Okay, it's that way!" Janson leaned back and crossed his leg over his knee. He took his John Deere ballcap off, brushed back his collar-length blond hair, and pulled at his Hawaiian print shirt. Janson had never spent a day of his life on the ocean, but he seemed to be a misplaced surfer everywhere he went. "It's just that, you know, my girl has been *pestering* me for an hour; she's heard about you and your psychic thing. She doesn't believe you."

"And you want me to prove her wrong, so you can get in her pants?"

"Is that so bad? C'mon, man, help a brother out!" Janson turned toward Andrew, ballcap now clutched over his heart, eyes pleading.

Andrew laughed, shook his head, and ran his hands over his face. He sat up quickly. "All right, you know the drill. Organize the troops."

While Andrew stepped inside to get prepared, Janson had several people lay personal objects—items that couldn't be readily identifiable—on the picnic table. Then the owners stepped off into the shadows to wait. When all was finally arranged, Janson shouted, "Showtime! Will the Amazing Andrew please appear!"

Andrew leapt through the French doors that opened onto the deck, pushing them aside with a flourish. He tossed his make-shift cape—a checkered tablecloth—on the ground and walked over to the table. There were four items: an autographed Atlanta Braves hat, a silver barrette, a set of car keys with a Corvette tag, and a sealed envelope that was postmarked in 2004.

"Ah, *magnifico!*" he said with a bad Italian accent as he circled the table. "With my hand-held, million-candle power spotlight, I will illuminate the owner of each object!" He powered the light, pointed it up, and the beam streaked skyward. "See how powerful it is; I have illuminated the moon!" His guests groaned and motioned for him to continue, while some tossed empty beer cans at him.

Andrew grabbed a greasy meat fork off the grill and waved it around like a musical conductor. He pointed the fork at the car keys, then picked them up. "Ah, this is quite easy. Ben Senior," he shouted, "you always wanted . . . ." Andrew paused, whirled around, and ignited his spotlight. He aimed it at a small patch of woods two hundred feet away. "This car, it belonged to your dad, didn't it?"

Ben stepped from behind the trees, his body practically glowing under the power of the light. He covered his eyes and walked back to the deck. "Damn, that's wild, man. I never told you my dad had a sixty-nine 'Vette. We were restoring it when he passed. How'd you know?"

Andrew tossed the keys to his friend. "Not quite sure. I twinged hard, saw two trails. One vanished, and one led right to you. Figured it was your father or grandfather. Your dad must have loved the car."

"You have no idea. It was his baby before he had babies, as he used to say." Ben held the keys in both hands. "Did you see anything—anyone else?"

Smiling, Andrew shook his head. "Sorry, I only see the owner's trail."

The hat and barrette were simple. Touch the item, see the trail, hand the item to the owner. But the envelope was different. It seemed to push him away, hold his hand at bay. *Shit, I'm hammered.* Andrew slammed his hand down on the envelope and dropped to the ground as if he'd been kneed in the groin. The twinge exploded out of him and accelerated away in a vertigo-inducing grayish-black streak. Through woods and over farmland he sensed the twinge's course. It swerved through town and over rooftops before plunging into an abandoned millpond. There the trail evaporated as if sucked into a vacuum.

Andrew started to rise, then vomited on the ground. His face paled to skeletal white. He dropped to all fours and dry-heaved.

"Andrew!" Vanessa screamed and rushed to him. "What happened?"

He shook his head and used the picnic table for balance. "Who– who brought this? And what in the hell is it?" Andrew groaned.

Janson stepped forward, his date trailing behind. She hid her face behind her hands as she stared at the ground. Her flip-flops made soft shuffling noises as she reluctantly followed.

"Andrew," Janson said, looking stricken. "I'm sorry, man, we didn't think anything like this would happen. I feel like shit."

"You feel like shit?" Andrew rasped. "At least you're not kneeling in your puke. *This* feels like shit." Vanessa took him by the arm and steadied him as he sat on the tabletop. He pulled his feet onto the long bench and rubbed his face.

"What in the hell did you do to him?" Vanessa snapped at Janson's crying girlfriend. She tried to step between the pair when Andrew pulled her back by her shirt.

"Vanessa, it's okay, they didn't know, couldn't have known. Not their fault." He grabbed a beer out of the cooler on the table, ran the cold can over his face, popped the cap, and drained most of it without stopping. He grimaced, then burped. His face regained some of its color from earlier. "Sorry, had to settle the nerves." He managed a weak grin.

Janson sat on the table beside Andrew, his date sitting below him, still refusing to make eye contact. "Andrew, what happened?"

Rolling his head on his shoulders, Andrew took a deep breath and let it out slowly. "I don't know. The last few years, my twinges have been coming on stronger, super intense. Sometimes they make me sick. I don't know if this is a symptom or a coincidence, but my writing has also gotten darker." He picked up the beer, leaned back, and finished it off. "The beer helps settle me down."

"So, what happens—or in this case—happened?" Janson asked, helping himself to a beer.

"I've explained my twinges to you, right?"

"Yeah, you said it's like a painful déjà vu. Like if you step on a nail, then almost do it again, you get a phantom pain that runs through you at the *anticipation* of stepping on the nail."

"That's it exactly. After I get the twinge, I see an invisible—" Andrew held his hands up. "I know that's an oxymoron; you can't see something invisible! But I see, sense, *feel* a trail rushing from the object. If I focus on it, it vanishes. But if I let it tease me just a bit, I can follow it, just like those old 3-D posters. Stare at it just right and an image appears. But move just a bit and there's nothing.

"And that's how these started originally. Kinda cool, just love giving someone back a lost earring, wallet, etcetera. Most of the deep feelings I get from an object are warm, almost nostalgic.

"But in the last year, year and a half, it's gotten really strong, from a twinge to a recoil." Andrew grabbed another beer, ignoring the reproachful expression of Vanessa. "I've started wearing gloves, and never, by God, go into an antique store."

"So, I guess you didn't get the warm-and-fuzzies?" Janson asked.

Andrew took a moment to answer as he stared across the tops of the trees that lined the river basin. Bats were diving through the air, turning incredible acrobatic maneuvers as they devoured the night insects that trespassed on their territory. "No. This one was so fucking cold I thought I was going to stroke."

"I'm so sorry, I really am," Kaylie Cantor, Janson's date said in a whispery voice. "I thought what you did was a put-on, a gag." She glanced up and pushed hair out of her eyes. "But you were my last hope." The woman pulled her dirty-blond hair back behind her ears, regained some composure, and continued, "The envelope has a picture of me and my brother when we were little, and a letter from my mom telling us how she couldn't wait to see us. Dad had visitation that summer. We're the only thing mom said she ever cherished. She always had the picture with her." Kaylie bit her lip as her emotions choked off her words. She swallowed several times. "Mom vanished almost fifteen years ago; we haven't seen her since."

"Andrew, man, I don't know what to say. I told Kaylie your twinge thingy only worked for people that were alive. If I had known it'd cause you to toss your cookies, I never would've put you through this." Janson ran a hand through his shaggy blond hair and stared straight ahead. "But Kaylie and her brother have been searching for their mom for years, and all they have are stacks of private eye bills and no luck."

"You're good." Andrew patted his friend's knee. "I've never had anything this intense happen before." He rocked forward, wobbled to his feet, and stood on the bench. "Okay, folks, that concludes tonight's festivities!" He tried to bow and almost took a header onto the deck.

Vanessa helped him down as his friends laughed and picked up the empty beer cans. Eventually, his guests exited through the house, all thanking him for the invitation. When Janson patted him on the shoulder and indicated he was leaving, Andrew pulled him back.

"Hang on a few minutes. We need to talk."

Twenty minutes later, the last of his guests' taillights turned onto the dark highway a quarter-mile down his long driveway. Kaylie and Janson waited in the cozy living room, the wide-screen TV on, but turned to the DirectTV programming channel. Vanessa closed the French doors to the deck and locked them. Andrew pulled up a chair to the edge of the couch and took Kaylie's hand in his.

"I'm not one-hundred percent certain, but I think I can help you find your mom."

Chapter Four

Less than a week after the party, Caleb and Andrew stood on an old rock fence running alongside the remains of a 150-year-old farmhouse. Janson and Kaylie stood on the other side of the structure, Janson's arm around Kaylie's waist, her head on his shoulder. The twenty-acre pond that once watered hundreds of heads of cattle was cordoned off. Warrenton County deputies manned a wide-bottom Jon-boat as divers repeatedly sank beneath the water. A county coroner van waited beside the pond.

"Correct me if I'm wrong," Caleb said as he kept his eyes on the bobbing divers, "Janson's girl gave you an envelope and you twinged on it. And that led you here?"

"In a nutshell, that's it," Andrew said. "The second I touched the envelope, the trail nearly took me off my feet. I've never, ever had one move like that, like a freaking cruise missile. From my porch to here." He made an arc over the land with his hand. "I've had them travel over water, but not *into* it." Taking his eyes off the divers, Andrew turned to Caleb, "For a moment, I couldn't breathe—like I was drowning. Scared the living shit out of me."

"I imagine. As bad as the depot?"

Andrew shook his head, the two-decade-old memory still entrenched in his mind. "Close, maybe. The first time I thought I was dreaming and having a nightmare. This time I thought I was dying."

Wispy clouds parted to let bright sunlight wash over the farm. Caleb cupped his eyes to block the glare off the water. "Do you think they'll find someone?"

Andrew was quiet for a moment, then took a deep breath. "I think they'll find *something*. I've never been wrong before. But what, I don't know. And, by the way, nice job getting the sheriff out here. I figured he'd rebuff you unless you had something solid."

Caleb took his county-issued ballcap off and scratched his close-cropped curly black hair. He laughed. "I'm not going to lie, at first I didn't think it was going to happen. Kaylie's mom isn't even listed as a missing person—not around here, that is. Her last known address was up in Fortner County. And, by all accounts, she was a bit flighty."

"And no records of her going missing in the past?"

"Nope, not a one," Caleb said, shaking his head. "A report might have been filed with another municipality, but not with the boys up there or around here."

"So, all you had to go on was a vision from your best friend?" Andrew asked, smiling.

"That's about it," Caleb replied. "Not a whole lot to go on. It was a hard sell."

"I'm surprised you were able to convince him."

"As they say, timing is everything, brother. Divers needed to have their certifications updated, and the county wanted to make sure their equipment wasn't gathering dust. Even though Sheriff Barnes thought I was nutty as a fruitcake for asking, he'd heard whispers about you."

"So, what you're saying is, I'm famous?" Andrew struck his Superman pose.

Caleb laughed hard. "Yeah, right. Maybe one day, if one of your little books becomes a movie." He curled the bill to his hat, then put it back on. "Think this piqued the good man's interest—kill two birds with one stone. Prove you're working some kinda hoodoo-voodoo on your friends and get the divers their necessary—" Caleb jumped from the wall. He pointed to a diver waving a red flag. "Yo, man, something's up. Could be your twinge paying off—or it could be bones from a dead horse. But the divers are excited about something." He jogged toward the shore

Andrew followed suit, sprinting after Caleb. Kaylie and Janson noticed the action, and reversed their path, though their progress was slow and apprehensive.

A sheriff's deputy was setting his tank on the shore when Andrew and Caleb reached him.

"Melvin," Caleb called out. "What'd y'all find?"

"Don't know yet," the deputy answered after unbuckling the last of his equipment. "But about thirty feet offshore there's a mess of chains wrapped around what looks like a roll of carpet. And it's all anchored to a chunk of concrete." Melvin rolled his wetsuit off his solid trunk, the material stretched to the edge of its limits. "Sheriff is calling in a backhoe to get it off the bottom."

"What's the ETA?"

"Should be here soon. We had it on standby."

Andrew pointed toward a red flag bobbing on the water. "That's a long way to throw a rolled-up piece of carpet. I wonder how it got out there?"

"There used to be a dock. It was rickety as hell, probably built in the forties," Deputy Melvin explained. "We used to fish from it as kids."

"What's your gut tell you?" Caleb asked.

Melvin snorted. "What does my gut tell me? Why in the hell would you chain up a roll of carpet and sink it to the bottom with concrete? I'd say the odds of a body being found in it are probably pretty good." The deputy pulled a tee-shirt from a duffle bag on the shore and pulled it over his head. He nodded toward Kaylie. "Whether it's your friend's mom, don't know. But your buddy was spot on, there's something here that someone didn't want to be found." His phone rang. "Sorry, guys, big-man's calling," Melvin answered the phone and walked forward along the pond's bank.

Caleb and Andrew followed at a respectful distance. Once they passed the old farmhouse, the whine of a diesel engine indicated the tractor had arrived.

Janson and Kaylie caught up with them by the shore. They watched the county-embossed construction equipment approach. "What's going on?" Janson asked quietly.

Caleb turned slightly and motioned for him to follow. When they stepped out of earshot, he filled Janson in.

"What do you think?"

"I think we're going to find remains."

Janson walked back to Kaylie, wrapped his arms around her shoulders, and spoke quietly. Tears began to slide from the woman's eyes. Andrew and Caleb watched as the tractor approached the water's edge, then spun around and backed in. The metal bucket, resembling a huge metal claw, was raised and extended over the pond A chain draped from the machine, disappearing into the dark water. A fresh set of divers disappeared beneath the windswept surface.

Every few moments, a wave of bubbles circled the chain before being swept away.

One of the divers reappeared and pointed up. The tractor's engine revved as the hydraulics lifted the bucket from the water. The man descended a second time and the machine paused. He returned moments later, pointed up and back toward the shore. The diesel revved even higher as the bucket's height increased and the loader began to drive out of the pond.

Andrew cut his eyes to Kaylie. She wasn't watching; she was now facing Janson, her face buried in his shoulder.

The wind calmed as the carpet—which resembled a drooping log—broke the surface. The equipment operator gently drove the tractor away from the shoreline, the chain barely swinging. Additional deputies staked down a large tarp by the shore. The coroner's van joined a cruiser by the tarp; the medical examiner parked, exited, and leaned against the front, a hand over his eyes to shield them from the sun's glare.

The sheriff directed the machine forward as if guiding an airliner to a gate, the carpet log swaying, the chain links rattling. Just as the backhoe reached the tarp, the roll split in half, water pouring from the center. One end dropped from the chain, while the other turned upright, and a tangle of gray sticks fell from the center.

Except they weren't sticks, Andrew quickly realized. He turned away in time to see Kaylie sink to her knees.

Caleb took Andrew by the shoulder and turned him his way. "Get them out of here," he said quietly. "Might be her mom, might not be. Either way, she's not in a good place mentally. And if a skull bounces out and rolls across the ground, she's going to have to be medicated."

Andrew nodded and tapped Caleb's shoulder with his fist. "No problem. I don't even want to be here."

"I hear ya." Caleb took a deep breath. "The medical examiner is going to set up shop here for a while—make sure we have all the, uh, parts—and then we'll categorize and catalog everything. I'll stay as long as I can and fill you in later."

"Thanks, man." Andrew put his sunglasses on and walked over to Janson. Before he was halfway, his friend was already guiding Kaylie away from the pond and toward their car. Andrew's phone chimed with a text from Janson: *Taking Kaylie home. Going to stay with her tonight. I'll call you later.*

Andrew's surfer-friend glanced over at him.

He gave Janson a quick thumbs-up and veered off for his car.

Chapter Five

Four days after finding the body in the pond, Caleb knocked on the door to the sheriff's office, was waved in, and motioned to sit. The sheriff was on the phone and scribbling notes. Taking a seat in front of his boss, Caleb checked his phone messages while the man across from him continued to write on a large legal pad. The man glanced at Caleb, rolled his eyes, and pointed toward the phone.

Barnes finally dropped the receiver heavily on the cradle and slumped back in the chair.

"Busy day, sir?"

"Son, you have no idea. We have an ID on that body we pulled out of the pond." He glanced down at the yellow pad. "M. E. says it's Kimberly Jones, like you suspected. Had to use dental records, since there was nothing else left of the victim."

"Have they been able to determine a cause?"

Sheriff Tim Barnes of the Warrenton County Sheriff's department and former Army Special Forces soldier leaned forward and put his elbows on the desk. His dark brown skin seeming to melt into the polished desktop, his skin resembling hardened mahogany. Though retired for a dozen years, the intensity projected by his body language and eyes constantly reminded Caleb that he never ever wanted to tangle with the man.

"Most likely we'll never know the exact cause, but coroner's office said the skull was cracked, possibly by a pipe or other heavy, narrow object." Barnes stared at the ceiling. "Unless we get a confession, we'll never know."

Caleb nodded, not knowing how they could get a confession when they didn't have a witness or any leads. "So, what did you need to see me for?"

Barnes clasped his fingers and stared over his combined fists. "How well do you know your friend?"

Caleb blinked. Not the question he was expecting. "Andrew?"

The sheriff nodded.

"Excellent, if not better. I've known him all my life. Can't remember a time I didn't know him."

"Has he ever shown any indication of violence?"

"Andy?" Caleb blurted. "He's about as calm, quiet, and timid as the proverbial church mouse, for the most part."

"And the part that's not timid? Has that part ever hurt anyone, shown any signs of violence?"

"No, of course not!" Caleb felt his blood heat; he gripped the arms of the chair tightly.

Barnes smiled and patted the air over his desk. "Relax, son. Just wanted to get a sense of your loyalty to your friend."

Caleb's blood perked up a degree or two as his jaw tightened. "Sir, you think I wouldn't turn in a friend who was a murderer? Best friend or not, murder is murder. Would I like it? Hell, no."

Barnes picked up the tablet he'd been writing on. "Tell me about his writings."

Caleb was stunned by the question. He shrugged a bit and sank deeper into the high-backed chair. Scrunching up his face and staring at the ceiling, Caleb was slow to answer. "I don't know, they're all right, I guess. He's landed an agent and is making a few bucks writing. I'm not much of a reader, and his material's definitely not my cup of tea. Most of it's dark, based around murder mysteries . . . ." Caleb stopped and laughed sardonically. "But you knew that already." Dropping his hands in his lap, he faced his boss. "You know Stephen King never set a rabid dog off on anyone or killed anyone in a hotel, don't you? It's his alter ego. He likes writing mysteries—has since he was a kid."

"You help him with the plots?"

"Me?" Caleb asked. "No, sir, absolutely not; we don't talk shop."

"So, where do you think he gets his ideas?"

"Sir, I really don't know." His eyes narrowed, not thrilled with the direction of the questions. "Local media? Television?"

The sheriff sat back in his chair and steepled his fingers. He favored his deputy with a lopsided smile. "Just making conversation, Deputy."

Yeah, just conversation. Right. "But this conversation *is* leading somewhere, yes? Sir, not to be disrespectful, but I've got a dozen reports to follow up on from our little flash-mob dust-up this past weekend."

Sheriff Barnes nodded slowly as he picked up his notepad. "In Jocelyn, Oregon, sixteen years ago, there were a series of murders, all unsolved. All involved young people—male and female— that were bludgeoned to death and dumped along the Greenbriar River."

"And you think those murders are related to the death of Kimberly Jones?"

"I do, in a roundabout way," the sheriff answered, rocking slightly in his chair.

"They were able to tie in a murder weapon?" Caleb asked, astonished.

"No." Barnes shook his head. "Don't think even the best forensics team could this quickly. But there is a loose connection, one I wasn't aware of." He paused and drew large ovals on his legal pad. "You ever read your buddy's stories?"

Caleb blinked. "Like I said, not my style. Why?"

"In an online magazine called *Tremors in the Dark,* a younger Andrew—Andy back then—Alewine posted a story—did quite well in a contest they were having—about a series of murders along the— " He paused to read his notes. "Greenbriar River in Jocelyn, Oregon." Dropping the notepad, he once again set his elbows on the table. "The story recounted how three women, two men—same as the actual murders—were killed with a 'hammer blow to the head' and buried in shallow graves along the river. In his story, as in actuality, the killer was never caught."

Caleb turned away and stared out the window. A shift change was in progress. Patrol cars were entering and exiting, fresh cops getting out of their personal cars, worn-down cops getting out of patrol cars. "Gotta be a crazy coincidence. Andrew would've been fifteen. No way in hell he could've traveled across the country to kill five people."

"It's here that we are in total accordance. But you have to admit, the coincidence is damn striking." The sheriff leaned further across the desk. "Any chance he had insight into the murders?"

"Andrew was afraid of his shadow back then," Caleb stated as he matched the sheriff's posture. "Maybe he read something, who knows."

"I'd like to know, that's for damn sure. I can tell you this—" Barnes casually pointed a finger at Caleb. "Your pal, while not a person of interest, is a *person of interest.*" He leaned back and put his hands on the arms of his chair. "That's all, Deputy. Thanks for your time." With that, Barnes picked up his phone and started dialing.

"Yes, sir," Caleb said flatly. "I'll let myself out."

Barnes flashed a large smile and gave him a thumbs-up, then started talking into the handset.

Caleb walked heavily through the building and glanced at his watch. Normally, he took lunch around one, but today he was going early. He needed to blow off some steam.

His phone rang the moment he stepped from the building. "Deputy Saunders," he said brusquely into the phone.

"Caleb, what's up? You sound tense."

"Double-A Copper Top, your ears must be burning." Caleb slid his silver shades on and marched toward his patrol car.

"Uh, sure don't like the sound of that," Andrew replied.

"Just office talk, my friend," he said, climbing into his car. "Got time for lunch?"

"Yeah, sure. Kind of early for you, isn't it?"

Caleb glanced at the clock in the car. It read 11:15. "Just a bit. You interested in Geddy's Deli?" He backed out of his parking spot as Andrew agreed. "Cool, see you in about ten minutes."

Traffic was light as Caleb drove through town. He thought about how he was going to broach the subject of his friend's writing and the murder in Oregon. He also wasn't sure how his friend was going to take being told he was a quasi-person of interest in the Kimberly Jones murder.

Caleb parked the squad car beside his friend's plain-jane vanilla Ford Taurus. *Nothing flashy about this boy.*

Andrew was waiting outside the deli when he approached. "So, what's going on? Sheriff thinks I have something to do with Kaylie's mom?"

Caleb laughed softly and shook his head, then nodded. "What he said is that 'you are not a person of interest but are *a person of interest.*'"

"How do they differ?"

"Hell if I know, man. In Barnes' eyes, there probably ain't no difference." Caleb held the door open and pointed to a booth in the rear. "Let's sit where we can talk without a thousand ears listening."

"Ooh, all cloaky and daggery!" Andrew stepped through the door quickly, turning fast left, then right, as if trying to spot an assassin. He slid behind a display cooler, peeked out, then pretended to scan the room intently. He jumped from behind the cooler to a small hallway that led to the bathrooms.

"Knock it off, fool. I was hoping to not attract any attention. You're doing the complete opposite."

Andrew stopped, stood ramrod straight, laced his fingers behind his back, and casually strolled to the rear of the building while whistling under his breath.

Caleb shoved him in the back. "Still drawing attention to yourself!" he hissed. "Go back to being an idiot. At least it was entertaining."

"Wow, this is serious. Should have said something sooner."

"What part of 'person of interest' didn't make you think this was serious?"

"I just thought you meant he was interested in me as a curiosity. Not like you meant it." Andrew dropped into the old faux-leather booth, grabbed a menu, and perused it.

Caleb dropped down opposite Andrew, facing the front of the restaurant.

Andrew put the menu down. "But why is he interested in me?"

Caleb stared out the front glass windows, the late-morning haze turning the glass cloudy. For the most part, they were alone in the half-century-old diner renowned for its chicken salad sandwiches and homemade fries. He cupped his chin and rubbed the stubble of a beard that was always trying to form. Turning toward Andrew, he kept a wary eye on the door. "It's those damn stories you write, that's why."

Andrew placed his palms on the table and leaned forward. "My books? Are you serious? They're just *stories*, no truth in any of them. Just random weird-ass thoughts. I blame them on that old chair you gave me. Creeped me out as a kid."

"I know they are. But that first short story you wrote—did you know it paralleled an actual murder? And that the coincidences are downright freaky?"

"What? No way! Just dreams I had." Andrew sat back and took a deep breath. "What are the similarities?"

Caleb told him.

"Well . . . shit," Andrew said.

Chapter Six

The lunch crowd and noise level increased while Caleb and Andrew ate in silence. After finishing his sandwich, Caleb leaned back and slid his glass around on the table, spreading the moisture ring in ever-widening circles. "Your other books and stories. Any chance they mirror any other killings?"

Andrew used his last fry to stir the ketchup on his plate. "How should I know? I see these images, write the stories, and get paid for them. Or, at least, try to get paid." He glanced up at Caleb. "Any chance your grandfather was an ax murderer? Maybe I'm channeling him."

"Oh, yeah, funny. You remember my grandfather was a preacher, don't you?" Caleb's eyes narrowed. "Not only was he not a murderer, but he was a borderline vegetarian. The man liked the sight of blood less than you."

Andrew continued to fidget with his food. "All I know is that the chair creeped me out when I first got it." He sighed and ate the ketchup-covered French fry. "But my writing got better, so there's that."

The waitress came by, dropped off the check, and collected the plates. Caleb waited until she was out of earshot before speaking. "What was the second book about and where was it set?"

"That would be *Highland at Dusk*. It was set in Utah. It's where the mysterious Dark Mule character shows up." Andrew sat up in his seat to explain the story.

Caleb waved him off. "Boil it down, tell me the main points."

Andrew slumped slightly as he thought about the plot. "Essentially, a really brutal killer is following hikers through the high mountains of Utah. He kills them one by one with a machete, picking them off as they try to hike out of the woods. He removes their skin, then hangs their bodies for bears and other scavengers to eat. A seven-year-old boy sees his parents murdered, escapes him, and runs for days trying to get help. That's when he discovers a man dressed in animal skins leading a mule. The man—called Dark Mule—saves the kid while fighting off the trail killer. A park ranger—who just happens to be in the vicinity checking trail cameras—hears a commotion, comes to investigate, and finds the kid. When they search for the other men, all they find are boot prints and the remains of the skins the man wore. They never find the trail killer or Dark Mule."

"How the hell do you sleep at night?" Caleb caught the waitress's attention and pantomimed asking for a refill on his tea.

"I sleep pretty good. Writing helps get these ideas and dreams out. Otherwise, I'm trapped with them."

Caleb started to ask about Andrew's next book when a familiar patrol car rolled through the parking lot. "Okay, we gotta get. Barnes is coming in. Don't know how much he wanted me sharing with you."

"Do you think he's going to call me in for a formal meet-and-greet?"

"I'd say it's a distinct possibility. Especially if any of your other stories mirror any other murders." The deputy reached for the bill.

"I've got it," Andrew said, sliding it his way. He started to walk off, then turned. "You do know I had nothing to do with anyone getting killed?"

Caleb laughed, flashing his wide smile again. "Of course I do. You struggle with killing spiders."

Andrew shrugged. "They, uh, wig me out. I'll call you later tonight."

"Sounds good. Take care, man."

Andrew nodded and headed to the front to pay. Caleb watched him go, then exited out a side door. He climbed into his patrol car and slowly pulled away. He wished he'd had a little more time to talk with his friend. For now, his officer duties called. But, later in the day, when his shift ended, he planned on checking with the authorities in Utah regarding a mountain trail killer.

It was after four p.m. when Caleb pulled into the Warrenton County Sherriff's Department. A quick scan of the parking lot confirmed that Barnes was gone, probably to one of his many association meetings. *How he gets anything done is beyond me.* He parked at the rear of the property beside a centuries-old water oak that had somehow survived the construction of the building. Every other tree for hundreds of yards had long ago been reduced to firewood or sawdust. The tree provided shade and partially obscured his cruiser. Caleb stepped out and entered the station through a rear door just in case the sheriff wasn't off-site. He wanted to do his research quietly without the thousand questions Barnes was sure to ask.

Once at his desk, he began searching law enforcement archives in the state of Utah, starting a dozen years ago. His search came up blank, as did the searches occurring over the last ten years. Three hours and one pot of black coffee later, he pushed back from his desk, rubbed his eyes, and leaned back in his chair. His search algorithm encompassed everything from mountain killings to hiking abductions to assaults on hiking trails. There were incidents with basic similarities, but nothing he could single out that would match the story Andrew recounted to him.

Between the hours of staring at the computer screen and the flickering fluorescent tube across the building, his eyes were shot. The clock on the corner of his monitor informed him it was almost eight o'clock. His little research project had taken over four hours and produced squat. He closed his eyes tight and sighed. "Ah, fuck it," he muttered, locking his terminal. Caleb pushed from his desk, letting the chair roll backward until it suddenly stopped. He glanced over his shoulder.

Sheriff Barnes stood behind him. "I sure like to see my deputies working late," he said with a wry grin. "This have anything to do with the Econo Inn robbery?"

Caleb shook his head, knowing full well Barnes knew exactly what he was working on. "No, sir." He stood and pushed his chair back under his desk. "I met with them earlier today and went over their statement. I reviewed the security footage from inside the lobby and outside cameras. Boys in forensics have it now." He pulled his badge and service weapon from his desk drawer and clipped them to his belt. "I was looking into Andrew Alewine's later writings to see if there were any coincidences with his next book and actual events."

"Find any?"

Caleb rocked his head back and forth and held his palms up. "There were events similar, but none that could be considered a DNA match," he answered.

"Give me the skinny on the story." Barnes took a seat on the edge of a desk behind Caleb's and crossed his arms over his chest.

After giving Barnes a quick synopsis of the book, Caleb sat on his desk and glanced at the clock on his computer. It was eight-thirty. If he left soon, he'd be able to get home and catch most of the Atlanta Braves baseball game. But Barnes was staring at him.

"Sheriff?"

Barnes didn't respond; his eyes were unfocused. They cleared and narrowed. "Did Mr. Alewine actually use the term 'Dark Mule'?"

"Yes, sir. Thought the name was pretty cool. Reminded me of an old Western character. Why? Does that mean something to you?"

Barnes stared over Caleb's head and toward the dark, empty parking lot. He nodded slowly, gently rocking as he did. "When I was in special ops, we did a good bit of high-altitude training. One winter, we spent a month in Kings Peak, Utah. Mountains get way the hell up there, well over ten thousand feet. We had a staff sergeant named DeMarcus White." Barnes's eyes lost focus again, and he allowed a thin smile. "You think I'm big? Sergeant White was huge. Everything had to be custom ordered for him. He was almost too big for the unit. Hard for a man that large to hunker down. The only thing going for him was that he could walk like a ghost, didn't make a sound. He was also damn-near jet-black. Make you look Caucasian!" Barnes chuckled, then took a deep breath. "When the sun set and until it rose again, he vanished, just melted into the shadows.

"And because he could carry a two-hundred-pound pack up a mountain without breaking stride, we called him our 'dark mule'."

Caleb stared back, unbelieving. "You're shitting me."

Barnes shook his head.

"What happened?"

"We were on a night reconnaissance maneuver, playing with some new night-vision goggles, some real slick equipment. Our CO was also a cousin of the local police chief. The chief reached out to our CO—how, I never found out, supposed to be a real hush-hush training op—to let him know that some hikers had gone missing over the last week or so and wanted us to keep an eye out for them. Not necessarily go looking, but if we spotted anything out of the norm to let him know.

"We were two days into the op, hiking along a ridge about six-thousand feet up, way above the tree line. There was nothing, and I mean *nothing* up there. Suddenly, DeMarcus advises we have movement about a hundred yards ahead and on our two o'clock. We figured it was the second squad trying to flank us. DeMarcus, in his ultra-quiet way, heads off to the right. Myself and another soldier continue straight. We're radio silent, so no communication between us. After about fifteen minutes we turn uphill, planning on catching up with Sergeant White." Barnes stops talking and clenches his hands into fists. His jaw muscles tense.

"I took point and flipped down my goggles. The second I do, I see two forms moving quickly across the ridgeline, one massive—DeMarcus—one slight. Thinking the hunt is on, we pick up the pace and close in on DeMarcus's six. We crest the ridge and see no one. Period. We search for another ninety minutes and never find anyone. Not DeMarcus, not the other person. We break radio silence and comm our CO. The rest of the squad reconvened on our location. We searched until dawn, then brought in 'copters and fixed-wing planes. We never found any trace of anyone."

"Damn, that's strange as hell. Did he have kids?"

Barnes nodded. "First one on the way."

"When did all this happen?"

Staring at the ceiling and closing an eye to concentrate on the date, Barnes said, "Bush had just been elected, so around 2000, maybe early 2001. When did Alewine write the story?"

"This has just got to be the biggest cosmic coincidence, but I think he penned it around ten years ago," Caleb answered. "About the time your friend's son would have been seven."

"Deputy Saunders, I want to have a conversation with your buddy—like tomorrow, at the latest."

"Yes, sir. I'll catch up with him tonight, see if he can swing by here sometime tomorrow." Caleb stood and pulled his keys from his pocket.

"Not here. That would make it too formal. I don't want your friend to think that he's a central focus of this investigation."

"Well, isn't he?" Caleb asked.

Barnes laughed. "He is, and he *isn't*. Like I previously stated; he's not a person of interest but *is* a person of *personal* interest. I mean, how do you explain him knowing of a body *no one* knew was missing? And then to use a name he couldn't know as a character in a book in the very same mountains he disappeared! I'm hearing the Twilight theme in my head as we talk." Barnes shifted off the desk. "Let's meet for lunch at the Culver Soccer Complex around noon. I'll spring for the pizza, ya'll bring the drinks. Let's talk this out."

Caleb nodded. "Sounds like a plan. If for any reason Andrew can't make it, I'll let you know."

"Very good. I'll see you guys then." Barnes slipped on his Ray Ban glasses despite the fact night had long ago fallen. "And Deputy Saunders," he said, leaning against an exit door. "If he can't make it, he needs a really good reason why." The sheriff pushed through the glass door into the waiting darkness.

Chapter Seven

It was twenty minutes before noon when Andrew met Caleb at the Culver Soccer Complex. They walked the bike trail paralleling the old railroad tracks. All that remained of the steel rails were the sections inside the park. The old tracks had been removed over a decade ago to make way for a new subdivision going in beside the park. The woods and depot were now bulldozed to facilitate the building of several hundred houses. The only tribute to the old depot and rail line rested in the names of streets and courts that made up the Central Station neighborhood. The park had been reconfigured to accommodate the influx of new families. Now soccer fields outnumbered baseball fields, and the football section was down to one far corner of the park. Caleb glanced up as a county-marked SUV drove around the Authorized Admittance Only sign and angled toward a pavilion covering a half dozen picnic tables.

Toting a small cooler full of drinks, Caleb pointed across the park. "Bossman's here," he said, indicating the red and white Tahoe. "Just relax, all he wants to do is pick your brain."

"So, no arrest warrant or funny reverse-strap white coat for me?"

Caleb snorted, then laughed. "Man, you watch too many cartoons. It's been weeks since we locked anyone up in a straight-jacket." He knocked Andrew's shoulder with his fist. "Chillax, dude, Barnes just wants to understand you a bit."

Andrew stared at the SUV as the sheriff climbed out, waved, then reached back in. "Dude's big. Wouldn't smart talk him ever."

"You got that right. He's ex-special forces and who knows what else." They angled off the path and toward the shelter. "He's a straight shooter—mostly. Doesn't like shit he can't understand."

"That's where I come in, correct?"

"I'm afraid so, Kemosabe." Caleb smiled.

Andrew pulled up his shirt collar, tightened the belt on his beige shorts, slid his glasses off his face, and rested his thumbs inside his belt loops. "Let's do this thang," he said with exaggerated gruffness and strutted up the sidewalk.

"As an officer of the law, I order you to stop whatever the hell you think you're doing before Barnes tases your ass out of the park," Caleb barked and made a mock attempt to grab his non-existent taser.

By the time they reached the shelter, Caleb had convinced Andrew to put his collar back down and quit walking as if he were a cowboy getting ready to draw at the O.K. Corral.

Tim Barnes was perched atop a table, his feet on the seat, a cold drink in his hand. Two large pizza boxes sat to his right. He smiled broadly and held out his massive claymation-sized hand to Andrew. "Nice to meet you, Mr. Alewine. I'm Sheriff Barnes."

Andrew shook the offered hand, his own completely dwarfed. "You too, Sheriff. But call me Andrew."

Barnes nodded and released the writer's hand. "I can do that only if you call me Sheriff Barnes."

Andrew froze and shot a glance at Caleb, who shrugged.

"Just kidding, son!" Barnes laughed and patted Andrew on the back, almost knocking him over. "Call me 'Sheriff'" He pointed to the white, flat boxes with Milo's Pizzeria on them. "Hope you guys are hungry. I have one pepperoni and one specialty. I figured we can chat and chow down at the same time."

Caleb set the cooler on the table and glanced over at Andrew. "Knock yourself out, Double-A Copper Top. Have you had a pie from Milo's? It is—" He kissed his fingertips, flicked them toward their air, and closed his eyes. "Divine!"

Barnes turned to Caleb. "What the hell did you call him?"

Caleb chuckled. "It's a nickname I've called him since we were kids. He used to be super skinny and always wore a black Star Wars shirt with lightning bolts on it. And with his red hair, he reminded me of a Duracell battery. Hence, the name 'Double-A Copper Top.'"

With a pizza in his hand and a resigned look on his face, Andrew said, "Thankfully, the name was too big to fit on my soccer jersey."

"Interesting," Barnes said, picking up a slice of pizza. He curled it up and polished it off in just a few bites. "Caleb tells me you have this sixth sense or something that helps you find people. Which I'm going to tell you upfront I think is horse shit. No offense."

Andrew smiled, turned toward Caleb, and rolled his eyes. "No offense taken. I think it's horse shit, as well."

Barnes was about to take a drink and stopped. "No need to be a smart ass, son. I just don't believe in any kind of psychic crap. If I can't see it, touch it, feel it, hear it, taste it, kill it, I don't believe in it."

"Man, I bet Santa brought you nothing!" Andrew winked at Caleb. His friend grimaced and tried to hide behind a table, doing a poor job of it.

A vein in the sheriff's neck pulsed. Barnes's hand crumpled the soda can he was holding.

"But to be honest, I feel the same way."

"How so?" the sheriff asked evenly.

Andrew sighed. "Because stuff like this isn't supposed to happen. There's no rational reason for it." He reached over and touched the table. "I get nothing from the picnic table." Moving toward the sheriff, he grabbed a can of soda. "Same for the drink." Andrew circled the table and found a chewed-up pen on the ground. He picked it up for the other man to see. "All I have here is a broken ink pen. Nothing more, nothing less. But if this pen had been used by a guy to ask out the woman of his dreams, and she said 'yes,' then the pen might become emotionally linked to him. If he lost it, the moment I touched it, my brain would start to sizzle."

Barnes stared at him hard, his eyes down to slits.

"Sheriff, I can't explain it. Random items light up my skull like strings of Christmas tree lights plugged into two-twenty volts."

"And that's how you knew about Kimberly Jones? Had one of your visions or something?"

Andrew nodded.

"What triggered it?"

"Her daughter handed me an envelope with a picture of her and her brother, said she found it in a box of her mom's most cherished possessions. It was all her mom had of the pair. She protected it like the Hope diamond. It was an extremely hard emotional connection, almost made me pass out. Did make me puke on my shoes."

Barnes stared at Andrew, his eyes now intense. He rocked slightly forward. "Okay, I believe you believe yourself. I still don't believe in this crap. But I don't think you're lying." The sheriff put both palms down on the table and stood. "Caleb, you haven't said anything. What's your take on this?"

"Sir, I've known this dude since we were kids." Caleb walked over and put a lean, dark-skinned arm around Andrew's shoulder. "I can still remember the first time it happened. Freaked me out then, freaks me out now."

Barnes picked up another slice of pizza, stood at the edge of the shelter, and stared across the park toward the far corner where the tracks used to be. He rolled up the slice and consumed it in seconds. He pointed with his drink toward the neighborhood. "And back there's where this all started?"

"Yes, sir. Right about the intersection of Reading Street and Canadian Pacific Lane. That's where the depot used to be and where I found the collar."

"Huh." Barnes sipped his drink.

"Something about that spot I should know?" Andrew asked.

"Not especially. When the surveyors worked the land, they found a fifty-gallon drum full of mostly animal bones."

"Mostly?" Caleb and Andrew said simultaneously.

"Yeah, they also recovered several human femurs, collar bones, a couple of jawbones, and lots of little piggies. But no skulls, which was a relief to everyone."

"Toes?" Caleb asked. "What kind of sick bastard collects toes?"

"Same kind of psychopath that stores bones in a drum," Barns answered.

"Any clue where they came from?" Andrew stepped to the edge of the concrete floor and turning toward the housing development.

Barnes shook his head. "No idea. But they'd been there a long time. The drum was almost rusted out. Could have been there forty, fifty years." He turned and walked back to the picnic table, rolled up another slice of pizza, and inhaled it as fast as the previous ones. He used a fresh soda to point back to the neighborhood. "I just find it ironic that you discovered the dead dogs where we discovered a drum of bones."

"Funny as in odd, I hope, and not humorous," Andrew said as he tried but failed to squash a shudder coursing up his spine. "I wonder if the folks around there ever hear screams in the middle of the night."

Barnes raised an eyebrow but didn't say anything. He waved at a quartet of young mothers that power-walked past the pavilion pushing toddlers in running strollers. Each one had a collar-length ponytail and expensive running shoes. The women smiled and waved back.

"Y'know, when I was first married, I don't think any of my wife's friends looked that good pushing a stroller," the sheriff said.

"I hated seeing the trees bulldozed, but the scenery around the park has definitely improved!" Caleb commented with a wide grin.

"Yes, it has." Barnes turned to Andrew. "Deputy Saunders told me about your book, *Highlands at Dusk*."

"Really? Why?"

"Well, son, since you've written another book that matches a series of murders, I thought we should get better acquainted."

Caleb stepped forward. "Sir, you were able to connect Andrew's stories to another murder?"

Barnes nodded. "And I still have two books to go through. Who knows what I'll find there."

Andrew dropped his face into his hands, then said hotly, "They're just stories I made up! They have nothing to do with any actual murders!"

The sheriff shrugged. "Maybe not. But, son, you've nailed, and I mean *nailed,* facts in your stories that weren't released to the press."

"It's just a coincidence. I think of a topic and who would do what, then I write about it."

"Is that so?" Barnes pressed. "In your book, *Highland at Dusk,* you called one of your characters Dark Mule. Why?"

"Why?" Andrew echoed, stammering a bit. "I needed a mysterious hero, bigger than life, one that would step out of the shadows to protect a kid."

"You didn't describe him in great detail. Why's that?"

Andrew fidgeted a bit. "I don't know. I never could see him very well in my 'writer's eye.' He just came to me as big, intimidating, shadowy." He stuffed his hands in his pockets. "I knew who he was going to be early in the book but could never get a solid fix on him. That's why he's covered in animal skins and barely speaks."

"Was he Black, white, Hispanic—what did you think?"

Closing an eye and staring at the shelter's rafters, Andrew took a moment to answer. "In the final edit, he was a Black guy. I always pictured him as a Black Mr. Clean from the cleaning bottles." He put his hands on his hips. "Sheriff, where are you going with this? You obviously read the book. Why the third-degree?"

Barnes told him of Sergeant Demarcus White's disappearance in the high Utah Mountains. "So, you can see my interest."

"I don't know what else to tell you."

Barnes sat on the table, dropped his hands in his lap, and sighed. "I'd like you to tell me where to find Sergeant White's body."

Chapter Eight

Caleb grabbed a slice of pizza, not because he was hungry, but because standing around in the uncomfortable silence was painful. Barnes was still staring at Andrew, who in turn found his own hands to be fascinating. Caleb grabbed a soda, popped the top, took a large drink, then set it down. "Gonna be a nice day today. Might go for a bike ride."

Barnes slowly turned his way, his intense scowl not fading. "What in the hell are you talking about?"

Caleb took a bite, then used it to point toward the park. "It's a beautiful day, warm, sunny. I feel like going for a bike ride."

"Deputy Saunders, you don't even own a bike."

"That is correct, sir. And Andrew doesn't have your answers. He's a writer, for Christ's sake. Not a murderer. He's never left South Carolina, and was a teenager when these murders happened."

Barnes barely moved, but his fist clenched, and he glared through Caleb. "I am aware of that, Deputy," he responded in a low, forced voice. "But he knows things that he shouldn't." Suddenly pushing off the table and making Caleb and Andrew dance to the side, Barnes grabbed another slice of pizza and stormed toward his vehicle. He stopped at the edge of the pavilion and turned. "Mr. Alewine, we aren't done here. I'll be in touch." He put his sunglasses on and stalked over to his county-issue Chevy Tahoe.

Caleb stood beside Andrew as they watched the SUV back out quickly, swerve around a toddler playground, slow, then accelerate forward, the tires spitting up dirt and gravel. The truck left the park with the engine howling.

"Well," Andrew said as he clapped his hands once, then rested his thumbs in his belt loops. "That went well."

"I thought so." Caleb chuckled. "I think the sheriff likes you."

Andrew nodded as he thought it over. "I concur. Definitely have a burgeoning bromance building. Think he'll have me over for tea and crumpets soon?"

"Most definitely. I'd be surprised if you didn't get a 'save the date' card soon."

Both men laughed hard, then stopped abruptly.

Andrew wiped his eyes with the back of his hand. "Oh, God, he's going to make my life miserable, isn't he?"

"Oh, yeah," Caleb said and nodded. "Going to be a bitch until he can wrap his head around what you do."

They laughed again, but this time not as long or as hearty.

"Andy-man, we need to get ahead of this quickly. We need to talk about your books and have some answers for my boss."

Andrew agreed with a slight tilt of his head.

"Do you plot out your books, do any research, or make notes of any kind?"

"All of the above."

Caleb rubbed his hands together. "Okay, let's strategize. Your place or mine?"

"Let's go to my house. Vanessa won't be home until late. We can have a beer or two, and I'll dig up all my old notes."

"That works. I'm out of here around five as well. I'll see you after that."

Andrew grabbed the last of the drinks as Caleb packed up the pizza. They walked quietly toward their cars, smiling and waving at kids on scooters and mothers with strollers, but not talking.

Andrew clicked the remote on his keyring and opened the door to his car. Caleb offered him the drinks. "Keep 'em. Take them along with the pizza to the station. I'm sure someone will polish them off."

"I can do that," Caleb answered. "Make a few brownie points with the ladies in dispatch."

"Cool. Hate wasting food," Andrew said, pulling his door open. "I'll have everything prepared when you get to my house."

"You want me to bring anything?" Caleb asked

"Yeah, bring a few beers. I think we'll need them."

"Will do, Double-A. See you in a few hours." Caleb tossed the pizza and drinks on the passenger seat of his truck, climbed in, and fired the engine. They pulled out of the park together but drove off in opposite directions.

Andrew's kitchen table was clean except for a couple of legal-size note when Caleb strolled in with a twelve-pack of Sam Adams and his laptop. Hp put the cold beverages in the refrigerator, the laptop on the table and powered it up. "Yo, Double-A, where you be?"

"Back here," Andrew shouted from his office.

Caleb stepped through the door and stopped. Practically every inch of the floor was covered with paper and notebooks. "Dude, what in the hell are you doing?"

Andrew was kneeling on the floor. He glanced up, wild-eyed. His hair was roughly brushed back, and he held a pen in his mouth. A dozen folders were scattered around his knees. The pen fell from his lips when he glanced up to talk. He caught it and tucked it behind an ear. "That talk with Barnes has me a bit freaked out." He leaned sideways so his knees were no longer under him and stretched his legs out. "When I got home, I took the details from my first book, *Shadows on the Creek Bank*, and compared them to events I could find online. Pretty close to some murders in Portland.

"Then I dug up my outline for *Highlands at Dusk* and did the same." Andrew stared directly at Caleb. "Like the sheriff said, another set of murders that my writing mirrors. Weird, huh?"

"Yeah, man, really weird."

Andrew pushed up on his knees again and stirred the folders below him, finally selecting one. "Now, this story's gonna make you hold onto your ass." He held up a folder. On the top was a cowboy carrying the body of a woman, the image roughly sketched in pen. "Remember when I wrote this?"

Caleb leaned forward until he could read the title. "Oh, hell, yeah, *Texas Moonfall*. That was the book that had me wondering how you sleep at night."

"For sure, had me wondering about my sanity. I began to wonder if my damn chair was demon-possessed." Andrew climbed to his feet and carried the folder to the kitchen table, first stopping by the fridge to grab a couple of beers. He removed the caps and slid one to Caleb.

"Do you remember the plot?" Andrew asked, taking a big pull off the bottle.

Caleb shook his head, then nodded at the same time. "Sorta. Kinda." He shrugged. "I do remember having a hard time getting it out of my head. How do you come up with this stuff?" He tipped up the bottle and removed almost half before setting it back down.

"Like I've told you, I just see flashes of images. Incredibly intense visions." Andrew drank from his bottle, then wiped his lips with the back of his hand. "I almost didn't write this one, but could hardly *not* write it."

"So why did you?"

Andrew opened the folder and spread out a dozen crudely drawn images of people being tortured. "Because they demanded it." The first picture was of a man in a business suit tied up in barbwire, his clothes on fire. A silhouette danced before the dying man. Another sketch was a woman looking up from below the bottom of a dark pond. Her face was just inches beneath the surface, her ankles chained to a concrete block. The same dark shadow danced on the shore. Andrew was about to turn over another picture when Caleb stopped him.

"If your book wasn't disturbing enough, these drawings are. I want to be able to sleep tonight. Why in the hell did you draw them?"

"He made me," Andrew said tapping one of the shadowy images.

"The thing—or whatever it is—made you draw the pictures?"

Andrew nodded. "Well, didn't make me *per se*. Just sort of bugged the shit out of me until I did."

"Seriously? A badly penned cartoon made you create these?" Caleb drew in a long, deep breath, then let it out slowly. "Double-A, I think you need professional help," he said with an uncomfortable laugh.

"That's what Mom said a long time ago." Andrew chuckled and finished off his beer.

Caleb stared at him, the smile now erased from his face. "What are you talking about?"

"That day we went to the depot and things got weird, remember?"

"Yeah, that's when you developed this *twinge* thing."

Andrew nodded. "Yep, that's it. Well, the night before I dreamed of the depot, of the animals, and of *him*." He tapped the ghost picture. "It was the first time he talked to me."

"Seriously talked to you? What do ghosts want to talk about?" Caleb leaned forward on the table, his arms folded before him.

Andrew hesitated. "He wanted me to watch him kill dogs with his bare hands. He beat them to death and laughed when they howled in pain."

"Goddamn, Andy-man," Caleb said in a rush, then pushed back off the table. "That's fucked up. That's a helluva nightmare."

Andrew slapped the table with his hand hard enough to make Caleb jump. "It has never been a damn nightmare! It's beyond that." He lowered his voice. "Sonofabitch has been torturing me since I was a kid."

Caleb held his hands chest high as if surrendering. "Yo, man, chill. I didn't mean to upset you. I'm feeling a bit like Barnes right now. This shit is from way out in left field. I'm having a hard time wrapping my head around it."

"So, what you're saying is, the twinges you understand. But me having hellish nocturnal conversations with a demonic-esq nightmare cartoon is hard for you to wrap your nappy brain around?"

"When you put it like that, it makes me feel kinda foolish." Caleb grinned, then let it fade. "Andrew, I've known you since forever, and you've always been different, talented, eccentric at times, and a totally bizarre friend. And now you tell me you've been hearing voices—"

"I *never* said I was hearing voices. I'm not that batshit crazy."

"Point taken." Caleb sat up straighter in the chair. "You're having demonic-esq nightmare cartoon conversations."

"That is correct," Andrew confirmed.

"Personally, I don't know which is worse. Either way, it scares me, man. Scares the hell out of me."

"You should be the one having cartoon demons talking to you all night. *That,* my friend, will scare the poo out of you." Andrew stood and walked toward the kitchen. "You want another beer?"

"Oh, hell, yeah." Caleb stood. "After what you just told me, I might need several."

Andrew returned with a couple more beers and a bag of chips. He pushed the folder to the side. He popped the top off the bottles and handed Caleb one.

"So, this cartoon crazy that talks to you at night, what does it look like?" Caleb asked, turning up his beer.

Shaking his head, Andrew shrugged slightly. "I don't know. It's hard to explain. It's like a shadow that I can see, but not see, bordering on a mirage." He set the beer on the table. "Sometimes it's like a person talking over my shoulder, whispering in my ear—to me, but not *to me*. Does that make sense?"

"Not in the least bit, but very little of what's going on does. Please continue, Kemosabe."

"Sometimes the *thing* feels familiar, like I know him extremely well," Andrew added.

"Well, you have been sleeping with him for, what, fifteen years? Sorry, that sounds kind of perverted!" Caleb laughed.

Andrew shook his head, tipped his beer at him, and shrugged. "Anyhoo, when I can see an image—which is always shadowy, ghost-like—it feels like he's older. Not much, just a bit, maybe as little as a couple of hours. But the thing always feels *dominant*, powerful. And no matter my age—ten, fifteen, twenty—it's always the same basic age I am, but like minutes or hours older. Still making sense?"

"Absolutely not, but still fascinating." Caleb leaned back in his chair, his arms crossed over his chest. "Do you hear from your spectral buddy every day?"

"God, no," Andrew said with a shudder. "It's pretty rare, maybe a couple of nights a year. Usually around the time—"

"You start a new novel. Correct?" Caleb interjected.

Andrew nodded, stared at the file containing horror pictures, and rocked his beer on the bottle's bottom, swirling the amber brew. "Yes. exactly."

"What happens?" Caleb asked, and set all four legs of his chair on the ground.

"Usually starts with an intense nightmare, and I'm talking damn-near bed-shitting bad. Most are heinous, bloody, worst carnage you can imagine, and then some. Television can't match the horror.

"The dreams intensify over several days, sometimes a week." Andrew stopped talking to finish his beer. He rubbed his palms together and closed his eyes. "If you ever see me with bloodshot eyes, shuffling like a zombie, looking like I haven't slept in years, you know I'm about to start a new novel." He tried a weak grin, but it never fully developed. "Not a damn thing I can do about it. Drinking, sleeping pills—nothing puts it on hold. I once drank until I passed out. Didn't help. The next night the nightmares intensified, almost as if they were pissed."

"When do the voices start?"

"Not long after the nightmares."

"What do the voices want from you?" Caleb was now leaning over the table, arms flat against the wooden top.

"They . . . want me to watch, to pay attention."

"Pay attention to what?"

Andrew swallowed a couple of times before answering. He took a deep breath, then leaned back hard in his chair. "To watch the murders."

Chapter Nine

Andrew slumped against the table, his face in his hands.

Caleb was quiet, the silence broken only by the sound of the laptop's fan engaging and pushing a warm breeze across the table. "I don't know about you, but I need another beer," he finally said as he slid his chair back.

Andrew stood and backed away from the folder containing the dark drawings. "Same here. Maybe something stronger."

"Do you have anything?" Caleb walked toward the fridge.

"No." Andrew shook his head. "I was hoping you could score something out of the evidence locker. Maybe some coke, heroin, or meth." He allowed a shaky laugh.

"Barnes frowns on me raiding the evidence locker. He's funny that way." Caleb cocked his head and turned to his childhood friend. "You're not having any bad vibes about dreams, are you?" Popping the tops off the beers, he handed Andrew one.
"No, thank God," he answered with a weak smile. "Let's sit on the deck. The house is feeling claustrophobic. I keep expecting that haunted chair I got from your grandpappy to come rolling out of my office." He turned the deadbolt on the French doors and pulled them open. The moon had fully risen with a blanket of stars in its wake. Warm, sweet early summer air swept in along with a chorus of crickets and bullfrogs.

Caleb followed Andrew through the doors to the custom-built cypress picnic table. When the land was cleared, several centuries-old cypress trees were pushed down along the edge of his property. Andrew didn't want their death to go in vain, so he had the kitchen and picnic tables cut from their trunks. "Feels good out here."

"Yeah, it does." Andrew said taking a deep breath, letting it out slowly and putting the beer on the table.

They sat on the tabletop with their feet on the seat.

A southwestern breeze carried the pungent smell of the swamp along with the call of a lonely night bird. Neither spoke as they drank. Caleb pointed toward the highway a half-mile away as a lone headlight flashed past, followed by a high-pitch whine.

51

"Hope your boss is running radar down there. I hear he loves to nail these kids on their crotch rockets. When he can catch them, that is."

Caleb nodded and finished off his Sam Adams. "Yep, speaking of my boss-man, you know he's scrutinizing all your books and looking for parallels with actual events?"

"Yep. Hope he buys them new so I can get a royalty off it."

"Don't count on it. What's the book after your novel *Highlands at Dusk?*"

"That would be the one we're looking at, *Texas Moonfall.* The one with the cheerful artwork." Andrew tossed his empty beer bottle at the garbage can by the door to the house. It missed and shattered on the brick patio. "Crap. Could have hit that one three beers ago." He leaned forward with his elbows on his knees, chin resting on his clenched hands. "Your boss is really going to like that one, particularly bloody. Essentially a coming-of-age story of a dozen at-risk youths at the Moonfall ranch in fictitious Diego, Texas. As with all my stories, it's all fun until things start going wrong—phones quit, horses disappear, then one by one the kids and counselors are attacked.

"First, just slashing events. Followed up with true carnage." Andrew paused and chewed his fingernails. "Kids are killed in their bunks, thrown into a well. Adults flattened with a tractor. You know, basic Stephen King stuff. In the end, out of twelve people—ten boys, adult male, and adult female counselor—five are dead, four are badly injured, two are missing, and one escapes and runs across twelve miles of desert in scorching heat to reach a town and call the cops."

Caleb glanced at Andrew as he studied his empty beer. "Why didn't he leave at night when it was cooler?"

"If you had read my stories," Andrew said with laugh and shake of his head, "you'd know the killer *always* attacks at night, dusk, or before dawn."

"Why's that?" Caleb stood and walked slowly toward the edge of the circle of light provided by the floodlights.
Andrew shrugged a little and climbed from the table. He joined Caleb at the light's border. The dark summer gloom pressed hard against the yellowish illumination. "Murder at night is more intense. I can

make the reader turn on another lamp to make them feel more comfortable."

"Your ghost ever talk to you during the day?"

"Ghost? Seriously?" Andrew shook his head and chuckled. "No one said nothing about no ghost. I said demonic-esq nightmare cartoon conversations. Ghosts are all warm and fuzzy. These voices ain't."

"Same question," Caleb said, staying serious. "You have daytime conversations?"

"Never. Why?"

"It's just that—now, don't think I'm crazy—but you have nightmares at night, evil conversations at night, the killer in your book strikes at night, and the real killer that parallels your story kills at night."

Andrew laughed. "What are you saying? I have a doppelganger or something?"

Caleb slowly shook his head. "Don't know, man. But you have to admit, those are some bizarre coincidences."

A bat passed over their circle of light, dipping and twisting as it chased invisible prey in the sky. It shot moonward and vanished. The men stood a bit longer as the river basin continued to serenade with bullfrog croaks and cricket buzzes.

Motioning toward the house, Andrew said, "Guess we might as well get to what we've been avoiding."

"Yeah. Let's see how close we can connect your Texas murders to the real thing."

"What do you think the odds will be?" Andrew said, swinging the door to the kitchen open.

"You've been damn near perfect so far." Caleb pulled the door shut and twisted the lock. "But knocking off teenagers—that's gonna be tough, even for you!"

While Caleb brought up a search page on his county-issued laptop, Andrew put in a delivery order for chicken wings and turned on the TV to a baseball game. He then organized the folder containing his notes for *Texas Moonfall*, instinctively leaving the drawings upside down. The food arrived a few minutes before his fiancé.

Vanessa walked in, her eyes taking in the empty beers, the blaring ball game, and a large bucket of wings from *Jo-Jo's Wings to Go-Go*. "You two are *so* stereotypical, guys. Beer, wings, and baseball." She walked over to Andrew, stood behind him, put her hands on his shoulders, and kissed him on the thin, bald spot on his head.

"Hello, Vanessa," Caleb said with a mouthful of celery and dressing. "How was your day?"

Vanessa pulled out a chair beside Andrew and sat heavily into it. "Oh, you know, rushing back and forth between the office and the courthouse, working up the legal papers for all those poor, innocent people you arrest daily."

Caleb flipped her off and smiled.

"You know." Vanessa sighed overly long as she ran a hand through her long, black hair. "Just another day in the office." She reached over and opened the wing box. "Seriously, nothing but buffalo wings? Jo-Jo's has, what, eighty flavors, and you get the very first one listed? You guys are so *bor-ring*." She grabbed a celery stalk and dipped it in the dressing. "What are you boys working on?"

Both men shrugged.

"Just hanging out, drinking beer, watching the Braves lose *again*," Andrew replied after a moment.

Vanessa leaned to her right with her elbow on the table and fingers resting beneath her chin, polished nails gleaming in the light. She glanced between the two. "Now, that is patently bullshit! The game's on, but neither of you has a clue of the score. Caleb has his work laptop here—I'm sure that's a no-no—and Andrew's bald spot is blushing. His head only blushes when something intense is going on." She leaned forward, wrists flat on the table. "So, Inspector Gadget, how close am I?"

"It's the wings," Andrew said. "They're way too hot, burning my head up."

"Yeah, right," Vanessa said, then noticed the folder. "What's this?"

"Don't open that!" both men shouted together. Before Caleb could stop her, Vanessa opened the folder, and a dark drawing of a person being sliced from stomach to throat, entrails leaking out, fell onto the table. She squinted as she tried to make sense of the drawing. She pulled out the rest of the pictures, gasped, and dropped the folder.

"Those are . . . horrible," she whispered.

Caleb grabbed another wing, pulled all the meat off with his teeth, then glanced at her. "We told you not to open the folder."

"Yeah, we did." Andrew leaned over to grab a wing. "Shoulda listened."

Chapter Ten

Andrew grabbed the remote control off the table and turned up the television. The TV announcer was giving a recap of the game against the Nationals. The Braves were winning, the pitcher throwing a shutout through eight innings. Vanessa had left the table and dropped onto the couch. The TV was on her left. She sat with her feet on an ottoman, head back, staring at the ceiling.

Andrew grabbed a fifth beer and slid in beside her. He was racing past his limit but needed the alcohol to get him through the night.

"You, okay?" he asked, his words starting to slur.

Vanessa shook her head and closed her eyes.

"They're just drawings. I doodle them to help cement the image I'm trying to create."

"They're horrible," Vanessa whispered.

"Yeah, I guess so." Andrew took a sip.

"Not to take sides, but they're pretty bad, Andy-man," Caleb said, walking past the couch and taking a seat across from them. "I've seen the real thing, and your drawings are pretty rough." He tore open a bag of chips and pulled out a handful.

"Have you always drawn like that? I've never seen you do it before." Vanessa covered her face with her hands, then glanced at him. "I can't get those images out of my head."

"No, not really. I've doodled a few stick-man mock-ups, just to get an idea to coalesce, but not this detailed." Andy drained more of his beer.

"I still don't know why you would draw them at all. They're *sick,*" Vanessa said with disgust.

"I told you why. They help me delve deeper into the darkness of the story. Helps me see the victims."

"Can't you just see the images in the 'writer's eye' you talk about so much?"

Andrew shrugged. "Yeah, to some degree. But the drawings are more visceral, intense."

"Plus, he has to," Caleb said between bites.

Andrew shot him a hard look.

Caleb grabbed more chips and stared back across the room.

"What is he talking about, Andrew?" Vanessa faced him straight-on, one leg resting under her.

"What he means is that I have to draw the pictures to help me write," he said to Vanessa, but his eyes were full-on Caleb.

"No, I didn't." Caleb rolled up the bag of chips and set them aside. His eyes were glassy from the beer, but his voice was solid. "Andrew, you gotta open up and tell her everything."

"Way to keep your mouth shut" Andrew snapped.

Caleb leaned forward, beer in one hand. "Andy, she's needs to know. You can't hold this level of shit back. Not with all that's going on. Vanessa needs to be looped in."

Vanessa cut her eyes between the men, landing on Andrew. "What is he talking about?"

Andrew continued to glare at Caleb, who responded by unrolling the bag and eating more chips. "I gotta pee," he said and left the room. "Ya'll talk."

After an awkward silence only broken up by the calling of balls and strikes on television, Andrew grabbed the remote control and turned off the set. He moved over to where Caleb had been sitting and stared at the dark TV.

"Andrew, what is going on?" Vanessa asked quietly.

"Okay, here's what's up." Andrew took a deep breath to calm himself. "I know you don't like the material I write, but have you read any of the books cover-to-cover?"

"No. The violence and graphic nature of them is horrible. I still don't know how you come up with your ideas."

Andrew smiled and shook his head.

"What's so funny?" Vanessa asked, her eyes narrowing with annoyance.

"There's nothing funny," he replied and began to laugh. He slumped back in his chair. "If you ever thought I was crazy before, when I get done, you'll have me institutionalized."

"I don't understand."

"You will. Maybe. Caleb is having a hard time with it, but he's coming around." Andrew sat forward and put his elbows on his knees.

Vanessa licked her lips and nervously brushed her hair behind her ears. "You're scaring me."

"That's why I wanted Caleb to keep his big mouth shut." Andrew picked up his beer and finished it off. "Hold on to your ass, 'cause I'm about to scare the bejeezus out of you." He set the empty bottle down and recounted the conversation with Caleb.

Ignoring the conversations going on across the room, Caleb powered up his laptop and began to search the Texas Department of Public Safety for any mention of murders at a camp. Within minutes of his search, he hit paydirt. Almost six years ago, nine members of the Hernandez family were attacked at a church retreat. Five dead, three injured, and one missing. The victims had been drowned, stabbed, and mutilated. Caleb glanced over to his best friend. Andrew was still laying out his story to a shocked fiancé.

While no more than eight miles out into the desert, not the twelve in the book, the event closely mirrored those in his friend's novel. The sheer number of dead was fewer, but the hand-drawn pictures were practically a confession. He'd have to keep the pictures to himself. Otherwise, Barnes would pounce on Andrew.

And there were two more published books, and one just finished to review. He glanced to his left. Andrew was finished with his explanation and sitting beside Vanessa, his arm around her shoulders.

"Andy-man, y'all done over there?" Caleb called across the room.

Andrew gave him a thumbs-up, then waved him over.

Caleb reclaimed his ottoman across from the couch. Vanessa's face was tear streaked. Andrew's eyes were stop-sign red. He couldn't tell if it was from crying or beer. "So," Caleb began, "Andrew tell you what's all going on?"

Vanessa sniffed back a few tears and nodded quickly.

"You do realize, and I think I'm correct here, that the boy didn't have any say in any of this. He's just a victim to something extremely weird."

"I know that," Vanessa said, her voice cracking. "I've known something was up for a long time."

"Really?" both men said at once.

Vanessa smiled, then laughed. "Yes, really." She wiped her eyes with the back of her hand. "Andrew talks, sometimes shouts, in his sleep. Has been for years. It used to scare me because it happens without warning. I thought he was going mental." Everyone laughed.

"No argument there!" Caleb said, still laughing. "But it has nothing to do with the ghosties."

Andrew shot him the bird, then threw a small decorative pillow at him.

Sitting up straighter, and with her eyes clearing, Vanessa continued, "Sometimes he talks as if he's arguing with someone. I can't understand what's being said, just that he is very defiant." She patted Andrew on the knee. "Sometimes he screams out as if he's in terror."

Caleb threw the pillow back at Andrew. "You didn't know any of this was going on?"

"First I've heard of it," Andrew said as he deflected the pillow with his hand. He looked at Vanessa. "Why didn't you say anything before?"

Vanessa sighed. "It only happens once or twice a year. Then Andrew would get up and start writing like crazy. I didn't want to stop his creativity. If I'd known the depth of the nightmares, I would've stopped him immediately. I'm so sorry." She pulled Andrew over and hugged him tightly.

"In other words," Caleb chimed in, "you wanted your golden goose laying more of his golden eggs. Just like a woman." He rolled his eyes and Vanessa smashed a couch cushion against his face, knocking him off the ottoman.

"I saw you at your laptop," Andrew said. "Find anything related to murders in Texas?"

"Andy-man, you're like a one-man homicidal crimewave. Or, at least your demon-spawn is." Standing up, Caleb backed over to the chair opposite the couch and dragged the footstool with him. He dropped heavily into the chair and propped his feet up. "Didn't find a complete match; this one only had nine victims, and the bunkhouse was less than eight miles out in the desert, not twelve. But the manner of deaths was spot on—drowned, beaten, fileted."

Vanessa closed her eyes. "Oh, God, how is this possible?"

"Sweetheart, God ain't got nothing to do with this," Caleb answered.

"Nope," Andrew said in agreement. "So far, Caleb's best theory is that I have an evil doppelganger following me around."

Vanessa sat up and faced Caleb. "What in the hell is that?"

"Just your garden-variety, run-of-the-mill, evil twin."

"Are you serious?" Vanessa blurted, turning from Caleb to Andrew, her eyes wide. "An evil twin? Is that the best you two alcoholics can come up with?"

Both men shrugged. "We don't have an explanation," Andrew replied. "Either I'm channeling some crazy dude or dudes, or someone is reading my books and acting out the storylines *before* I can write them."

Chapter Eleven

Vanessa hadn't slept well. The conversations from last night had her tossing and turning. Putting on a robe, she stood in front of the mirror in the master bath. Dark circles ringed her eyes and her shoulder-length black hair hung in knots as if a depraved hairdresser had been teasing her hair all night. She glanced over at Andrew. Her fiancé was blissfully sleeping off a six-pack of beer, four more than he normally could handle. His best friend was most likely still sprawled on the couch where he'd crashed shortly after finishing off the twelve-pack. She stepped from the bedroom into a house bathed in the blue light of early morning.

She padded quietly across the hardwood floor toward the kitchen for a badly needed cup of coffee. She'd always thought Andrew's ideas came from his buddy. Caleb was always going on about crimes in the big city, who got shot and who got the stuffing beat out of them, and the gruesome injuries and assaults he saw. Now she knew better.

While the coffee pot worked its magic, she checked the constant stream of emails hitting her phone. So far, she could ignore all the messages until Monday. Thankfully, last night had been quiet, and she wasn't going to have to visit anyone in jail. With the coffee finished, she could now savor the cool morning air on the back patio and watch the swamp come alive. With a magazine cradled under her arm, she pulled the door open with her free hand.

"Need some help?" Caleb asked.

Vanessa's first instinct was to run in seventeen different directions at the same time. Instead, she threw her coffee in Caleb's face, screamed, and danced a high-stepping jig. She watched in horror as Caleb tried to jump out of the way of the brew. The coffee splashed his face and neck. He cried out in pain, wiped his face clean of the coffee, then quickly pulled his shirt away from his skin.

Vanessa sprinted across the room, grabbed a dishtowel from the kitchen and raced over to dry the remaining coffee off Caleb's face. "I am so sorry!"

Caleb took the towel and dabbed his face and hair. "I'm just glad you were holding a coffee cup and not an armload of steak knives."

Vanessa pulled her hair back with one hand and took the towel from Caleb. "Are you okay?"

"I'm fine." He held his shirt by the collar. A large wet stain started at his neck and ran down the front of his shirt. "Luckily, most of the coffee hit me in the face."

"I said I was sorry!" Vanessa cried holding her hands against her chest. She took a long deep breath, and let it out slowly, hands still clutched tightly. "Would you like some coffee?"

"Yes. And if it's not too much to ask, I'd like it in a cup. The free-floating form is hard to drink."

"All right, smart ass." Vanessa said with a laugh and turned toward the kitchen. "Cream or sugar?"

"A little of both, thanks."

He held the door to the back patio open for Vanessa and faked ducking as she approached. Vanessa stepped on his barefoot as she passed, pausing a bit to grind her heel into the top of his foot. She smiled at him, then put the cups on the picnic table. They sat on the same side, eyes gazing out over the river and swamp below.

"Caleb, what do you think is going on?" Vanessa sipped her coffee while her fiancé's buddy stared at the growing sunrise.

"I have no idea." He slowly shook his head. "Initially, I thought the twinge thing was some kind of clever trick I couldn't figure out. I've never been a strong believer in ESP, but when he finds things and returns them to their owner . . . ." He shrugged. "Okay, I can almost wrap my head around the twinge thing." Caleb blew softly across his coffee cup and swirled the dark drink. "But these new developments blow me away. I can't even begin to understand it."

"You don't think he committed the murders, do you?"

"Andy-man?" Caleb sputtered. "There ain't no way in hell he killed anybody. Plus, the first killing happened when he was about fifteen. And the murder was over two thousand miles away." He sipped his coffee, then glanced Vanessa's way. "You don't think he had anything to do with them, do you?"

Vanessa laughed hard and spilled her coffee on her robe. She wiped it away with her hands. "God, no, not a chance. I just don't know what to think about the connection between his books and the true events.”

“Me, neither.”

They quit talking to concentrate on their morning brews. The sun was now completely over the horizon and approaching eye level. The back door opened, and Andrew shuffled onto the deck, rubbing his eyes. “What are you guys up to?” He picked up Vanessa’s cup and took a deep drink. “Why does your coffee always taste so much better than my own?”

“Because you didn’t have to make it!” Vanessa leaned forward to accept his morning kiss.

Andrew patted Caleb on the back. “You’re not out here trying to steal my woman, are you?”

“I keep trying, but she keeps resisting me,” Caleb said with a grin.

“Try harder,” Andrew encouraged, then ducked out of Vanessa’s arm reach.

“Now that you’re up—” Vanessa stood. “I’m going to take a shower. I wanted to take one last night, but our talk and your pictures had me too keyed up.” She kissed Andrew on his bald spot, rubbed Caleb’s back quickly, then disappeared through the patio doors.

Andrew watched Vanessa slip through the French doors, then turned to Caleb. “What time do you go in today?”

“Taking a few personal days. Barnes has been all up in my ass the last few weeks, and I need a break.”

“Got any interest in going to the park and shooting baskets, maybe playing a little twenty-one?”

“Tons!” Caleb replied. “I need to blow off a little steam, and whipping your scrawny ass is just what the doctor ordered.”

“In your dreams!” Andrew said and jumped from the table. “How about nine-thirty, before it gets too hot?”

“Done. I’ll go home and take a quick shower. See you in a few hours.”

Andrew walked his friend to his car, then stood on the drive until Caleb turned onto the highway and disappeared. Vanessa was just stepping from the shower when he walked back in. “You got any plans?”

“Me?” Vanessa asked, caught off guard. “No,” she said hesitantly. “Why? What’s in that crazy head of yours?”

"Gonna meet Caleb at the park to shoot some baskets. I was just thinking you might want to ride with me." Andrew slipped an arm around her and dragged her toward the bedroom.

"Uh-huh. The last time you invited me to town to watch you and your juvenile buddy get all lathered up on the court, you then hit Jimmy's Ale House for a 'beer or two,' and I had to drive both of you home." She spun out of his arm. "Thanks, but I think I'll sit here in the quiet of your house and enjoy some me-time."

"Alrighty, then. You don't know what you're missing." Andrew stripped out of his tee-shirt and tossed it at her. Vanessa batted it away as if it were a stink bomb.

"Oh, I know what I'm missing—peace and quiet, if I go with you!"

"Suit yourself!" He blew her a kiss and stepped into the shower.

Two hours later, Andrew pulled into the Culver Soccer complex. He parked beside Caleb's truck and grabbed his water bottle and basketball. He exited his car and walked toward the four outdoor courts. Normally, there'd be at least one pickup game going on, but today the courts were empty. *That's odd.* Andrew made a slow one-hundred-eighty-degree turn. He cupped his eyes and studied the grounds beyond the courts. Fifty yards away, yellow crime-scene tape fluttered near the pavilion where he previously met with Barnes. He was unlocking his phone when it began to ring. "I was just about to call you."

"Sorry, man, games gonna have to be rescheduled."

Loud, agitated voices sounded through the phone. "Caleb, what's up?"

"I don't have all the details, but it looks like we might have a missing kid."

Andrew heard the mic being covered, muffled, and Caleb answering rapid-fire questions.

"You being called in to help?" Andrew asked.

"Not yet. We've got enough cooks running around the park and not enough chefs. Gonna hang loose until they decide whether they need me or not. Parents are freaking out."

"Definitely a parent's worst nightmare. Anything you can tell me?"

The speaker muffled again as if the phone were in a pocket. Then the sound cleared. "Okay, gotta be fast, but here's what I know," Caleb said quickly. "Last night, a trio of ten-year-old kids—boys—were riding their bikes through the park, goofing off and whatnot—when they realized one of their friends was missing. They circled back but didn't find him or his bike. They assumed he went home, since it was getting late. This morning, the boy's mom started calling his friends, looking for him. That's when they realized he had vanished."

"So, not at any of the other boys' homes?" Andrew asked.

"Nope. Parents canvassed everyone. Kid hasn't been seen since around eight forty-five last night."

"Kid have a phone?"

"Yes. But it's off; they can't ping or call it."

Andrew walked slowly, giving the yellow tape and congestion of officers a wide berth. He took a seat in the pavilion facing away from the investigation but with enough of an angle to casually watch the action. "What's with the crime-scene tape?"

"Found a bunch of scuff marks in the dirt and a pocket knife the kid was known to carry."

Oh, shit. "Caleb, the knife, how important is it to the kid?"

The phone went silent for a moment, then Caleb's voice returned in a hush. "Man, I wouldn't go there. Barnes is here, the parents are here. Helluva lot of emotion currently."

"Trust me, I wasn't overtly offering, but you know—" Andrew paused and walked away from the roped-off area. "The first twenty-four hours with a missing kid . . . ."

"Don't have to tell me, man."

"Okay, then. I'll let you get back to it. If anything changes, I'll be on the court chunking some shots at the basket."

"Sounds good," Caleb said and was gone.

Andrew retreated to the basketball court and shot free throws with no enthusiasm. Most of the shots clanged off the basket or missed entirely. After twenty minutes he quit, grabbed the ball, and stashed it back in his car. He returned to the park and walked toward the asphalt track that ran the perimeter of the green space. He followed it until the path crossed the old rail line, the metal now rusted and, in some places, coated with a multitude of pastel-colored chalk.

Smiling at the simple, colorful artwork, Andrew stepped on a rail, balancing on the narrow beam like a high-wire walker. Soon he reached the end of the line. Fifteen years ago, the old tracks continued through the fence and into the forest beyond. Now the tracks ended at an ornate metal fence and pedestrian crossing. He exited the park and walked into the neighborhood, all the streets and signage having a railroad motif.

Grand Central Avenue was the main drive. He walked past upper-middle-class homes until he was deep in the subdivision. Near the center, three acres of land—enough space for six homes—sat undeveloped. The land, originally cleared, was now in the process of being reclaimed by nature. Brambles and small trees covered the lots. At the front of the land stood a small playground with a wooden fort resembling an old steam engine and several smaller buildings constructed to look like boxcars. He pushed through the gate and walked to the center. Despite being a sunny weekend morning, the park was silent, chilly.

Andrew made a slow three-hundred sixty-degree pivot. The air suddenly felt unsettled. Studying the park, he noticed the assorted swings and slides showed limited signs of use, the ground beneath was grassy, and the dirt wasn't even scuffed.

Kids don't like it here. Andrew turned back toward the soccer complex, letting his mind insert all the trees that had been there a decade and a half ago, and realized he was standing where the old depot had been. He shivered. A gate in the rear of the playground led out to the empty, unbuilt lots. A creek flowed along the far edge of the green space. He ambled over to the gate and stared at a knot of trees near the stream. Light bounced off an object in the water.

Andrew pushed through the gate, the rusty hinges resisting his effort. Near the creek was a mirror. When he got closer, he realized it wasn't a mirror but a phone. He pulled out his cell and dialed.

"What's up, Copper-top?" Caleb asked quickly, quietly.

"What kind of phone did that kid have?"

"Phone? I don't know. Why?" Caleb's voice dropped to a whisper.

Andrew left the playground and angled toward the stream. "I'm in the neighborhood behind the park. There's a small creek. I think there's a phone in the water."

"Where exactly are you?"

Caleb's voice sounded as if he were walking fast.

"Go down the main entrance, past the first road. There's an overgrown field behind a playground."

"I know where you are. Keep your distance. I'll be there in a few minutes."

Andrew heard the phone click off and did as instructed. He walked out to the front of the park. Within a few minutes, he could see his friend running full tilt in his direction.

Caleb sprinted to the entrance and stood with his hand on his hips, breathing hard, heavy sweat streaming from his face.

"S-show me." Caleb took a deep breath and motioned for Andrew to lead him.

Andrew stopped twenty feet from the creek and pointed. "See, by the half-buried Coke can. I don't think it's been there long."

"That's definitely a phone." Caleb wiped the sweat from his face. "How close did you get?"

"No closer than this."

"Good." Caleb walked along the stream but kept his distance. His eyes were focused on the far edge of the water. After a moment, he came back.

"See anything else?" Andrew asked.

"Not from here, no. I'd need to get closer." Caleb focused on the object. "I don't think anyone's walked or run through the area today."

"So, what do you want to do?" Andrew stood with his hands on his hips, eyes on the phone.

Caleb held his jaw tight, then took a deep breath. "Barnes has his hands full at the moment. If we call him down here and it's nothing, he's gonna blow his stack and give false hope to the parents. But if this belongs to the kid. . . ." He walked away, pulled out his phone, and dialed.

Chapter Twelve

Andrew took a few steps back as several cop cars drove rapidly through the neighborhood and slid to a stop in front of the playground.

Barnes was out of his car before the engine died. He left the door open and stormed over to Caleb. "What do you have?"

"Might be nothing, sir. But we found a phone in the creek. Don't think it's been there long."

"Who's 'we'?"

"I found it, Sheriff," Andrew said. "I was waiting on Caleb and decided to take a walk. I glanced through the gate and saw it. Thought it was a bottle or a mirror."

Barnes spun around and stalked up to Andrew. He had a good six inches and forty pounds on the writer and stared down at him. "Mr. Alewine, nice of you to assist. But I don't think we requested a psychic."

"I'm not a psychic," Andrew bit back.

"Of course not," Barnes said, dismissing him. "They don't exist. Now, if you don't mind, please step out to the road and don't interfere."

The sheriff waved at a pair of men with cameras slung over their shoulders. "Carlton, Massy, over here." He pointed toward the small stream of water. The officers changed direction and angled his way.

"Andrew, c'mon, hang back and make yourself invisible for a while—or, at minimum, stay out of Barnes' line of sight," Caleb said ushering Andrew across the playground. "Once we retrieve the phone, we'll ask the parents to identify it. I don't know if the parents know about your twinge thingy. Sorry, man." He escorted his friend through the front gate and then secured it.

"You're good," Andrew said, stepping back onto the street. "I'll just take a little walk. Call me if you need me."

Caleb gave him a thumbs up, nodded toward Barnes, then jogged over to his boss.

Andrew stayed where he was for a few minutes. The men huddled and pointed toward the stream. Flashes of light let him know the investigators were recording every inch of ground around the phone before reaching for it. One of the men gingerly picked up the device and dropped it into a clear zip-lock bag. He then wrote on the front of the clear plastic, walked briskly to Barnes, and handed over the phone.

The sheriff retreated to his vehicle, backed out with a squeal of his tires, and sped away.

The officers remained behind, stringing additional crime-scene tape before returning to their vehicles and leaving.

Several neighbors drove by, made eye contact with Andrew, pointed at the tape, and mouthed, "What's going on?"

He shrugged as if he didn't know anything, then turned his attention to the neighborhood park entrance. The gate was now secured with zip ties, the remaining officers standing by the creek talking quietly. With the thought of spending the morning trading baskets with his best friend kaput, Andrew drifted toward the soccer complex. He was just stepping onto the property when his phone buzzed.

Caleb texted one word: *Bingo.*

Another text came through seconds later. *Guess who's VERY interested in you now?*

Andrew shook his head and moved away from the crime scene. He sent back the following message: *Tell him I don't put out unless he buys me dinner.* Despite the tense situation, he laughed. His phone buzzed a minute later.

Lol. Fortunately/unfortunately that's not the interest. Don't take any long trips. Expect a call from Barnes.

Oh, joy, Andrew replied. He walked to his car, climbed behind the wheel, cranked up the radio, and was just beginning to relax when his phone rang. He glanced down and sagged against the seat. He didn't recognize the number, but the final four digits matched the sheriff's department. He watched the phone vibrate on the console as it rang once, twice, three times, before he reluctantly grabbed the phone. "Hello?"

"Good morning, Mr. Alewine. This is Sheriff Barnes with the Warrenton Sheriff's Department. Do you have a moment?"

I know who you are, you prick. "Yeah, I guess so." Andrew switched phone hands so he could look up the hill toward the yellow crime-scene tape. Except for one cruiser, everyone else had left. *I wonder where Caleb is.*

"First, we would like to thank you for the tip on the cellular device. We were able to recover it, and once we dry it out, we're going to see who it belongs to."

Bullshit, you know whose it is. "Well, that's great. Glad I could help."

"If you could, we would like you to come down to the station so we can take a statement."

Andrew sat up straight in his seat. "You need me to make a statement? What kind of statement do you need?"

Barne's chuckled with zero mirth. "Just procedure, Mr. Alewine. Just want you to go over the day's events while they're still fresh in your head—how you found yourself in the neighborhood, how you spotted the cellular device, etcetera. That's all."

"What if the phone doesn't belong to the missing kid? Do I still need to make a trip into town?"

"So, I'll see you around two this afternoon?"

Andrew glanced at his phone. It was almost eleven. Vanessa would be expecting him home around twelve-thirty. "I'll have to check with my fiancé."

"Two o'clock, Mr. Alewine. I'll see you then." The call ended.

"You piece of shit!" Andrew shouted at the now-silent phone. He slammed it down on the seat beside him, then gripped the steering wheel hard and shook it.

Moments later, his phone buzzed again. A text message was waiting for him from Caleb. *Call it a gut feeling, but I don't think Barnes likes you much.*

"No shit," Andrew muttered and tapped hard on the phone. *What the hell's wrong with him?*

After a few moments, Caleb wrote back. *More than we have time to go into. See you at 2.*

Andrew collapsed into the seat and cranked the radio up until the welds of his car vibrated. The music did little to alleviate the dread he felt. He down turned the radio and called Vanessa. It took a good twenty minutes to explain the events of the day so far.

"He's a jerk!" Vanessa shouted. "Every time I see his smug face around the courthouse, I want to smack him."

"Yeah, probably not the wisest move." Andrew smiled. "But one that I think would be roundly approved of by your friends and co-workers. They might even take up a collection to bail you out of jail."

"Do you want me to meet you at the station?"

"Nah. Don't think I need my fiancé-slash-fiery personal attorney at the meeting. If he already suspects me of being involved somehow, you being there doesn't paint a very innocent picture. Now, if you get a collect call from the Warrenton Sheriff's department, please take it."

"Okay." Vanessa sighed deeply. "I'll be arranging bail just in case things go south."

"Thanks. Love ya." Andrew hung up and pulled out of the park. He turned right and slowly drove along the boundary. The yellow tape still twisted in the wind. The lone forensics agent now retired to his vehicle protecting a patch of land not that much bigger than half a volleyball court.

Andrew pressed the accelerator down and sped past the soccer complex and toward town.

Caleb made it back to the precinct before the sheriff. It was his day off, and he was none-too-happy to be sitting behind his desk. Technically, he didn't have to be here. The officers that took the initial report were required to follow up on the morning's events and co-ordinate with the department's forensic investigators to get the search started. *Damn it! Should have turned around when I saw the forensics van.* He was supposed to be dripping sweat on the basketball court and whipping his best friend's hide. But there was no way he was going to leave his buddy in Barnes's cruel hands—not that there was much he could do.

A shadow fell across him. He glanced over his shoulder to find Barnes standing behind him, arms crossed over his muscular chest, staring down. "Saunders, what in the hell are you doing here? Thought it was your day off."

"Yes, sir, it is. But looking for that Hanover boy got my detective juices flowing." Caleb spun his chair around to face his boss, then reclined until it stopped against the desk. "I wanted to look at the responding officer's notes—didn't want to come in Monday morning and have to play catch up. If that boy doesn't show up soon, Monday's going to be rough."

"Uh-huh." Barnes eyes focused on Caleb. "Doesn't have anything to do with me bringing your boy in for questioning, does it?"

Caleb considered how to answer his boss. With Barnes, honesty was the only way. The man could smell a weak excuse from a country mile. He nodded slowly. "Sheriff, despite what you think, Andrew's a good guy. There's no way he's involved in any of this. Hell, I spent the night at his house last night. I know he didn't go anywhere."

Barnes's expression didn't change—it remained steady and flat. His dark eyes reflected the glare of the overhead fluorescent lights. "Have you read his book, *Bayou Mist?* It's an intense read about drownings in Baton Rouge, Louisiana. All the victims are taken off boats—shrimp, house, sail—as they sat at anchor. All the murders happened about four years ago during a rainy, misty couple of weeks. Local PD nearly caught the perp, but he escaped by diving out of a boat anchored several miles offshore."

"And you're telling me this because . . . ." Caleb raised his eyes to meet his boss's, his palms resting on his thighs.

Barnes leaned forward, his hands now on his hips, his nostrils flaring. "Because in all the murders, and in all his books he has written, the killer has *always* escaped. And no one has seen much more than a silhouette of the killer." The sheriff paused to watch a car slowly circle the parking lot. "Until the Baton Rouge murders. A surveillance camera caught the guy hopping a gate. The individual was approximately five-nine, one-seventy. Had shaggy red or light brown hair. He also appeared to have a thinning or bald spot."

Caleb sat silent, slowly shaking his head. "Sir, there is no way in hell Andrew is involved."

"Well, we will know soon enough. I checked with the boys in Baton Rouge, and they have a DNA sample from one of the murders. I'm gonna take a DNA swab of Mr. Alewine, and we'll find out soon enough."

Jumping to his feet, Caleb stepped just short of his superior. "Sheriff, he hasn't done anything. You just can't take a DNA sample without his permission."

"If he has nothing to hide, he shouldn't care."

"You're going to violate his civil rights," Caleb countered, glaring at Barnes.

Barnes focused hard on his deputy floor and. He then stepped around Caleb and toward his office. "And, Deputy, if you don't want to lose your job or be arrested for obstruction, I suggest you take the rest of the day off and have no contact with Mr. Alewine unless it's to bring him in for questioning." Barnes looked back over his shoulder. "Do I make myself clear?"

"Crystal," Caleb snapped.

"Good. Now go home," Barnes barked and slammed his office door.

Chapter Thirteen

Andrew drove around town for an hour before heading toward the Warrenton Sheriff's department. He thought about calling Vanessa back and having her with him when he met with the sheriff, but that would be kind of wussy. *Just need to buck-up and take no prisoners.* He pulled into the parking lot, looking for Caleb's truck, but didn't see it. *Probably on his third beer somewhere.* The parking lot was mostly vacant. Andrew steered his car into the first visitor spot and shut off the engine.

The clock ticked over to two p.m. He stared at the double-glass doors, each one tinted to block the view from outside. Warrenton Sheriff Department was stenciled across the front glass. *Screw it. Just wants to ask me questions.* Andrew left the protection of his car and walked toward the building. As he was reaching for the door, it opened.

Barnes stepped out and held the door for Andrew. "Thanks for being prompt, Mr. Alewine."

"You didn't make it sound like I had a choice," Andrew said with a snort.

Barnes ignored his comment and followed Andrew inside. "If you will, turn left and cross the lobby, please." He led Andrew through the darkened sheriff's department, the normal hustle-and-bustle of the week now subdued.

An officer manned a small information desk. A couple more talked in the back of the building, holding white Styrofoam cups and watching him. The sheriff's office was walled by tinted glass with blinds closed to block curious stares. The door was propped open. Barnes motioned for Andrew to sit in a high-back, well-appointed chair as he moved around his large desk and stood behind it.

"Is there anything I can get you? Water, Coffee?"

"I'm fine, thanks," Andrew replied. He put a hand on the chair but remained standing. "I'm still a little confused why you asked me to come down here."

"Sit, please." Barnes motioned to the leather chair as he sat and leaned forward over his desk.

Andrew sighed and allowed himself to warily drop into the seat.

The sheriff stretched his heavily muscled arms before him, then steepled his fingers in front of his chest. He smiled, though the expression did little to warm his face. "This is all procedural, Mr. Alewine. Can I call you Andrew?"

"Sure," Andrew said, still sitting mostly upright in the chair.

"Relax, son, this isn't an inquisition!" Barnes laughed. "I just wanted to talk to you about today."

"I thought we covered everything this morning." Andrew now wished he'd let Vanessa join him. *Stupid, stupid, stupid.*

Barnes rocked his head from side to side as if thinking over the question. "Well, yes and no. Things were heated and moving fast. When a kid goes missing—" He slowed and stared right at Andrew. "And I'm positioning officers around the chessboard, if you will, I don't have time to digest all the smaller, minute details."

"So, you're saying I'm a pawn?"

Barnes smiled his non-warming smile again and chuckled. "No, Andrew, not a pawn. I just want to compare what you told me earlier to what you remember now."

Andrew leaned forward, his blood spiking. "Are you insinuating that I *lied?*"

The sheriff's jaw clenched as he leaned back slowly, his chair creaking. After a moment, he let out a slow sigh and leaned forward. "Mr. Alewine, if I thought you were lying to me, we wouldn't be having this cordial chat. I'd have a patrol car pick you up and escort you in. Handcuffed, if necessary. Are we clear?"

Andrew nodded curtly. "Yes, sir."

"Excellent," Barnes said, though his eyes didn't reflect this positive assertion. "Now, tell me about your morning."

Andrew took a deep breath, let it out slowly, and settled deeper into the chair, now feeling like a kid being excoriated under the withering glare of a parent.

Barnes relaxed his posture, let his arms rest in his lap.

Sonofabitch has already written off what I'm about to tell him. "I met Caleb at the park—"

"That would be Deputy Saunders?" Barnes questioned, with a raised eyebrow.

Andrew smirked and rolled his eyes. *You cold bastard, you know who it is.* "Yes, sir, Deputy Saunders." He took another deep breath and again wished Vanessa was by his side. "We were going to play basketball before Caleb got pulled into the investigation. Not being of any help, I decided to go for a walk until he could play; the morning was too nice to go back home or sit in the car."

"Did you intentionally head toward the neighborhood park?"

"Specifically? No. Just started walking aimlessly, kind of imagining where the tracks ran and thinking how dark and scary the woods felt when I was a kid. And I know this is going to sound cliche-ish." Andrew sagged and stared at the ceiling. He shook his head slowly. "But the next thing I knew, I was standing in front of the playground."

"Just like that?" Barnes asked, snapping his fingers, his eyebrows rising in mock belief.

"Yes, just like that." Andrew sat up and pressed back against the chair. He fixed Barnes with a firm stare. "You notice kids don't play there?"

"I'm sorry, I don't follow," Barnes said, now sitting forward.

"The park. It's where the old depot was. That's why it has a train motif. Kids don't play there—don't like it."

"Really?" Barnes said, now easing forward. This time his eyes squinting accusingly. "And you know this how?"

If you didn't have your thumb up your ass, you'd noticed it too! Andrew shrugged just a bit. "Did you notice the swings? There's grass underneath them—it's not worn down from swinging. Same with the slides. If this was a brand-new park, maybe. But this park has been there for years. Also, the gate hinges are rusty and the ground around it is not scraped up. Kids don't play there. Guarantee it."

Barnes picked up a pen and chewed the cap. "Huh, fascinating. You hang out in playgrounds a lot?"

Andrew slammed a fist down on the chair's arm. "What in the hell is that supposed to mean?"

"Just that we have a missing kid, his phone is found by you, in a playground that you say kids avoid." Barnes set the pen slowly on his desk and arranged it with several others so they were lined side by side. "And because you're a fucking weirdo."

"Fuck you!" Andrew snapped. "If you weren't such a half-assed rent-a-cop, you would've noticed the things I did about the park!" He pushed out of the chair hard enough to knock it over. "We're done here." He turned to storm out when an officer stepped into the doorway blocking his path.

"Sir, parents confirmed the bike is the boys," the deputy said over Andrew's shoulder, not giving him the chance to leave.

Andrew put a hand out to force the deputy out of the way.

Barnes growled, "I wouldn't do that, boy. Assault on an deputy is another charge you don't want."

"Are you saying you're charging me with something?"

Barnes ignored the question. "Where was it found?"

The officer stepped into the office and shut the door behind him. "Vacant house fairly near the park, maybe eight blocks from the neighborhood. The area was scuffed up, lots of footprints. Looks like the kid fought back or was dragged off the bike."

"Has forensics been over it?"

"Yes, sir," the deputy confirmed. "They finished up about thirty minutes ago. Didn't find any prints. They pulled some partials off the handlebars, but those were badly smeared and probably the kid's."

Barnes nodded. "Mr. Alewine, please follow Deputy Gentry. We would like you to take a ride with us."

Andrew backed away from the door and stood at an equal distance between the men. "No way in hell. I'm done here!"

Barnes slammed his heavy fist on the desk, making the pictures and decorative clock jump. "You'll be done when I say you're done!" he growled. "You can either come willingly, or I can have my deputy cuff you and leave you in a holding cell until Monday when I haul you up in front of a judge."

"What the hell did I do?" Andrew shouted, his voice rising slightly as panic took over.

"One, you show up at a park where a kid has just been abducted. Two—" Barnes continued rounding the table. "We find you at another park where his phone has just been found." The sheriff stood almost on Andrew's feet, towering over him, glaring down, his hand on his holster. "Three, I don't like you. You're involved somehow. I can smell it."

Andrew shook his head and took a step back. "Fine, whatever. If this will satisfy your psychotic ass, I'll take your little ride. But first I'm going to call my fiancé and let her know I'm going to be late."

"Put that away," the young deputy snapped and stepped forth. He attempted to take Andrew's phone from him.

Barned motioned for him to stand down. "That's not necessary, Deputy Gentry. Let the man make his call."

The deputy glared at Andrew, then stepped back with a subtle nod of his head, giving Andrew the room he needed to move past and into the lobby.

Andrew was barely able to slide his finger across the phone and unlock it. His hand was shaking as he tapped in Vanessa's number. She answered on the third ring.

"Hey, babe, what's up? You and Caleb still—"

"No, listen up," Andrew barked harsher than he wanted, his throat tight, emotional tears positioned on the edge of his eyes.

"Andrew, what's going on?" Vanessa asked, her voice quiet, worried.

Biting his bottom lip, Andrew held the phone tight to his head as he hunched over and walked a tight circle. "That kid that went missing," he said slowly. "They think I'm involved."

"They *what?*" Vanessa shouted. "That's insane! I'm coming down there right now."

"Vanessa, don't do that." Andrew glanced over his shoulder. Barnes caught his eye and tapped his wrist, indicating it was time to wrap it up. He recounted the conversation to her quickly. "They're taking me to another crime scene. I need you to stay close by and not come down here and get yourself arrested." Andrew chuckled lightly, trying to end the conversation upbeat.

"They're taking you to a crime scene? Why?"

Barnes walked slowly toward Andrew. He held his hand out, fingers flexing in a 'give it up' motion.

Andrew walked across the room putting additional distance between them. "I think they are taking me to the kid's bike."

"Why?" Vanessa said, then answered her own question. "They want you to *twinge*, don't they?"

"That's my guess," he answered. "Gotta go." Andrew ended the call and slid the phone into his pocket.

Barnes waited a dozen feet away, sitting on the edge of a desk. He glanced up with a sarcastic smile. "Everything okay at home?"

"Awesome," Andrew said flatly. *I can't wait until the day Vanessa turns your ass inside-out on the witness stand, you peckerhead.*

"Very good!" Barnes stood, straightened his slacks, and pointed toward the door. Waiting outside was a red and white Dodge Charger with Warrenton Sheriff's Department stenciled on the side. "I believe our ride is waiting."

The captain walked ahead of Andrew and held the door for him. Barnes walked around to the front passenger seat, and Andrew took the driver's-side rear. He climbed in and the door was shut for him. He noticed there was no inside handle. *Great. Trapped with this jerk.*

Chapter Fourteen

Less than ten minutes after they departed the sheriff's department, the driver pulled up to an abandoned, ranch-style house. Two additional patrol cars were already parked on the long, cracked driveway that climbed a slight hill to the early seventies brick home. A rusted, listing basketball hoop hung from a pole at the top of the drive. Most of the paint around the home's eaves was peeling and mildewed, and the roof was covered with a thick mat of pine straw. Many of the windows—the ones not boarded up—were shattered. The broken panes reflected the strobing police lights like jagged blue and red teeth.

A pair of investigators with blue latex gloves exited the dark home and moved toward the street. Barnes waved to a tall, thin man wearing a windbreaker with "Forensics" stenciled across the front. The man snapped off his gloves and headed in their direction.

Barnes stepped from the car, meeting the investigators at the curb. "Whatcha got for me, Sweeny?"

Charles 'Sweeny' Sweeneyhoffer took off his department-issued ballcap, shook his head, and shrugged. He then ran a hand through his thinning gray hair. "Not a lot. The bike didn't have much for prints. Most were so smudged they were useless. We'll take what we can and compare them to that of the missing boy.

"We also canvassed the home," Sweeny continued. "We've got prints everywhere; the house was a transient dumping place. Every square inch is coated with prints." He glanced at Andrew and raised an eyebrow.

"Consultant," Barnes said with a smirk.

"Really?"

Barnes nodded, walked around to the rear of the car, and opened the door for Andrew. "Yes. He has an interesting insight into these matters."

Andrew hesitated and glanced between the men.

"Mr. Alewine, this is Charles Sweeneyhoffer; he's the lead forensics investigator. I was hoping you could assist him."

"Assist?" Andrew asked, staying put in the car and edging away from the door.

"That's what I said." Barnes stared over the top of the car and pinched the bridge of his nose. "We could use your expertise on the bike." He pushed his sunglasses up tight on his face.

Charles glanced over at the sheriff, then into the car. "Mr. Alewine, I'd appreciate any help you can lend. If you don't mind me asking, are you F.B.I. or with a state agency?"

Andrew shook his head and grinned. He knew his next words were sure to make Barnes more excitable than ever. "No, nothing so lofty," he said with an eyebrow raised. "Ain't that right, Sheriff?"

Sweeney stared at Barnes. "Sir, I'm confused. I thought you said he was a consultant." He nervously pulled at his windbreaker.

"Mr. Alewine's position is—" The Sheriff shook his head and glanced toward the house.

"Is what, sir?" Charles took a step back from the car, now holding his clipboard and notes against his chest. A bead of perspiration dribbled down his temple.

"He's a psychic," the sheriff growled in a low voice.

Charles's eyes grew large with surprise. "Sir, did I hear you correctly?"

"Yes!" Barnes bellowed. "Little sonofabitch is a goddamn psychic, or something close," he snapped. An uneasy silence settled between the men penetrated only by the sound of a passing car, the driver slowing to rubberneck.

"Maybe physic is a stretch," Barnes said after a moment. "But Mr. Alewine has a unique talent that might aid us. Is that not so, Mr. Alewine?"

Andrew scooted toward the door and glanced up at the men. He shrugged. "I don't know about having a special talent, though my fiancé thinks I'm pretty good in the sack. So, if that's the talent you're thinking—"

A large fist grabbed him by the shirt, jerked him from the car, and threw him to the ground.

Barnes stood over him, fist balled up, veins in his neck and forehead pulsing. "Listen here, you little prick!" he spat. "I don't give a shit about you or what you do. But I have a missing kid out there, and I don't need any of your smartass comments." He stormed over to the car, slammed the rear door, then spun back around. "Get your ass off the ground and go with Mr. Sweeneyhoffer." Barnes's eyes narrowed to cobra slits.

Andrew scrambled away, climbed to his feet, and brushed himself off. "You ever touch me again like that, I'll have your goddamn badge!" He walked quickly past the forensics officer. "Take me to the bike," he demanded over his shoulder.

Sweeneyhoffer hurried to catch up. He glanced at Andrew. "So, you're not a psychic?"

Andrew forced himself to slow his pace. His blood was spiking, his fist clenched hard enough to crack bone. "No, I'm not a psychic. I'm—" He paused and took a deep breath. "I'm sensitive, I guess is the best word." He turned back toward the vacant, ranch-style brick house. The blank windows leered down at him. "Where's the bike?"

"Around the corner, by the garage," Sweeneyhoffer said and took the lead. "What do you mean by 'sensitive'?"

They crossed over to the driveway and veered toward the garage. Near the basketball goal, lying on its side by the rotting garage doors, was the kid's mountain bike. Crime-scene tape was suspended on poles around it. Andrew walked to the circle and slowly measured the perimeter.

There was nothing special about the bike. It was just a scratched, scuffed, cheap bike. A few stickers adorned the frame, and a dirty orange Clemson ballcap was hooked to the handlebars.

"Best way to explain it is this: I think people leave their 'essence' on things they cherish. Can be a set of car keys to jewelry. If they have an emotional attachment to it, I can sometimes 'feel' it, but not always." Andrew stared down at the bike, noticing all the black dust from the forensics team. "If you carry a pen and just write with it, I'll get nothing. But if that pen belonged to your father and meant the world to you, and I touch it, I'll see a mist or trail running from it to wherever the owner is."

"Interesting," Sweeneyhoffer said. "I've never heard of anything like that. Never been a big believer in the paranormal." He stood to the side as Andrew made another circuit of the bike.

"Neither have I," Andrew agreed in a soft voice.

"But this 'talent,' as Barns calls it, is essentially a paranormal event?"

Shaking his head slowly and holding his hands palms-up as if he didn't have an answer, Andrew didn't comment further. He ducked under the tape and hovered over the two-wheeler.

"So, what do you do, touch it?" Sweeny followed Andrew to the edge of the tape and stood behind it.

Andrew nodded.

"Do you want gloves?"

Andrew shook his head and stared at the bike. He crouched down and noticed for the first time how quiet the world had become. There were neither birds chirping nor insects buzzing. The air was flat. He lifted his eyes and saw Barnes was still down at the street, standing behind his cruiser but looking his way.   Four officers stood within a dozen feet of him and were respectfully staying out of his line of sight. Sweeny was hovering nearby, a clipboard gripped in his hand.

He would get no indication of the power of the twinge if there was one until he grabbed the bike. Andrew closed his eyes, took a deep breath, and put a hand on the handlebar.

Nothing. No nausea-induced trails streaked out and flew through the woods.

"So?" Sweeny asked. "Anything?"

Shaking his head, Andrew put the kickstand down and stood the bike up. He straddled the seat, then sat on it, both hands on the rubber handlebar grips. Sitting flatfooted, he rocked the bike back and forth. When he did, the clip holding the hat let loose, allowing the ballcap to fall to the ground. Andrew stretched to reach for it. When his fingertips brushed the button on top of the hat, a bolt of electricity shot through him. The world tilted crazily, and he began to fall. His breath was driven from his lungs and he dimly felt his head strike the concrete drive. The red and blue strobe lights faded away.

Chapter Fifteen

The world returned in the form of intense red flashes and a coppery taste in his mouth. Andrew felt himself being lifted and pushed quickly toward the flashing brilliance. He tried to sit up but found his arms and legs strapped down. Fear surged through him as he realized he was on a gurney and being wheeled toward an ambulance. Fully opening his eyes was nearly impossible. The flickering light felt like nails being driven deep into his skull. He moaned and tried to cry out, but an oxygen mask covered his face. Andrew pulled at the bindings with his right hand, attempting to free himself. The gurney came to an abrupt stop.

Even though his vision was murky, he could see a tall, thick man pushing through the paramedics.

"He's back with us," Barnes stated in his 'don't question me' voice. "Get him up."

Andrew felt the straps on his arms come loose, then the front of the gurney rise, lifting him into a sitting position. The oxygen mask was pulled from his face, and he took a deep breath of the warm, humid air. So much different than the cool, antiseptic smell of the bottled oxygen. He rubbed his eyes and face to clear his head.

"Sheriff," Andrew croaked, "we've got to talk."

Barnes leaned over him, staring down at him with hardened, distrustful eyes. "Shut your mouth and listen to *me!* That was a helluva stunt. Nice acting job you pulled back there." The officer leaned closer. "Once they release you from the hospital, I'm charging you with obstruction of justice!"

Moving quicker than he thought possible, and on an instinct that scared him, Andrew reached up, grabbed Barnes by the front of the shirt, and pulled him down. "No, *you* shut up and listen!" His voice was primal, angry. The other man tried to pull back, but Andrew would have none of it. "Go down to lake Sinclair, all the way to the end of Fisherman's Cove Road." His head swam. He felt bile push up from his gut. "They're in a pale blue van. Can't tell the model." The world was becoming watery, the image burning up in his brain, being consumed as quickly as he could remember it. "Hurry, they're—" He let go of Barnes's shirt and slumped against the gurney.

Barnes glared down on Andrew. "Boy, don't do this!" He grabbed Andrew by the shoulders and shook him. One of the paramedics stepped forward and pulled the sheriff away, then put the oxygen mask back over Andrew's face.

"He's passed out, you idiot!" the EMT snapped. "Now, clear a path!"

The sheriff retreated and watched Andrew get loaded into the back of the ambulance. "Gentry!" Barnes shouted. "Did you get what he said?"

"Yes, sir," Gentry answered, hustling over to the departing ambulance. "I just brought up the street on my phone. It's about thirty minutes from here. I'm ready to roll when you are."

"Contact dispatch. See if anyone else is in the vicinity, redirect them there, and advise we are in route. Relay everything you heard. Give me a minute, and I'll meet you at the car."

"Yes, sir," the deputy responded. He was on his phone and relaying the order as Barnes walked over to Sweeny.

"Wrap everything up here, then bring your team out to Fisherman's Cove Road. We're not done yet."

"You believe him?" Sweeny asked, then motioned toward several of his techs. He twirled a finger in the air to wrap it up.

Barnes leaned forward, eyes narrowed, hands on his hips. "That he had a vision or some kind of crap? Hell, no! Do I think he might be trying to pull something off to save his ass? Damn straight."

"Understood. We'll be about ten minutes behind you guys."

"Make it five," Barnes ordered and spun away from Sweeney.

Gentry jogged to catch up with Barnes, reaching the vehicle at the same time, and slid behind the wheel. He fired the engine, dropped the car in gear, and raced out of the neighborhood.

Gentry followed the navigation beacon on his phone until they were out of town and racing toward Lake Sinclair. The sparsely populated, twisting body of water was a favorite of anglers due to the tight, tree-lined coves and secluded location. Tall cypress trees grew along the shoreline, their gloomy shadows turning the water into a black mirror. This section of the lake was the most secluded, far up the Socastee River. Access to the lake was limited. Places to dispose of a body were limitless.

Gentry exited Highway 196, a wide-open, four-lane expanse of asphalt that bisected the state and ran to the coast, for a narrow two-lane road that was ten years late in repaving. The deputy held the accelerator of the county-issue car down, letting it race down the cracked asphalt a tick under eighty miles per hour, the sedan swaying and rocking.

Barnes shifted suddenly and snapped his phone off his hip. He lifted it to his ear. "What did you find?" The sheriff was quiet as the other party spoke. "How far out? He asked, then waited for the reply. "Absolutely! Get a wrecker and divers out there now!" Barnes ended the conversation and turned to Gentry. "We found a blue van submerged on the ramp about forty feet out and under about ten feet of water. If it had rolled a bit farther, we wouldn't have seen it."

Gentry glanced at the GPS on his phone. "We'll be there in seven to eight minutes."

"Make it seven," Barnes said and felt a gentle push in the back as the car accelerated.

Gentry did better than seven minutes and had them at the landing in a bit over six. A Warrenton County Sheriff's Department car was parked in the middle of Fisherman's Cove Road, blocking access to the landing, its lights on and flashing. The deputy slowed and pulled up beside the opposing cruiser. Gentry lowered the driver's side window and Barnes leaned across the seat.

"Jasper, what can you tell me?"

Deputy Owen Jasper, a rookie on the force, his face still fresh and unscarred from lines of fear or worry, leaned against his driver's door and spoke through the open window. "Not much, sir. I've been on scene for about twenty minutes. Deputy Coleman rolled in just ahead of me and is securing the ramp. We didn't want to step off the pavement until forensics got here."

"Good thinking, son. Did Coleman spot the van?"

"Yes, sir. Could just make out the taillights in the water. Any deeper, or if the sun hadn't been so bright, he wouldn't have noticed them."

Barnes nodded, then pointed down the long asphalt drive toward the boat launch and parking. "Any civilians?"

Jasper shook his head. "No, sir, the parking lot was empty when we arrived."

"That's good. One less thing to deal with." Barnes tapped the dash and pointed forward.

Gentry put the cruiser in gear and drove down the long ribbon of asphalt toward the lake. They parked a distance from the ramp, exited, and walked across the paved slope. Yellow crime-scene tape fluttered in the breeze, suspended by portable barricades set up a hundred feet from the water. The air was heavy with the melodious chirps of crickets as the dark water lazily drifted by.

Coleman waited for them at the park's water access. He nodded as they approached.

Barnes stepped over the tape, carefully walked to the water's edge, cupped his eyes to block the glare, and stared at the barely visible gray-blue box sitting under the cove's dark surface.

Gentry stood beside him. "Well, Sheriff, there's a blue van just where Alewine said it would be. Is he psychic or involved?"

Barnes snorted but said nothing.

Chapter Sixteen

Vanessa, notified by Caleb of Andrew's situation, arrived at the hospital shortly after the ambulance pulled into the trauma center. She paced fitfully outside the emergency room, trying her best not to barge in and demand to know his condition. She brushed tears off her cheeks, unaware she was crying.

Caleb jogged up the corridor fifteen minutes later, breathing heavy with sweat on his brow.

Vanessa marched up to him. "What have you been told?"

Caleb shrugged. "Not a ton, but a little. I talked to a buddy on the force who said Barnes dragged Andy to an abandoned house a half-mile from the park. That's where they found the kid's bike. Barnes—who doesn't believe in Andy's gifts—wanted him to touch it."

"Why would he do that if he doesn't believe him?" Vanessa's eyes began to blaze again.

Caleb shook his head and then spread his arms wide, palms up. "I have no idea. But at first, nothing happened. Then the hat, that was hooked to the handlebars, fell off. When Andrew touched it, all hell broke loose."

"What do you mean, 'all hell broke loose'?"

"Just what I said. Andy touched the hat and damn near went into cardiac arrest. I heard his back arched, and he screamed like he was being electrocuted. He stumbled a few feet, crumpled over, and went head-first right onto the concrete." Caleb made a motion with his hand arcing in the air then diving straight down. "And it gets crazier from there."

Caleb paused as the doors to the emergency room opened, and a tall, middle-aged doctor stepped out. He pulled the gloves off his hands and stuffed them in a pocket of his coat. "Ms. Kirk?"

"Yes," Vanessa said quickly, breathlessly.

"I'm Dr. Ives; I'm the physician on call."

"How is Andrew? Is he okay? Can I see him?" she asked rapidly while pulling at her dark black hair for the fiftieth time.

Dr. Ives smiled and held a hand up. Despite having more than a little silver in his once-brown hair, his eyes lit up and danced a bit, making him seem much younger than his sixty-odd years.

"Soon, Ms. Kirk. Except for a serious bruise and laceration over his left ear, he seems to be fine. His vitals are strong—blood pressure is a bit low—but he's breathing well, eyes are clear, and he doesn't seem to be in much discomfort. But due to the severity of the head wound and the EMT's report, we've ordered a CAT scan. After the scan, he'll be admitted for observation. I'll have a nurse come for you when we have a room for him."

Vanessa reached out and gave the doctor an awkward hug. "Thank you!"

Dr. Ives smiled and pulled away. "He's going to be okay. Just want to make sure he didn't fracture his skull. I'll check in with you later. If you will, kindly have a seat in the waiting area until someone comes for you." His beeper began to chime. "Sorry, duty calls." He waved with his clipboard, then stepped back through the doors to the emergency room.

"C'mon, Vanessa, let's have a seat. I believe we're going to be here a while." Caleb slipped a strong arm around Vanessa's shoulders and guided her toward the rows of chairs in a softly-lit waiting room.

Vanessa dropped her face in her hands, her dark hair spilling over her fingers. After a moment, she took a breath, brushed her hair out of her eyes and glanced at Caleb. "That man is going to be the death of me!" Vanessa made claws out of her hands and reached for Caleb.

Caleb leaned back with his hands out. "Hey, girl, you can have your way with Andy-man when the doc releases him. Just don't mess up my pretty face." He smiled.

Vanessa's eyes narrowed and she took a step forward. She poked him in the chest. "And where were you, Mr. Don't Hate Me Because I'm Beautiful? That crazy boss of yours put my fiancé in the hospital!"

With his hands still raised and in full retreat with Vanessa bearing down on him, Caleb darted around a length of chairs in the waiting room. "Hey, now, Barnes didn't put him in the hospital. It was the blow to the head that got him the nice ambulance ride." He finished with his disarming million-watt smile.

Vanessa's stony expression vanquished it like a fire hose dousing a cigarette. "And his head wouldn't have hit the concrete if Barnes hadn't made him touch that damn bike!" She clenched her fist and growled. The half-dozen people waiting on word of their loved ones turned her way. Vanessa glared at them with wild eyes, sending them back to fumbling with their magazines and phones.

"You're his best friend!" she continued. "Why'd you let this happen?" Her tone softened; her eyes changed from a fiery glare to one edging on disappointment and bitterness. Vanessa dropped into a chair. "He's just a little boy in a grown-up man's body."

Caleb walked around the row of chairs, grabbed one, and pulled it close so they could sit kneecap to kneecap. "Hey, now, you know I love that man like a brother, like a very *pale* brother!"

Vanessa smiled just a bit.

"But." He held a hand up to stop her from interrupting. "There's only so much I can do. Barnes is running the show and following the law, more or less, the way it's intended. I did what I could to soften his approach, but, you know, he's—"

"A dick."

Caleb laughed, leaned back hard, and stared at the ceiling. He sat forward again. "I was going to say *ass*, but your description is apt as well. Anyhoo, there's more I need to tell you, some of it is really hard to believe, stranger than strange."

Vanessa began to cry again; this time, she was aware of it.

Caleb licked his lips and took a deep breath. "Andy started to have a seizure, and an officer ran over to hold him down, to try and prevent him from further hurting himself." Caleb leaned forward, voice dropping in volume. "When he touched Andrew, he said it felt like he put his hand into a 'bucket of electricity.' He said he's been shocked many times, but nothing like this. It was as if Andrew *pulled* power out of him."

Caleb composed himself. "The deputy was thankful the contact made him puke. He wasn't sure what would have happened if he hadn't broken the connection. After that, Andy became still and didn't move or speak until the ambulance loaded him onto a gurney."

"But he was talking at the end?" Vanessa asked, rubbing her eyes with the heel of her palms.

"Well, sort of. He came around enough to give Barnes a description of a van and where to look for it, then passed out again."

"Why is this happening to him?" Vanessa asked, wiping her eyes.

Caleb moved to sit beside her. He put an arm around Vanessa's shoulder and pulled his best friend's fiancée close. "Girl, I wish I had an answer for you, but I don't."

"It's that damn chair of yours!" Vanessa cried through her hands. "It's haunted!"

Caleb suppressed a laugh, rolled his eyes, and shook his head. "Now, now. Let's not blame my grandpappy's chair."

Chapter Seventeen

What had promised to be a quick examination turned out to be considerably longer. The sun's light streaming through the windows became less intense, and the waiting room shadows lengthened. Caleb passed the time by checking his phone a thousand times an hour and by watching a custodian meticulously clean the floors.

Vanessa was curled up on a small sofa, her head on a pillow. She stirred when Caleb walked past. "What time is it?" she murmured.

"It's closing up on seven." Caleb picked up her legs, took a seat on the couch, then let her legs fall across him. They were now the only ones in the waiting room.

"Has anyone checked in with you?" Vanessa asked, still curled up as best she could, her head on a pillow.

"A nurse came by about thirty minutes ago. Said they would be with us soon." Caleb caught her eyes focusing on him. He patted her on the arm. "I didn't wake you 'cause you were out cold, and the conversation was only in passing."

"Shoulda woke me up," she said grumpily, the pillow muffling her voice.

"Nurse said they were waiting on a room and would come get us," Caleb paused as a nurse walked purposely toward them. "Looks like it's show-time, sleepy-head."

Vanessa sat up and put her feet on the floor. She ran a hand through her hair and pulled loose strands of hair from her eyes. They stood simultaneously when the woman angled their way, her soft white shoes barely making a whisper on the floor.

"Hi, I'm Nurse Harmon," she said amiably and held out her hand. "Are you Vanessa?
"Yes, ma'am," Vanessa replied.

"Just wanted to let you know that we just got Mr. Alewine settled into a room."

"How is he?" Vanessa said in a rush.

"He's still fairly sedated. He was getting agitated in the CT scan, and since Dr. Ives was concerned about scarring on Mr. Alewine's head, we had to sedate him just a bit."

"Can we see him?" Caleb asked.

"That's why I'm here." The nurse nodded. "He's in room 302." Using her clipboard as a pointer, she stepped around the chairs they had been sitting in and motioned down the hall behind them. "Just go to the end, turn right, go past the nurse's station, then back to the left. It's the first room on the left."

Vanessa thanked the nurse, then set a mad pace down the hall. Caleb had to pull her back twice to keep her from flattening an orderly rounding a corner. After reaching the room, Vanessa knocked softly and pushed the door open. Dr. Ives was by Andrew's bed speaking in hushed tones with a nurse. He smiled and nodded toward Andrew, who was lying on his right side. A small patch on the left side of his head was shaved, cleaned, and dressed. His eyes were closed.

Dr. Ives broke from the conversation, put a hand on Vanessa's elbow, and gently led her from the room. Caleb followed. When the door shut, Ives guided them to another small waiting area.

"I'm truly sorry to keep you waiting, Ms. Kirk." He held a metal notebook binder against his hip. "Anytime we have someone brought in with a head injury, I like to run a thorough battery of tests. The initial report is that he had a seizure, collapsed, and lost consciousness. My main concern in these situations is an aneurism or other brain bleed." Ives paused after noticing their concern and smiled comfortingly. "Just want to assure you we didn't find anything."

The doctor lifted his metal notepad holder, flipped the lid off, and began reading through the notes. "Vitals are fine, blood pressure was initially low, but last time we checked, he was fine. Lungs sound good, eyes, reactions—all look fine." Ives snapped the binder closed. "He's probably going to be out of it for a bit. Seizures take a lot out of you, and then we had to get him a bit more relaxed for the scan."

Vanessa nodded vigorously. "Thank you! I was so worried about him." Tears slipped from her eyes again.

Ives reached out with one hand and gave her a friendly squeeze on the shoulder. "He's going to be fine. Wouldn't have bothered with the CAT scan if I hadn't seen the prior skull injury. Just wanted to make sure we didn't miss anything." The pager on his hip chimed. Dr. Ives glanced down. "Well, duty calls once again. I'll check in with

Mr. Alewine later this evening." He turned to leave when Vanessa put a hand on his sleeve.

"Dr. Ives, what prior injury are you talking about?"

The doctor glanced at his watch, then looked up. "I'll talk with you in detail about this later. I'm needed in the ER. But he apparently had a very serious injury many years ago. We'll talk soon." Ives excused himself and hurried down the hall, his white coat floating out behind him.

Vanessa followed the physician from the waiting room, watching until he disappeared toward the elevators. She turned slowly to Caleb, her brow furrowed as she bit her bottom lip. "Huh," she said flatly. "That's odd."

"What's odd?" Caleb leaned against the doorway to Andrews room.

"Did you know Andy has an old head injury?"

Caleb pursed his lips as he thought it over. "Not that I know of. We've been best friends since we were in grade school, maybe before that. But I don't know of any accidents or injuries. Hell, I can't remember the last time the boy physically hurt himself." He snorted. "Short of falling out of his chair, I've never seen this kid have a bruise—ever."

"Me, neither," Vanessa added, wishing she'd had more time to talk to the doctor. "It's weird he never mentioned it."

"Maybe he doesn't know," Caleb said.

"A prior head injury that the doctor is concerned enough about to run more tests?" glanced at her sleeping fiancé'. "He's gotta know about it."

A young nurse stepped out of Andrew's room, caught their eye, and motioned them to come on in. "He's coming out of it now," she said in a low voice as they walked over. "Just ignore anything silly he says—sometimes the meds scramble them for a few hours. But, just in case, keep your phones out and recording!" She winked.

"The boy is always silly," Caleb said. "We might not be able to tell the difference." He grinned.

"When they come off this stuff, you'll know the difference." This time they all laughed. "If he needs anything, let me know. I'll be on the floor all night." She smiled and pulled the door shut behind her.

Andrew's eyes were fluttering when Vanessa pulled a chair over to the bed. She patted his arm and ruffled his hair, paying close attention to the thinning spot on the back of his head where the hair was very thin and wispy. On his scalp was a scar about twice the size of a silver dollar.

"See anything?" Caleb asked. He stood at the foot of the bed.

"There's definitely a scar here. I guess we'll have to wait until he wakes up to ask about it."

Caleb walked around the bed and stared at the spot on Andrew's head. "That weird. I've known him all my life and never noticed it before. He must comb his hair over it."

"Never saw what before?" Andrew asked in a quiet, slurring whisper.

"Hey, the man of the hour awakens!" Caleb squeezed Andrew's shoulder.

Andrew glanced between Vanessa and Caleb, his eyes wide with confusion and failing to focus. "What's going on? Am I in the hospital?"

Vanessa reached down and brushed his cheek. Before she could speak, Caleb cut her off.

"Sorry, man. You fell and hit your head. What do you remember?"

Andrew shook his head slowly. "I hit my head?"

"Yeah, man. Hit it hard. You've been in a coma for six years. The doctors will be thrilled to see you're conscious!" Caleb winked at Vanessa, who scolded him with her eyes.

"I've been in a coma?" Andrew's eyes grew ever wider. "For six years?"

"Yeah, man, sure have. Lots of things have happened," Caleb said quickly. He sat on the side of the bed and started counting down events on his fingers. "Where do I begin?" He stared at the ceiling before speaking. "The Chinese have a man on the moon, the French completely surrendered to the British after their war, we have our first android president. Oh, and me and Vanessa got married three years ago and are expecting our first child. Ain't that right, Sugar Bear?"

"Y'all got married?" Andrew rocked to his side, struggling to sit up.

"Honey, Caleb is just messing with you!" Vanessa cut her eyes to Andrew's best friend and glared at him. She took her fiancé's hand and kissed it. "You did fall today, but you've only been in the hospital for a few hours." She pointed at Caleb, then stabbed a finger toward the door.

Caleb shook his head vigorously, his wide grin growing larger.

"So, no coma?" Andrew asked quietly.

"No, sweetheart."

"And no android president?" Andrew's eyes were clearing and his voice getting stronger.

"No, baby." Vanessa kissed the back of his hand.

Andrew managed to sit up. He turned to his best friend and slurred, "You're a jerk!"

Caleb walked over to the bed, laughter tears still streaming down his face. "Sorry, man. I couldn't resist!"

"You're a very bad man, Mr. Saunders!" Vanessa said sharply, but the corners of her mouth were slowly evolving into a smile. She gently ran her fingers through Andrew's hair. "What we were talking about before that lunatic of a friend got us off track was the injury to the back of your head, and what caused it."

Andrew sat up straighter, eyes still mostly unfocused, his words slow to form. "What head injury? I've never been hurt bad in my life."

"Honey, you have a scar on the back of your head. That's why your hair is so thin."

Caleb sat on the edge of the bed; his laughter finally quieted. "What about your mom? Think she would remember?"

Andrew shrugged. "She might. Just depends on how much she can remember. Her dementia has gotten worse. I can't even guarantee she'll remember me."

"When's the next time you plan on seeing her?" Vanessa asked.

Andrew leaned back and stared at the ceiling as if trying to remember. He shook his head slowly. "I was thinking Monday morning, providing the sheriff doesn't have me locked up."

"We'll make sure that doesn't happen." Vanessa ran a finger through his hair. "In the meantime, let's get you out of here as soon as we can."

Chapter Eighteen

Caleb excused himself, leaving Andrew and Vanessa to talk in private. He walked past the nurse's station to the end of the hallway where a bank of high windows overlooked the hospital grounds. The sun was setting just above the pines, coating the trees in orange and yellow. Stonework paths wound through the lawn, giving patients and visitors cozy, secluded benches to sit on. Being the weekend, the lawn was empty, with only a couple of people making use of the greenery. Caleb pulled his phone from his pocket and unlocked the screen. Two new voicemails were waiting to be heard. Sitting on the couch facing the wall of glass, he played the voice mails.

The first message was from his mother, asking how his "little scarecrow friend" was doing. Caleb laughed. His mom loved Andrew, but refused to call him anything but "scarecrow," mostly in homage to his bright red hair and to the fact he wore flannel shirts almost year-round as a kid. The second was from Barnes, asking when Caleb thought Andrew would be available for further questioning.

"Fuck you," Caleb muttered. He was sliding his phone into his pocket when it started to vibrate. Annoyed, Caleb looked down. The call was coming from the station.

Caleb stared at the display as the number flashed and the device vibrated. Right before the voicemail picked up, he unlocked the phone and lifted it to his ear. "Deputy Saunders," he said quickly.

"Yo, Caleb, it's Eric."

"Well, hello, Deputy Mosh. What's up?" Caleb let out a deep breath and relaxed just a bit, allowing the over-stuffed couch to swaddle him. His mind flashed to the new officer on the force—tall, thin, and Black. *Finally getting some athletic guys on the force I can shoot hoops with!* Caleb smiled, thinking about how bad Andrew was on the court.

This new guy was barely out of the academy, but already pulling his weight. Still green around the gills but with great instincts and would become a fine deputy. That is, if Barnes didn't run him off.

"I didn't know if you heard or not, but your boy was spot on. They pulled an early nineties Dodge van out of the lake," Mosh said quietly.

Caleb glanced around the sitting area making sure he was still alone. "No, I hadn't heard. I'm not surprised. My friend is usually correct." He pushed from the couch and walked to the windows. Streetlights now glowed as the sun dropped below the evening clouds. "They find anything?"

"No bodies, if that's what you mean. From what I heard the van was pretty clean."

"And no blood?"

"Not so far. Forensics has it now. Hopefully, we'll know more soon."

"Eric, thanks for keeping me looped in."

"No problem. How's your buddy?"

"Seems to be okay. They're keeping him just for observation—probably go home tomorrow." Caleb continued to stare at the clouds, which were now ramping up to fiery purple and orange streaks.

"That's good," Eric said. "One piece of advice for your buddy—stay clear of Barnes. That bastard is on some kind of weird-ass witch hunt."

"You know it. Thanks again, Eric."

Caleb ended the conversation, clipped the phone to his belt, and idly walked the halls to give his friend some alone time with his girl. An hour later, the hospital was nearly deserted, patient rooms were shut, and non-family visitors were encouraged to head home. At around eight-thirty, he found himself in the cafeteria, the food lines long closed, but vending machines still in operation. He grabbed a well-read newspaper, the pages creased and out of order. He was flattening out the sports section when a white coat swirled past, then spun around at his table. Caleb glanced up to see Dr. Ives' blue eyes looking down at him.

"Deputy Saunders?" Ives asked.

Caleb started to slide from the booth when the physician shooed him back. "Please, don't get up. Sit." The physician dropped into the bench across from him, leaned back, and released a long breath.

"Been a long day?" Caleb asked, folding up the paper and sliding it to the side.

"It's been a day, I assure you. And it's not even a full moon!" Ives laughed softly, stretched his arms wide, and sat forward in the booth, putting his elbows on the table while clasping his fingers together.

"Doctor, is there something I can help you with?" Caleb asked.

Ives yawned hard and shook slightly. "Sorry, Mr. Saunders—"

"Just call me Caleb. Mr. Saunders was my father."

"Duly noted," Ives said with a slight tilt of his head and sat up a bit straighter. The physician fumbled with a saltshaker for a moment before continuing. "You and Vanessa are listed as contact persons on Mr. Alewine's admittance papers. And somehow, I feel this is something I should share with you before I share it with her."

Caleb was now at full attention. "Is this one of those 'I should be sitting down' kind of info dumps? 'Cause I'm already sitting."

Ives shook his head and smiled. "Maybe this is nothing. But has Mr. Alewine talked with you about any problems sleeping?"

"Sleeping?" Caleb asked, dumbfounded. Not the question he was expecting. "As far as I know, he hasn't. This is something I think Vanessa would be more privy to than me."

Dr. Ives nodded slightly. "Well, sort of. When the EMTs were driving him in, he was unconscious. Suddenly, he sat up and began screaming like a banshee, according to the EMT's notes. When one of them tried to sedate him, Mr. Alewine grabbed him by the shirt and said something like, 'Tell Caleb the boy is back' then fell unconscious again. Does this mean anything to you?"

Caleb pressed hard against the rear of the booth, his eyes wide, his heart beginning to race. The room seemed to chill but he never heard the AC pushing cold air through the vents. "Yeah, it means something, and it isn't good."

"I don't follow," the other man said, now no longer playing with the saltshaker.

"It's kind of complicated. You might not be aware, but Andrew is a writer—a really good writer, by some accounts. But his books are dark—in the horror genre. He said he gets his ideas from his nightmares. When he starts having them, he writes feverishly." Caleb didn't like misleading the doctor, but he couldn't tell him of Andy's dark dream-world shadow.

"And this worries you?" Ives asked.

"Big time. I know it's rough on his body. And with him collapsing yesterday—" Caleb sighed and slumped a little. He folded his hands on the table. "The dreams concern me."

The doctor leaned back, stared at the ceiling, and partially closed an eye.

"What are you thinking?" Caleb asked as the doctor continued to gaze at the acoustic tiles lining the ceiling.

Ives brought his eyes back down, shook his head, and put his hands on the table palms down. "The x-rays and CAT scan on his head are just . . . odd. Looks like he has an old cranial injury. With that prior injury and him hitting his head again, I was just being cautious. The old injury could be putting pressure on his brain and causing nightmares."

Caleb now sat with his elbows on the table, arms straight out. "How old does the injury look?"

"If I had to guess, I'd have to say it's been there since birth."

Chapter Nineteen

Dr. Ives patted the table twice and excused himself to finish his rounds.

Caleb watched the man whistle and rock slightly as he made his way down the hall. *What an odd bird.* He glanced at his watch. It was now nine o'clock. Vanessa would probably be wondering where he'd wandered off to.

The corridors were abandoned by the time he made it to Andrew's room. Caleb tapped lightly on the door before entering.

Vanessa was stretched across a chair and ottoman beside the bed, and Andrew's eyes were closed. The TV was on with the volume too low to hear.

She glanced up when he closed the door. "So, what have you been up to? Harassing the nurses?" She grinned and swept her hair out of her face.

Caleb smiled. "That was my plan, but someone must have tipped them off." He dragged a chair beside Vanessa so he could share her footstool. "They don't lack for beauties, that's for sure. If Andy-man gets a look at the nurses manning the floor above, you might never get him out of here."

Vanessa slapped him with a small pillow from her chair. "Well, if he continues to sleep, I don't think it will be much of an issue."

"How long has he been out?" Caleb asked, his smile dimming as concern took over.

"He was up for about thirty minutes before he began to fade again." She slid out of the chair and stood beside Andrew and ran a hand through his hair. Then she leaned forward and kissed him on the forehead. "Whatever they gave him knocked him out."

Vanessa caressed Andrew's face, sliding her palms along his temples, jaw, and down his neck to his shoulders. She kissed his nose. "I'd sure like to know what they gave him," she said quietly.

"I don't know," Caleb answered, "But I'm sure it was for the best. With a head injury, you just don't know how bad they are."

"Maybe so," Vanessa said as she let go of Andrew's arm and retreated to her chair. "I didn't get to talk to him much. He was pretty loopy, and a lot didn't make sense."

"Loopier than he normally is?" Caleb said.

"Much," Vanessa said. "He was like a bad cartoon."

They quieted for a moment as Caleb picked up the television remote and searched through the channels. He put the TV on the hospital information page and glanced at Vanessa. "I ran into the doctor," he said almost as an aside. "He's an odd dude."

"Really? Where?"

"Down in the cafeteria. I was in there reading the paper, and he plopped right down on the opposite side of the booth."

"And . . . ?" Vanessa faced Caleb.

Caleb sat up in the chair, then leaned to see Vanessa. "Well, he had some interesting things to share. One is the injury to Andrew's skull. He thinks it came from when he was a toddler—maybe even a newborn."

Vanessa nodded. "Did he have anything else to say?"

Caleb rocked forward, his head bobbing slightly. "Yeah, he asked if we knew of any sleeping problems Andrew might be having. Have you noticed anything?"

"No, absolutely not. He's been going out like a light. I haven't noticed him so much as twitching or moving. Boy sleeps like a log. Does he think the head injury might be causing sleeping issues?"

"Don't think so. He was just curious."

"About what?" Vanessa asked, now lines of worry showing around her eyes.

Caleb took a deep breath and let it out very slowly before answering. He cocked a thumb at his friend. "Well, on the ride over, while still unconscious, sleeping beauty came back to life, started screaming, and told the EMT to tell me 'the boy is back,' then passed out again. Apparently, the episode was in their notes."

"Are we talking about *the boy*? The one from his dreams?"

"That was my take on it."

"The EMT must have been mistaken," Vanessa said emphatically. "Andrew has been in a great mood and sleeping well. I remember the last book—he went through a spell where he barely slept and looked horrible. I thought it was just part of the writing process."

Caleb shrugged and stretched his legs out onto the footstool. He settled back in the chair. "I do remember him being moody, but Andrew has *always* had mood swings. It's what makes him such a swell guy!"

"Yeah, try living with him when he's in his moods." Vanessa pressed back, stared at the ceiling, and sighed deeply. "I just thought it was a natural part of the writing process. It doesn't appear so benign now."

Caleb looked toward Vanessa. "No, definitely not. Do you think it's possible he's not aware of the nightmares? I mean, what if they manifest on some unconscious level that he's currently not aware of."

"You mean nightmares that he's doesn't know he's having?"

"That's exactly what I mean." Caleb said.

With her head still on the back of the chair, she rolled her face toward Caleb, her eyes wide. "That's a scary thought."

"Yeah, it is," Caleb replied nodding.

Vanessa massaged her face with her fingertips, concentrating on her temples, and sat up straight. "I know it hurts Andrew when he visits with his mom, but we need to talk to her and see what she can tell us about his head injury."

"Yeah, watching your last parent waste away from dementia is horrible." Caleb slid the footstool away from him and stood. He straightened his shirt and tucked it in. "Do y'all want me to go?"

Vanessa smiled. "She responds to you the best."

"I know. It's kinda weird." Caleb pulled his keys from his pocket and motioned toward the door. "I'm going to take off. Do you need anything?"

Vanessa stretched, yawned and pushed herself out of the seat. "No, I think we're good." She walked over and put her arms around Caleb's neck and hugged him. "Thanks for keeping an eye out for my Andy-man."

"Ain't nothing." He pointed toward Andrew and his expression turned serious. "Keep an eye on yonder sleeping man. Try to note any changes in his sleep patterns."

"I plan on it," Vanessa promised and yawned again. "Sorry, I'm tired, and I have a feeling I'm not going to get the best sleep tonight."

"Call if you need me." Caleb exited the room, hoping his phone wouldn't ring in the middle of the night.

<h2 style="text-align:center">Chapter Twenty</h2>

Caleb's phone didn't ring in the middle of the night, but it was ringing like crazy around six in the morning. He ignored it the first two times, letting the call go to voicemail. On the third set of rings, he rolled over and picked up the device.

"Hello," he mumbled into the phone.

"Deputy Saunders," the voice on the other end began. Caleb fell against his pillows with one arm over his eyes, the other holding the phone as far from his head as he could. He took a deep breath and brought the phone back up to his face.

"This is Sheriff Barnes."

I know who in the hell you are. "Sir, it's just after six in the morning, and I was with my friend at the hospital until after midnight. Is this something that can wait until later in the day?"

"It could," Barnes replied with more than a hint of irritation in his voice. "But since you're awake, I thought I'd bring you up to speed."

Caleb clenched the phone in his fist and reached back as if he was going to throw it against the wall. He relaxed his hand and sat up. "Sir, I'm only up because you called me."

"Be that as it may," Barnes continued without taking notice of the umbrage in Caleb's voice, "I wanted to talk to you about the events from yesterday. How soon can you be in my office?"

"Sir, I've only had five hours of sleep, and yesterday was a long, tiring day. Can I meet you around noon? Today is a scheduled day off."

"Deputy, I completely understand. Get some rest, I'll see you at eight a.m."

Caleb was left to argue with a dial tone. He screamed invectives at his boss, clenched his phone hard enough to elicit cracking sounds from the handset, and this time did throw it.

According to the digital clock in his car, it was 8:07 when he pulled up in to the sheriff's department. He parked in a visitors only spot, not caring who he pissed off. He sat for a few minutes listening to the tinkling sounds of his cooling engine. At 8:10, he climbed from the car, sunglasses glinting in the early morning sun, and walked in the main entrance.

Barnes stepped out, held a door open, and said flatly, "You're late."

"Bite me," Caleb muttered.

Barnes let the door shut on its own and followed his deputy close, almost stepping on his heels, practically breathing on his neck. "Deputy, I don't think I heard you correctly. Can you repeat yourself?"

Caleb's first instinct was to repeat himself along with all the varied places on his ass his boss could kiss. But he liked being a cop and held his tongue. "I said 'getting up early is a bitch', sir."

"Yes, it is," Barnes agreed almost jovially. He moved around to the backside of his desk and dropped casually into his chair.

Caleb sat across from him, arms folded over his chest. "So, what's so important that I needed to come in on my day off?"

Barnes leaned back in his chair, one leg crossed over the knee, a pen clenched in his teeth. "Forensics has been examining the van since we pulled it from the river," he said conversationally, the pen slightly muffling his words. Barnes let the pen fall, caught it, and set it on his desk in perfect alignment with the other writing instruments. "They've done an amazing job of drying it out and going over every inch of it. I think we're going to have a report very soon."

"I see," Caleb said and yawned. "And this was the important news that you said couldn't wait? News so damn important you dragged me in on my day off?"

"Oh, this news is just conversational chitchat until your morning coffee throws off the cobwebs in your brain." Barnes lifted a black mug with the department's logo embossed on it. He took a sip, then lowered it. "I'm sorry, Deputy, have you had your morning coffee?" The mug lingered beneath his chin.

"No, sir. I'm fine. I'm trying to cut back," Caleb replied evenly.

"Pity. I truly don't understand people who don't start every day with it." Barnes swirled his coffee and breathed in the aroma. "Well, let's get on with the facts of the day." He spun around to the cadenza behind his desk and retrieved a manila folder. He turned back to face Caleb, put the folder on his desk, and opened it.

Caleb knew the game being played. He stared at the ceiling for a moment and worked up the brightest "Oh, gee!" smile he could. He locked in the expression and faced his supervisor. "Sir, what might you have there?"

"As I'm sure you're aware, the initial sweep of the van found little, if any, evidence. Forensics is still going over it as no one can completely erase all evidence." Barnes thumbed through the contents of the folder, found what he was looking for, and held a finger on it. "But it's usually not what the person leaves behind that gets them caught—it's what they don't expect." The sheriff held his fingers on the leaf of thick paper in the folder. "I assume you're aware that where we found the van is an animal refuge?"

"Yes, of course."

"Right, I'm sure you do. But did you know there are game cameras lining the river and interspersed through the woods?"

The cobwebs in Caleb's brain dissipated immediately as his heart rate increased. "Sir, what do you have?"

Barnes smiled broadly and tapped the folder. "You tell me." He slid a series of eight-by-ten black-and-white pictures to Caleb.

Caleb grabbed the photos by the edge, careful to avoid smudging the images. The first was too blurry to make out much more than two people walking through the woods. But the second was much sharper—a cross-angle picture of a young woman with her head partially turned away from the camera.

The third picture was along the water's edge. The girl's features were murky, but from behind her was a clear, close shot of an individual holding a machete. It was a man, a touch under six-foot-tall, thin, wearing jeans and a flannel shirt unbuttoned at the cuff.

The photos were black and white, and Caleb couldn't tell the true color of the man's hair, just that it was shoulder length and shaggy. "Sir, uh, are you sure these are the pictures you wanted to show me? This could be anything. The male doesn't seem to be wielding the machete in a threatening manner. That brush is thick—maybe he was clearing it. What about the boy?" Caleb pushed the pictures back toward Barnes.

"This is our man!" Barnes almost shouted. He stabbed a finger down on the glossy image hard enough to make his coffee cup dance. "The date stamp is shortly after the van arrives at the boat ramp.

Whomever this is, he matches the basic description of your pal. We don't have an ID on the woman, but we're checking missing person databases."

Caleb remained sitting despite wanting to jump from his chair and argue that Andrew has been in the hospital for the past eighteen hours. "Could be nothing—just a couple walking in the woods."

"Nothing, my ass!" Barnes snapped. He grabbed the clear picture of the man and flung it at Caleb. "I'll stake my career on the fact that this is our abductor and he's taken another victim."

Slowly rising, Caleb picked the picture off the floor and studied it. The man shared Andrew's build, but so did a million other guys. "I don't know, sir." He sighed, stared intently at the picture, and scratched his head. The fluorescent lights from the ceiling cast a glare on the back of the man's head.

Caleb glanced up. "Sir, do you still keep a magnifying glass on your desk?"

Barnes kept a wary eye on his deputy as he slid his center draw open, reached in, and brought out a magnifying glass big enough to make Sherlock Holmes envious. He handed it across the desk. "Mind sharing what you're looking at?"

Caleb held the picture and ran the glass over it, paying attention to the hairline. As he did, his mouth went dry. Casually, he slid the picture back on the desk along with the magnifying glass. His heart was beating in his throat when he sat back down. "Sorry. Thought I saw a shadow or tattoo on the man's neck."

The sheriff grabbed the black and white photo and placed it with the others. The glass he left at the corner of his desk-pad. He leaned back hard, making the chair creak on its springs. "And?"

Caleb shook his head. "Nothing, sir, I didn't see anything." He shrugged. "I was hoping to get lucky."

Barnes sat forward, rested his elbows on the desk, and steepled his fingers. He rested his chin on the top of his fingertips. "Well, if you don't see anything, then I guess we're done here." He smiled broadly, his eyes reflecting no humor.

"Yes, sir." Caleb stood.

"Deputy, if you will be so kind, please close my door on the way out." Barnes reached over, lifted his desk phone off the cradle, dialed, and turned his back to Caleb.

Chapter Twenty-One

Caleb fought the urge to pull his phone and call his best friend's fiancé as he walked across the lobby of the sheriff's department. He moved slowly, deliberately, to his car, casually opened the door, and slid behind the wheel. His pulse continued to race. Caleb cranked the car, checked his mirrors, and backed out of his spot. He waited until he pulled out of the station before retrieving his phone and dialing.

Vanessa answered on the fourth ring, sounding tired. "Caleb, good morning. I'm surprised you're up."

"Mornin', girl. How was your night?"

Vanessa yawned into the phone. "Okay, I guess. Just hard to sleep in a recliner."

"Andy-Man sleep through the night?"

"Mostly. He tossed and turned some—also mumbled in his sleep."

"No night terrors and screaming?" Caleb asked.

"Not that I'm aware of. The doctor came by this morning and said they're discharging him. Did you need to speak to him?"

"No, I wanted to speak with you."

"With me?" Vanessa sounded puzzled.

"Yeah, I think it's important that we talk to Andrew's mom about his childhood." Caleb paused when a local patrol car pulled up behind him. The car followed for a moment before turning down a side street. "Tell you what. I'm beat, and I think I'm about one yawn away from falling asleep behind the wheel. Can you call me later today when you get a chance?"

Vanessa readily agreed and the connection ended. Caleb dropped the phone on the passenger seat and drove home. After the days events he wasn't sure how well he would be able to sleep with his mind currently in overdrive. But his bed drew him in as if it had cast a spell. He fluffed his pillows, stretched out on the bed, two a deep breath and was asleep within minutes. He woke up for the second time that day to the sound of his phone ringing. It took a herculean effort to drag himself to consciousness and out of the gauzy clouds of hard slumber. He rolled over and grabbed the phone off the nightstand.

"Vanessa, what's up?" he managed to say once he had the phone oriented correctly to his mouth.

"You asked that I call?"

"Yeah, sorry. I'm exhausted. Barnes called me at six this morning, wanted me to come down to the station."

"And . . . ?"

"I told him to 'pound sand' and find himself another sucker to browbeat."

Vanessa gasped. "Are you serious?"

"Hell no!" Caleb laughed. "That psycho would have reached through the phone, grabbed me by the throat, and dragged me back through the phone line."

"So, what's up? What did you need to talk about?"

Caleb sat up straight in the bed, swung his feet onto the floor, yawned, and stretched. "As far as you know, did Andrew have a sibling, a brother?"

"Did he have a brother?" Vanessa repeated, then laughed. "Caleb, you've known him longer than me. Have you ever seen another little kid running around his house? I'm pretty certain he's an only child."

Caleb chuckled. "I guess that was a dumb question. And, no, I never saw another kid running around the house. Just Mr. Coppertop." He quieted for a moment. "What about cousins? Andrew ever mentioned any other relatives?"

"Again, you've known him longer than me. I think he has some much older cousins, but no one his age. What is this all about?"

Caleb stood, walked out of the bedroom and into the small kitchenette of his apartment. He pulled a Coke out of the fridge, opened it, and took a deep drink. The coldness of the soda helped push the sleep out of his head.

"We found the van Andy mentioned, where he said it would be. We didn't find anyone or anything inside. But near the boat ramp are a series of trail cameras. They are triggered by movement. They were installed by a conservation group a few years back to capture wildlife pictures."

"What did they catch, Caleb?" Vanessa asked quietly.

"One camera caught a man and a woman just as they stepped into view. The first couple of pictures were blurry or from a bad angle."

"But one wasn't," Vanessa said as a statement.

Caleb nodded subconsciously. "That is correct. One camera caught a clear image—albeit it from the back—of the couple. The man was tall, thin, looked a bit under six-foot. He had shoulder-length hair."

"What color hair?" Vanessa asked, a nervous tremble in her voice.

"Can't tell—cameras are black-and-white." Caleb drained the rest of the Coke before continuing. "Vanessa, the male's build, the way he stood in the shots that were clear, resembled Andrew."

"Caleb," Vanessa said quickly, "that could be any number of men—hundreds or thousands!"

"I agree," Caleb said quickly. "But, Vanessa, this guy's hair was thinning, going bald on the back of his head, just like Andrew's."

"But he's been in the hospital or with one of us for the past few days. It couldn't be him!" Her voice became shrill.

"I know that," Caleb answered calmly. "That's why I asked about cousins, close relatives, any blood relatives."

Vanessa was silent, but Caleb could hear the hitch in her voice as she breathed. "Andrew hasn't mentioned anyone, not to me."

"Me, neither," Caleb agreed. "That's why we need to talk with his mom."

"You know his mom's getting harder to talk to every day, don't you? More of her mind slips away as the months go by."

"Yeah, Andy-man told me. That's why we need to go see her soon—today, if possible."

"I'll talk to him in a few minutes. I know he won't mind. But sometimes his mom gets upset when people visit her. The facility then calls Andrew, and that *does* upset him. So, I know he'll want to be with us."

"Where are you now?" Caleb asked.

"I walked down to the cafeteria to get us both coffee while we wait on the discharge paperwork. I'm on my way back now." Vanessa stopped talking and Caleb heard doors opening and closing followed by voices echoing down a hallway. "He hasn't seen her in a week. It hurts him to see her mind disappearing more and more each day."

"I know it does," Caleb replied as a memory of their last visit to his friends' mom unspooled in his mind. Mary Beth Alewine sat on her bed, her once thick, dark brown hair now solid gray and in disarray, the light that always seemed to permanently radiate from her eyes dimmed. Andrew held her hand in his and talked soothingly to her. She would occasionally smile, but not make conversation. Mary Beth turned his way, noticed him, and her eyes cleared a bit, taking on some of the familiar radiance. "Caleb, it's good to see you again! How's your mom? Are you boys staying away from the depot?" she asked.

"Caleb, you still there?" Vanessa asked, her voice taking on the edge of someone who'd been waiting for an answer.

"Sorry, Vanessa, got kinda lost in my thoughts. What did you say?"

"Just wanted to know if you wanted a ride. Hopefully, we'll be out of here in another fifteen minutes. Then run home quick to shower and change, then back on the road."

"That sounds good. While I wait, I'm going to see if any additional pictures have been uploaded. Oh, and one last thing."

"And that is?" Vanessa answered hesitantly.

"Y'all shower alone. I know how goofy Andy-man can get when y'all have been in a marital way, as they say. I need the man clear-headed and serious."

"Oh, good grief," Vanessa groaned into the phone. "Can't you live vicariously through anyone else's life?"

"Nope, just you two!" Caleb laughed. "I can't afford HBO, so I have to get my Sex and the City—" The phone went dead in his hand. He danced over to the refrigerator again, retrieved another soda as well as lunch meat and mustard. He laughed harder. *Andy-man, you are the best friend—white, black, silver, or green—ever. And I'm going to protect you, brother. No matter what it takes.*

Chapter Twenty-Two

Andrew pulled into Caleb's driveway ninety minutes after Vanessa's and Caleb's conversation

Caleb glanced in the car's window.

Andrew was beaming. And singing.

"Dang girl, you got him all goofy again," Caleb said, climbing in the back of Andrew's car. In his hand was a valise. "Now be a good girlfriend and crush his spirit a bit. I need him to be serious."

Vanessa half-heartily slapped at Caleb. "You know I have a weakness for mysterious men!" She winked at Andrew, who sang louder with the radio.

"You two are the whitest white-folk I know." Caleb sighed and leaned back against the seat. "When your boyfriend comes back down to earth, I want to show him some of the pics we pulled from the trail cams. We gotta couple more about a half-mile from the ramp. I printed them all."

"Okay-dokey," Andrew sang and rocked back and forth. He pulled out of Caleb's house and onto the highway. "Are you going to share those with Mom?"

Caleb pursed his lips and closed one eye as he thought it over. "I'm not sure. I don't know if it will register with her or confuse her. But I wanted *you* to see them. You and Vanessa."

"Why?" Andrew asked, glancing up in the rearview mirror.

"Didn't Vanessa fill you in?"

"Yeah, sort of. Said you found the van and some dude that looks like me."

"Well, 'looks like' is a misnomer. Let's just say he favors you in a few ways."

Andrew's giddiness faded.

"In what ways?"

"Well, the biggest one is his hairline—or lack thereof." Caleb opened his briefcase, thumbed through reports, then pulled out the best pictures. He handed them to Vanessa. "Unfortunately, the trail cam picture quality isn't as good as an iPhone, but they give us something to work with."

Vanessa sorted through the pictures, nodding slowly. She pulled one out of the stack, held it up, and shook her head. "This is uncanny."

"That the one with a dude standing beside a tree with his hands on his hips?" Caleb asked, leaning forward.

"Yes," she said in a voice just over a whisper. She placed the picture on her lap and pulled another from the stack.

"Stands just like our Andy-man, doesn't he?"

Vanessa nodded and stared intently at the next picture. She reached over and fluffed the hair at the back of Andrew's head.

"If you only had those two pictures, who would you think you would be looking at?" Caleb asked.

Instead of answering, Vanessa turned to Andrew and touched him on the arm. "Sweetheart, we *really* need to speak to you mom."

The drive took twenty minutes, and the conversation ended. Caleb slid the black-and-white photos back in his case and rode with his eyes closed, fatigue still hovering nearby.

Andrew steered the car through the entrance and up the long, tree-lined drive. He parked in front of the Lillywood Manor Assisted Living Facility and shut the engine off.

"Okay, people, we're here," he said quietly.

Vanessa put her phone in her purse and ran her left hand down her fiancé's arm. "Do you want to go talk for a few minutes and look at the pictures?"

Andrew shook his head. "Not really. I could see them fair enough while I drove. If you say this guy looks like me—" He shrugged.

"Andy-man, it's spooky how much you guys look like each other from behind. Even have the same thin spot on the back of your head."

Andrew looked at Caleb. "Thanks, buddy. Nice of you to bring up something I'm already insecure about."

Caleb grinned. "No problem! Let's go talk to you mom."

All three exited at the same time and shut their doors in unison. Vanessa caught up with Andrew and slipped her arm inside his.

The main lobby at Lillywood Manor was warm and inviting. The building was spacious, lined with a variety of potted plants, all growing well under the natural light of the high-ceiling atrium. Several elderly couples shuffled past holding hands and smiling.

Andrew's mother was on the Alzheimer's wing. Though not guarded, the doors were secured to prevent residents from wandering away. Caleb and Vanessa waited on an overstuffed couch surrounded by ferns and backed up against a massive saltwater aquarium. Soft big-band-era music drifted down from recessed speakers in the ceiling. Andrew walked over to the reception desk while Vanessa and Caleb waited in a secluded alcove.

"This place is really nice," Vanessa murmured as she turned and gazed at the fresco relief paintings.

"I hope my kids do well enough to put me in a joint like this," Caleb said in agreement. "With my luck, I'll be chucked into a single-wide mobile home on some farmer's back-forty. Me, an old hound dog, and a dozen chickens. I'll be the crazy old Black man who sits on his front porch in his boxers while talking to his birds."

"And you'd be in your element." Vanessa said grinning.

Caleb nodded. "Pretty much." He glanced up when Andrew walked over.

"So, Mom's in her room and seems to be having a good day." He stuffed his hands in his pockets and slumped his shoulders. He resembled a tall twelve-year-old boy who'd just found out that his best friend couldn't come over and he'd have to go clothes shopping with his mom. "But she didn't seem to recognize my name when they told her I was here to visit." Andrew paused. "Don't know what we'll get out of the visit."

"You'll get to see your mom again," Vanessa said and kissed his forehead. "C'mon, let's go spend time with your mother."

An elderly nurse, appearing older than the residents, waited for them by the doors to the Alzheimer's wing.

"How long has Ms. Ida Mae been working here?" Vanessa asked as she waved to the nurse.

"Since way before we brought Mom here," Andrew replied. "I think she's been associated with the facility since it originally opened in the sixties on Silver Street."

Caleb nodded. "That's what she told me once. Said it all started back in the late forties when she was a candy-striper helping out wounded soldiers. She's been here—and on Silver Street—ever since."

"Hello, Andy and Vanessa." The nurse reached forward and lightly hugged them both. "And how are you, Deputy Saunders?" Ida Mae hugged him as well, but this embrace was stronger.

"I'm good, Ms. Jeffers," Caleb said, smiling and pulling away.

"And your mom?"

"Mean as ever!" Caleb replied, laughing.

"I know that's right!" Ida Mae replied, her old warbly voice cracking with delight. "Tell her I said 'hi' and that we missed her at poker night."

"I'll tell her, don't you worry." Caleb's smile was set on maximum intensity.

"Well, it's good to see you, folks," Ida Mae said, her thin, nearly translucent fingers pressing the button that opened the door to the Alzheimer's wing. "Most parents only see their children once in a blue moon. It warms my heart to see y'all visiting Mary Beth. She's a sweet lady. I know your mom misses you, Andrew."

Andrew smiled but shook his head. "I just wish she remembered me."

The nurse let the group step through the door, then closed it behind them. "She does, sweetheart. All mamas remember their children." Her eyes twinkled in the subdued lighting of the hallway. "They might not be able to say so, but they do."

"I don't know, she hasn't recognized me in months."

"But she remembers me!" Caleb added with a wide grin.

"Mr. Saunders, how could anyone ever forget you? You've been a rascal since the day you were born!"

"He's still a rascal." Vanessa laughed.

Ida Mae patted Caleb on the back. They reached Mary Beth Alewine's door, and the nurse stepped back to let them enter.

Mary Beth's room was simple. There was a bed to the left, a couch, chair, and coffee table against the far wall. A television was mounted on the wall across from the bed. Mary Beth sat on the couch in a simple pair of pants and a cotton shirt. Her hair was combed, and she was leafing through a magazine. She glanced up, then returned to her article.

"She still has a gleam in her eyes from your visit last week."

"That was two weeks ago," Andrew corrected Ida Mae.

"Are you sure? I could have sworn you were here. You were sitting on the couch talking. I was busy with another resident, so I didn't have time to stop and chat. But I did peek in on you two. Your mom's eyes were very clear, and she seemed to enjoy your visit immensely."

A cold shiver ran down his spine. "Ida Mae, what did this man look like?"

Ida Mae glanced from Andrew to Mary Beth, and paled. "Why, son, he looked just like you."

Chapter Twenty-three

"Andrew, quit teasing Ida Mae!" Vanessa said quickly. She turned to the nurse. "I don't know what gets into this boy. I think it's the time spent with his n'er do well best friend. He pulled this same stunt on me earlier this week, tried to make me think I was crazy!"

Ida Mae worked up a shaky smile and glanced over her shoulder at Andrew. "You tell that man of yours, next time he pulls a stunt like, that I'm gonna whop him good and hard on the head!"

"Ms. Ida Mae, if he pulls a stunt like that again, we're both going to whop him on the head, whop him something good!" Vanessa hugged the nurse, then watched her slowly leave the room and down the hallway. When Ida Mae turned the corner, Vanessa ducked back into the room.

Andrew sat beside his mother on the couch, talking quietly to her.

Caleb sat on the edge of the bed, his valise held against his stomach.

Vanessa sat down beside him. "Caleb, what in the world is going on?"

He shook his head slowly. "I have absolutely no idea."

"What does your gut tell you?"

"My gut tells me nothing. I don't have any plausible speculations."

"What about crazy, non-plausible, way-off-the-beaten-path speculations?" Vanessa asked feeling her blood beginning to chill.

Caleb pulled a pen and the pictures out of his case, put the base of the pen in his mouth, and began to chew it. "Well, if I had to foster a guess, I'd say Andrew has a sibling that looks very, very much like him." He glanced at Vanessa. "But that's just a wild-ass guess."

"And you think this long-lost brother is the same one from the trail cams? And he has now come to visit his mom?"

Caleb shrugged, shook his head, then nodded. "I don't know. Maybe." He placed the black and white pics on the bed. "I mean, what in the hell do you make out of these? Super crazy coincidences?"

Vanessa spread the pictures out and glanced between her fiancé and the mystery man. "This is unbelievable. If I hadn't known Andrew was with your boss or on the way to the hospital, I would have sworn this was him." Vanessa tapped a finger on the clearest pic caught on the trail cam, the one showing a clear, partial profile. "Do you want to have Mary Beth take a look at these?"

"Possibly, but let's see if she'll talk to me. Andrew appears to be striking out." Caleb motioned toward his friend.

Andrew sat beside his mom, hands in his lap, talking quietly to her.

Mary Beth continued to turn the pages in a magazine without acknowledging her son.

"Wish me luck," Caleb whispered and walked over to the coffee table. He pulled an extra chair over and sat.

"Hey Mrs. B!" Caleb said, using the nickname he had called Andrew's mom since they were kids. He ignited his intense smile.

Mary Beth stopped thumbing through the magazine, closed it, and glanced up at him. For several moments, she just stared blankly at Caleb, her eyes washing over him, no recognition forming. Then she reached out and patted his head. A smile formed slowly. "Caleb?" she asked haltingly. "Shouldn't you be working today?"

Caleb glanced at Andrew, who gave him a subtle thumbs-up gesture. "No, ma'am. Boss let us all go early today, said it was 'go visit a grandparent day.' And since my grandparents have already gone to heaven, I thought I'd come visit you!"

Mary Beth snorted and her eyes flared. "Your boss sounds lazy."

"Yes, ma'am. That's what my mom says as well. I was hoping to run into your son. Is he here?"

"My son?" Mary Beth asked as her brow furrowed. "I haven't seen Andrew today." Her gaze drifted off, as her hands shook slightly. She quieted for a moment before a spark returned to her eyes. "But he was here just the other day. We had a good talk!"

Caleb glanced past Mary Beth to Andrew who shook his head and indicated the statement was false.

"Well, that's good! What all did y'all talk about?"

At this, Mary Beth stared directly at Caleb. "Well, he wanted to know how I was doing, if I needed anything, and about the hospital he was born in." Andrew's mom closed her eyes, tilted her head and rubbed the edge of her chin with her index finger. She began to laugh lightly. "I think I told him too much." Mary Beth dropped her hands to her lap.

"What did you tell him?" Caleb asked, forcing a grin, resisting the urge to try and press for information. "That he was getting a puppy for Christmas?"

Mary Beth's smile faltered and her eyes narrowed. "No, of course not." She held her gaze on Caleb.

"I'm sorry Mrs. B, I was just teasing."

"Not very funny, Mr. Smarty Pants. But you've always been a smart-alecky kid." She reached forward and pinched his cheek. "But I love you just the same." Mary Beth leaned back and sighed. "I don't think he was very happy after we talked."

"Mrs. B, why would Andrew be unhappy? What could you possibly say to Andy-man that would upset him?" Caleb tried his wide smile, but could only work up a pale version of it.

"I told him about the adoption."

Caleb flashed another glance over to Andrew whose eyes were wide and face pale. "Andrew was adopted?" He didn't have to feign being shocked. "He never told me."

Mary Beth nodded and leaned in close, her voice dropped to a whisper. "We couldn't tell him!" She glanced around and stared through Andrew as if he didn't exist. "You know how he is, so sensitive. His father, God rest his soul, said it would be best if we just kept it a secret. Besides, we couldn't tell him everything."

"Mrs. B, why was that?"

Andrew's mom sat up and backed away from Caleb. She bit her bottom lip as her eyes began to water. She put her hands over her face and slowly shook her head. "I don't want to talk about it."

"But Mrs. B, if Andrew was upset, I might be able to talk to him, help him understand. He's my best friend and sometimes listens to me." Caleb turned on his bright smile.

Mary Beth's lips trembled as a tear trickled down her cheek. She regained control over her emotions, sat up straighter, and ran a finger through her hair. "You're a good friend, Caleb. My boy is lucky to have you." Mary Beth said and patted him on the knee.

"So, Mrs. B, what couldn't you tell him?"

"That he had a brother." She said quietly.

Caleb leaned in closer, sensing Mary Beth was pulling back. "Mrs. B, was it an older brother?"

Mary Beth shook her head.

"Younger brother?" Caleb pressed.

Again, Mary Beth shook her head and withdrew farther into herself.

"Were they twins?" Caleb asked, his voice quieter, mirroring Mary Beth.

Andrew's mother nodded, her eyes now on her hands and the magazine was fumbling with.

Caleb caught Vanessa out of the corner of his eye rising from the bed and beginning to pace around the small room. Andrew was motionless. "Mrs. B, why couldn't you adopt both?"

"Because we could only afford one child."

"You didn't have enough money to take care of two children?"

Mary Beth shook her head. "We didn't have enough money to *pay* for both."

Chapter Twenty-Four

No one spoke for several minutes. Mary Beth fumbled with the magazine and stared at the floor. Andrew and Caleb turned to each other, then shrugged at the unspoken question: *What now?* Both looked up when a shadow crossed the doorway and entered.

"Hello, how is everyone?" Ida Mae stood just inside the door with a small tray of food and drink. She smiled, seemingly dismissing the heavy atmosphere.

"Mary Beth, are you ready for your afternoon snack?" Ida Mae poured Kool-Aid into a small plastic cup. She unwrapped a sandwich and cut it into sugar cube-sized bites. "Did you guys have a nice talk?"

Mary Beth stood, using Caleb's shoulder to push off from, and shuffled across the room. "We did!" she responded in her quiet, shaky voice. "My son's friend came to visit, and we had a wonderful talk."

"Did your son also come to visit?" Ida Mae asked as she put the sandwich bites on a small plate. The nurse turned to Caleb and Andrew, then subtly motioned them to sit still.

Mary Beth's eyes darkened. "No, he did not. He said he was coming back. I think he's going to look for his birth-mother, that tramp."

"Well, maybe he'll still stop by. You know young people can't sit still for more than a few minutes at a time."

Vanessa grabbed a memo pad beside the bed and wrote furiously. She showed it to Ida Mae. The old nurse's face tightened, then she slowly nodded.

"Mary Beth, do you remember his birth mother's name?"

Andrew's mom stopped nibbling at the sandwich cubes. She twisted around in her chair to glare at the old nurse. "Why would I want to remember her name? She was a druggie, a total junkie. Probably dead anyway!" Mary Beth turned back to her food. "Only good thing she ever did was give up her babies."

"Everyone has a little good in them," Ida Mae replied. The nurse caught Caleb's eye and motioned toward the door.

Mary Beth continued to nibble on her snack and ignored Andrew and Caleb as they quietly slipped out of the room.

Ida Mae stepped a few feet down the hall, then allowed a small chuckle. "My, that is some imagination your mom has!" she said, directing the comment to Andrew.

"Yes, ma'am, it is," Andrew answered quickly.

"If y'all want to stay a bit longer, that's fine with me. But the medication I'm about to give her will make her sleepy. She usually takes a nap afterward."

Andrew's mom was still nibbling at her food like an aging rabbit when he stepped back into the room and gave her a quick kiss on the cheek. She startled, relaxed a bit, then went back to eating. He stepped out of her room, brushing a tear off his face.

"Son, she has her good days and bad." Ida Mae Jeffers reached out and gave him a quick hug. "Come back any time you can. She might not show it, but it does warm her heart."

Caleb slipped an arm around Andy's shoulders and gave him a brotherly squeeze. "C'mon, Andy-man, your mom's got to take her meds. We'll come back again next week."

Andrew dropped his head and nodded. Vanessa took his right hand, pulled him in close, and kissed him on the nose. He glanced up and allowed a brief smile. "Watching mom eat made me hungry. Anyone down for tacos?"

Vanessa let go of his hand and playfully pushed him away. "Is that all you think about, food?"

"I can't help it!" Andrew shrugged and smiled sheepishly. "I got hungry watching mom eat."

Caleb shook his head. "Son, you never cease to amaze me." They reached the doors to the main lobby. "Monterey Cabana good for you guys?"

Vanessa and Andrew nodded eagerly, waved to the front desk nurse, then walked briskly to Andrew's car. Twenty minutes later Andrew pulled into a TexMex restaurant as the lunch crowd was thinning. They asked for a booth in the rear of the restaurant and were seated under a mural of the Texas-Mexican border. The Rio Grande river ran down the wall to the floor and halfway across the restaurant. Patrons sitting to the left of the line, to the north, received a traditional American food menu. Those sitting to the south, a menu listing Mexican entrees. Since their booth straddled the blue line, they received a menu for each.

A young, blond waitress took their drink order, promised to be back soon, and disappeared down the row of booths and tables. Caleb watched her leave before turning to the sound of Vanessa clearing her throat in an unapproving tone.

"Sorry, but this place hires some of the best-looking women," Caleb grinned.

"She's like, what, twenty—barely," Vanessa said, rolling her eyes.

"What's the big deal? I liked girls when *I was* twenty."

Vanessa crumpled up a napkin and threw it at him. "You know what the deal is. Tell him, Andrew."

"She wants you to be like me," Andrew said, playing with the saltshaker, "and date old women."

Caleb laughed hard enough to rock the booth.

Vanessa turned on Andrew and wrapped her hands around his throat.

"Never thought an old woman would be strong enough to strangle me." Andrew fake wheezed as if his air had been cut off.

Vanessa pulled Andrew in close, kissed him playfully all over his cheek, then licked his forehead. "Next time I do that after eating Brussel sprouts!"

"God, no, not that." Andrew faked horror. "I like young women, not old biddies." he said quickly as he escaped the smooch attack. he glanced up to see the waitress now standing at the table with a tray of drinks. "Piece of advice, if you want a good tip, don't call her old."

The drinks were passed out and their orders taken. A second waiter stopped by and dropped off chips and salsa. Vanessa grabbed a chip, dipped it, then looked up at Andrew and Caleb. "Okay, boys, we need to talk about what went on with Mary Beth." She paused to eat the chip. "Do y'all think her mind has slipped more, or is she telling the truth?"

Caleb shrugged, grabbed a chip, and followed Vanessa's example. He ate it whole and turned to Andrew. "What do you think?"

"I'm hoping she's telling the truth. Then I can *finally* have someone to blame for all the crap I was supposed to have done as a kid. And let me tell you something, that would be a *huge* relief!"

Andrew spread his arms wide and stared at the ceiling. "Man, I feel better already!"

"Be serious, silly man," Vanessa said with a snort. "Honestly, what do you think? That was a lot to digest. I'm sure some of it hurt."

Andrew dropped his hands in his lap and shook his head. "I don't know, really. On one side I hope she's slipping. I know that sounds horrible, but if she's telling the truth . . . ."

Caleb nodded and squeezed the lemon floating in his tea. He glanced up, his expression no longer jovial. "Let's say we take her words at face value. Are we to believe Andy-man was adopted . . . illegally? Hells-bells, Andy is evidence of a crime." Caleb barked a quick laugh, then sobered. "This is messed up."

Glancing up, Andrew sipped his Pepsi. "If I'm evidence, can you put me in the narcotics lock-up room? I mean, that's where you keep the good stuff, right?"

Vanessa's eyes flashed at her fiancé and she elbowed him hard enough to make him spill his drink. "Boy, I'm going to beat you black and blue if you don't take this serious!"

"Yeah, Andy-man," Caleb said, "this is a ton to deal with. I'm having a hard time processing it, and it's not even my life. It's yours and it's got to hurt like hell."

Andrew quieted and stared across the room. He then grabbed a stack of napkins and mopped up the table. "I am taking this serious—or as seriously as I can," he said slowly, but with harshness to his words. He slid the stack of wet towels to the side, put his elbows on the table, clenched his hands together, and stared over his knuckles. His hands shook, and his knuckles turned white. "How would you feel if you found out the novels you had been writing mirror murders across the country, that you're being pursued by a nut-case sheriff and, just to add a bit more to your mental plate of fucked-up shit," Andrew's voice rose and diners glanced his way, "your parents purchased you like a goddamn puppy! Probably kept me in a crate to keep me from peeing on the floor." He picked up his drink, his arm was shaking, and he sloshed tee on the table. Andrew gave up on trying to drink from the glass and placed it back on the table. "Kinda having a bad week, so excuse me, I'm not handling it well!" Andrew practically shouted. He unclenched his hands, put his palms flat on the table, and leaned back. "I'm fucking handling it the best I can," he said softly, and closed his eyes.

A soft cough made Andrew look up. The waitress stood at their table with her order pad in hand, pen hovering slightly above it, and an uncertain gaze in her eyes. "Are you guys ready to order? I could come back."

Caleb turned on his smile and removed some of the anxiety from the waitress's expression. "Yes, we are!" He handed the waitress the menu. "I'll have the lunch special just as it is on the menu."

The waitress hesitantly turned to Andrew.

"And I'll have the complete mental meltdown with all the trimmings, and a house salad, easy on the dressing." Andrew slid his menu across the table. "I'm trying to eat healthy." He folded his hands together and smiled.

The waitress cringed slightly and turned to Vanessa.

"What the asswipe beside me meant to say is that he, too, would like the lunch special, we both would. And that he's sorry for being such an *ass*!" Vanessa reached down and pinched Andrew's side, just above the belt, hard enough to make him yelp.

The waitress's hand was still lingering above the order pad, her eyes flickering back and forth between Andrew and Vanessa.

"Yes, the lunch special, for both of us," Andrew said.

The waitress began to write slowly, the tension in her face palpable as she backed from the table.

"And a house salad!" he added as the woman walked away.

The waitress stopped and turned slowly. "Light on the dressing?"

"Yes, indeed, that's an excellent suggestion! As you know, I'm eating healthy."

Caleb stared at Andrew and shook his head. "Man, you are one weird-ass dude." He stifled a quick laugh with his hand. "You've got some serious issues."

"Runs in the family," Andrew replied as he pulled the basket of tortilla chips in front of him. He wrapped an arm around the basket and leaned over to it to guard his possession. When Vanessa attempted to wrestle them from him, he barked and tried to bite her.

Chapter Twenty-Five

By the time the frazzled waitress dropped off the check, there were four empty beer bottles and two empty margarita glasses. Caleb and Vanessa only had tea to drink. Andrew lounged against Vanessa, his eyes glassy.

"You feeling better?" Vanessa asked.

"Very much so greatly," Andrew slurred.

"Are you going to apologize to the waitress?"

"Yeah, probably should." Andrew sat up and leaned against the table using his elbows to support him. "I'll give her a good tip as well."

"Well, I guess that concludes the *Andy Show*. Let's leave before they call my buddies," Caleb advised and pushed back from the table. "Can he walk?" He directed his question to Vanessa.

"If I time my sways with the rolling of the restaurant, I'll be fine." Andrew slid from the booth, staggered, and grabbed the table for balance. "Do y'all want me to drive?"

"No!" Caleb and Vanessa said together.

"Sheesh, y'all didn't have to shout," Andrew muttered.

Vanessa looped an arm around Andrew's waist, steered him between the tables, and to the front of the restaurant. A restaurant manager held the front door open for them, glanced at Andrew, rolled his eyes, and shook his head.

"He'll be all right," Caleb said, helping Andrew through the exit. "He had a bad reaction to his medicine."

"I take it the medicine was the almost six-pack of beer and two margaritas?"

"That'd be the medicine, yes, sir." Caleb nodded.

"Maybe the doctor should change his prescription."

"I was going to suggest the same thing." Caleb patted the man on the shoulder. "Sorry for the mess. We left a nice tip for the waitress. Hopefully, with time and professional help, she can put this behind her."

The manager of Monterrey Cabana smiled. "It's all good. Not often does the afternoon crowd get lunch *and* a show. You guys take care."

Caleb saluted the man, then hurried across the parking lot, reaching the car in time to help Vanessa pour Andrew into the backseat. Vanessa handed Caleb the keys and climbed into the front passenger seat. She slumped, buried her face in her hands, then sat forward, and stared out the windshield.

"Have you ever, in all the years you guys have spent doing stupid things, seen him like this?"

Caleb started the car, put it in reverse, and backed out of the parking spot. He dropped the transmission in drive, glanced at Vanessa, and shook his head. "Never . . . ever." Caleb into the rearview mirror. "Boy's passed out."

"No, I'm not," came the muddled protest from the backseat.

Vanessa turned around, reached back, and patted his knee. "Go to sleep, silly man. When you sober up, we'll talk about your mom."

"If I stay drunk, can we ignore the subject?"

"No, sweetheart. We'll just talk about her without you." Vanessa turned back around.

"I'm good with that," Andrew replied.

Caleb drove toward his friend's home, turning the radio up to cover Andrew's snoring.

Andrew slumped on his couch and sipped coffee from a trembling mug while Vanessa leaned against him, thumbing through the TV channels. Caleb sat across from them, steadily writing notes on a yellow legal pad.

Caleb set the pad down. "So, how does the Amazing Andrew feel? How's your head?"

"I still can't believe I had the staff calling me the Amazing Andrew. How many readings did I try to do?"

"Just one, sweetie. You grabbed a customer's phone off their table, tried to 'twinge' on it, tripped, and knocked an entire tray of food out of a server's hand."

"Yeah, Andy-man. Not one of your finest moments," Caleb said.

"God, I'm not going to be able to show my face in there for years," Andrew moaned and slumped further into the couch.

"I don't know about that." Vanessa sat up and took the coffee cup out of Andrew's hand. "The management said they'd like you to do two shows next Friday, and one on Saturday."

Caleb laughed hard, leaned forward, and high-fived Vanessa.

"Ha-ha, very funny," Andrew groused. "Kick a man when he's down and drunk."

"Hopefully, the kicking will sober you up a bit. We need to talk in a serious, sober way about today." Caleb picked up his notepad. "Something is going on here that I'm having a hard time wrapping my head around. I've been making some notes that should finish sobering you up."

Andrew pushed himself off the couch and stumbled around it. "Let me take a shower and clear my head. Then we'll talk."

"Sounds like a plan, Andy-man." They fist-bumped when Andrew passed.

Vanessa returned to her spot on the couch with a fresh glass of tea. "So, what're your thoughts on the situation?"

Taking a deep breath and releasing it slowly, Caleb stretched his feet out on an ottoman and shook his head slowly. "This is going to sound crazy as hell, but this is what I believe." He retrieved his notepad and started reading from the bullet-point items he had compiled covering the last thirty-six hours. Several times he stood, walked around the small den and asked if she still followed. Each time she nodded but didn't speak. He'd then sit and continue to read until he felt he needed to stand once more. It took him about forty minutes to illustrate his ideas.

"So, what do you think?" Caleb asked when he finished.

Vanessa leaned back against the cushions, stared at the ceiling, and ran her fingers through her long dark hair. "I think—" She balanced her hands in front of her face as if trying to weigh the difference between two major decisions.

"She's trying to decide if you're as crazy as I am," Andrew said for her. He now stood in the room wearing shorts and tee-shirt. He toweled his hair and wiped moisture out of his ears.

"Crazy? You two passed nutty some years back. You're both now certifiably insane!" Vanessa said laughing. "You can't expect me to believe this...any of this, can you?"

Andrew dropped down on the far end of the couch from Vanessa, leaned against the armrest, and glanced her way. "So, what are you having a hard time believing? That I have a twin? Or that I have an evil twin?"

"Both!" Vanessa practically shouted. "I mean, how in the hell can you believe it?"

"I didn't say I believed it, per se. It's just that—" He shrugged and sagged on the couch. "How do you make sense of everything we've seen and heard?"

Vanessa jumped up and paced. "There has to be a simple explanation, one we can all wrap our heads around."

"There is." Caleb stood and stretched. "Andrew's mom bought him from a crack whore and left his brother behind. Brother is insane, gets his jollies by killing people, and Andrew is reliving these murders through his dreams. The dreams are expressed in his writings. See? Very simple."

"Makes sense to me." Andrew fist-bumped Caleb, then opened his fingers and let them flutter in the air as if his fist had exploded.

"You two wouldn't know 'sense' if it jumped up and bit you in the ass." Vanessa continued to pace while rubbing her palms together. "Okay, there's only one way to settle this. We need to find Andy's birth mom."

"And how do you plan on doing that?" Andrew asked.

Vanessa stopped pacing, ran her hands through her hair, and pulled it hard behind her head. "I have no idea. Let's let the detective boy figure it out."

Caleb leaned forward and tapped his chest. "You want *me* to find his mom?"

"Well, who else has the resources?" Vanessa countered.

"I'll do what I can." Caleb said. "But I'm also helping the investigating into a child's abduction and a dozen other less serious crimes. Not to mention the fact that Barnes would blow his stack if he knew how much we had discussed."

"But you're his *best friend!*" Vanessa shot back. "I'd think you'd want to do everything you can to help him."

Caleb stood and took Vanessa by the hand. He held it in both of his. "He is my best friend, and I will do everything I can, but I also have a boss to answer to that is not convinced of Andrew's innocence. I could lose my job—my badge—and then we'd all be working blind."

Vanessa's eyes teared up.

Caleb wrapped her in a quick hug. "C'mon, girl, relax. We're going to figure this out. We just need to be careful and not step on Barnes's toes."

"You're right." Vanessa wiped her eyes with the back of her hand. "I just feel so helpless."

Caleb hugged her again. "It's all right, counselor. We'll figure it out."

Vanessa nodded but didn't answer.

"Hey, guys, either get a room or step away from the TV. *Cops* is coming on in a few minutes, and it's always fun to see Caleb's profession in action." Andrew powered up the television behind them.

"I say we get a room," Caleb cooed in Vanessa's ear.

"That's fine," Andrew said as he leaned over to see around them. "Just don't wear my pajamas."

Vanessa pulled loose from Caleb, grabbed a pillow off the couch, and held it over Andrew's face. "We might make you watch!"

"That's fine." Andrew's reply was muffled by the pillow. "Just leave my pajamas out of it. They've done nothing wrong."

Chapter Twenty-Six

Caleb arrived an hour early at the Sheriff's Department for his morning shift. He was already logged into his computer when Barnes strolled in through the rear door, whistling. The sound made Caleb's skin crawl.

"Deputy Saunders, you're here early." Barnes stopped beside Caleb's desk and glanced down at him.

"Yes, sir," Caleb replied and turned his chair to face his boss. He leaned back and rested an ankle across his knee, leaving one foot on the floor. "I thought about the trail cams and wondered if other cameras captured any photos."

"Forensics' was out earlier checking all the cameras but I haven't heard back. Any luck?"

"No, sir. Just a few blurry pics of deer and a very curious bobcat."

Barnes nodded, pursed his lips as if he were going to speak, then walked off whistling. Caleb stood and watched the man greet several arriving deputy's, enter his office, shut the door, and pull the blinds. *What is that obnoxious ass up to?*

Caleb settled back into his chair and turned his attention to the never-ending flow of reports and emails. It was nearly 11:00am, he'd already burned through several hours of his workday and was pouring his fourth cup of coffee in the breakroom when a tired, exhausted couple walked past and sat on a couch in a secluded corner of the building. The wife, petite and slender, sat with her arms wrapped tight across her chest. A man with wide, strong shoulders and thick arms sat beside her, one arm around her shoulders, his free hand nervously sliding a ballcap back and forth on his head before curling the bill of his hat in his hands. *The parents of the missing boy. Shit, there's not a damn thing they can do, and it's killing them.*

Taking a cautious sip of coffee, Caleb turned to find Barnes standing in his path, staring at him. Caleb startled, staggered back quickly, and sloshed coffee over his hands and onto his Warrenton Sheriff's Department pull-over dress shirt. "Damn, Sheriff, you shouldn't sneak up on people like that!" Caleb held the cup at a distance as brown rivulets ran down the cup and off his hands.

Barnes didn't react, just stared at him through piercing dark eyes.

"Deputy," Barnes said flatly. "You appear jumpy. Any reason why?"

"Jumpy, sir?" Caleb switched the coffee cup to his left hand and shook the drops off his right. "I didn't expect to find you looming over my shoulder like a gargoyle. Kinda spooked me, sir." He smiled broadly and held his free hand up like a claw, hoping his grin would diffuse the situation.

"You think I resemble a gargoyle, deputy? Is that how you see me?" Barnes turned his head and called across the room, "Deputy Saunders thinks I resemble a gargoyle. Anyone else see me that way?" The only response was the soft buzz of the lights and bland acoustic music from the recessed ceiling speakers.

Caleb stared over Barnes's shoulder and sighed. "Sir, you don't resemble a gargoyle. It was a poor attempt at humor." He put his gaze back on his superior and locked eyes. "I apologize for demeaning you."

The sheriff held Caleb's gaze, then stepped aside to let him pass. "My office, Mr. Saunders. Five minutes."

"Yes, sir," Caleb said quietly and exited the break area. *Peckerhead,* he thought as he crossed to his desk. No one would make eye contact; all kept their face neutral as if he didn't exist and that the brief stand-off with their boss hadn't happened.

He swung his chair from his desk, dropped into it, and was tapping hard on the keyboard by the time he pulled up close to the desk. "What kind of shit is this," he muttered. The intra-department website that contained the trail-cam photos was now password secured. Caleb attempted a couple of runs at it. When those failed, he slumped in his chair. His desk phone chimed. He let it ring several times before reluctantly picking it up.

"Yes, sir?"

"My office. Now." Barnes said and broke the connection.

Slapping the keyboard away from him where it fell in a clatter, Caleb stood and made the short walk across the floor to his boss's glass-fronted office. The blinds were already pulled—not a good sign.

Rapping on the door frame, Caleb stepped through and closed the door without being asked.

Barnes was staring at a new collection of black and white photos. "Have a seat," he said without taking his eyes off the pictures.

Caleb sat.

"Deputy Saunders, did I not give you explicit instructions to not discuss this investigation with Mr. Alewine?"

Leaning forward with his palms on his knees, Caleb said, "Sir, I haven't discussed the investigation with Andr—Mr. Alewine."

Still shuffling through the pictures, Barnes continued, "Your login was used to access the department's trail camera downloads."

"I did, yes, sir. I wanted to see if anything new had been posted."

"You have also spent an inordinate time with him over the past few days and have logged in remotely with your county-issued laptop."

Caleb clenched the sides of the chair and was tensed to stand. "First, Andrew Alewine is my very best friend. Second, I have never and would never compromise this investigation," he said sharply. "My best friend hit his head and was hospitalized because you ordered him to use his talent to help in the investigation." His voice was down to a growl. "I spent time with him at the hospital and then went with him to visit his mother. Nothing there would compromise the investigation."

Barnes straightened the pictures in his hands, tapping them lightly to make sure they were all aligned. He sorted them in his hand as if they were an eight-by-ten deck of cards, selected two, and dropped them on the edge of his desk. He slid them toward Caleb.

Caleb picked up the pictures. The first one was of Andrew's ghost—a profile shot—and the same female in the earlier pictures.

"Still haven't identified the female in this picture." Barnes said then tossed him a second photo.

This one was of a young male, about age ten or eleven. Caleb cupped his chin, nodding slightly. "The Hanover boy."

"Correct. Missing over forty-eight hours now. The only leads we have are the boy's phone and bike. So far, the van has been a bust, wiped clean." Barnes held onto one more picture. "Those and these trail-cam pictures. The first set was taken about the time your *friend*—

" Barnes said "friend" as if the word were toxic, moving from it quickly. "Woke up and told us about the van."

Barnes sifted through the trail cam shots before handing more to Caleb. "The pictures you are holding—the ones clear enough to share—were taken around seven this morning, four miles from the landing."

Caleb leaned forward, anticipation igniting deep inside his head. He studied the photos, trying to read their angle to the rising sun. "Which way are they heading?"

Barnes laughed hard and with little enjoyment. "Heading? They aren't heading anywhere. If you can believe it, they are traveling in a circle!"

"A circle?" Caleb stammered. "Are you sure?"

Leaning over his desk, Barnes planted his elbows and clasped his hands. "Quite. This fool even scuffed up the dirt to make sure we didn't miss the fact he was making one big-ass circle."

"He's toying with us," Caleb said and sat back in the chair. "Why would he do that?"

Barnes released his hands and held them up in a "your guess is as good as mine" gesture.

Caleb glanced back down at the pictures. The woods were very dense, the sun's light barely filtering through. The woman wasn't tied or restrained. Her hair appeared tangled, and her jeans had dark stains Caleb hoped was mud. In one clear photo her face was drawn, eyes barely open.

The camera didn't catch a picture of the boy with his head up. The child's eyes were on the ground in all the pictures. Caleb could just make out smears that could be mud on his face. But it had to be Lance Hanover—he was still wearing the clothes his parents described.

Their abductor never looked directly into any of the cameras. All the pictures were partial profiles, or his head was down. Regardless of the camera angle, if Caleb hadn't spent the last couple of days with Andrew, he would have sworn that the thin man in the grainy black and white photos was his best friend.

"What do you make of this, detective?" Barnes asked in a softer, almost subdued voice.

Shaking his head, Caleb was slow to answer. He steepled his hand, covered his mouth, and slowly shook his head. "Sir, it's . . . bizarre. Why kidnap a kid and a young woman, then parade them around where we can see them?"

"Hell, if I know." Barnes leaned back in his chair, the springs creaking under the load. "At least we know the pair are alive—for now."

For now, Caleb thought. *But for how long?*

A snapping noise caused Caleb to look up. "Detective, back with me, son!" Barnes said with a note of irritation in his voice.

"Sorry, sir. Kinda got lost in my head there for a moment."

"Don't get too lost. I need some answers, and I don't need to tell you that I need them as of this morning." Barnes picked up the handset for his phone, signaling the meeting was over, then paused. "And, Deputy, once again, do not share any of the details of this investigation with your friend, no matter how much you feel you need to. I want the flow of information to go from your mouth to my ears—or Sweeny's. Nowhere else. I have requested additional assets from the State, and they will be on site soon. Until then, our forensics team is working their ass off and I need you to on top of all developments. Am I clear?"

"Yes, sir." Caleb stood and pulled the door shut behind him, paused, and glanced at a large clock hanging over the reception desk near the front door. The red numerals indicated that the time was 11:18 am. It was way too early for lunch, but not too early to walk out back, throw an armload of shadow punches, maybe pull out some of his tight-cropped hair. He grabbed a coke out of the department's refrigerator, then set a mad pace out the back door.

Chapter Twenty-Seven

The day was heating up fast, the humidity climbing. Caleb sat at a picnic table under the remaining water oak tree behind the station. The long, spindly limbs stretched fifty feet in each direction, casting leafy shadows over the table and a handful of prime summertime parking spaces which were occupied nearly twenty-four hours a day. His truck was currently sitting in the middle of the parking lot, baking on the asphalt stovetop.

Caleb used the Coke from the department fridge, chilled almost down to almost slush, to cool his brow. A 1970s-era gold-colored Buick Electra 225 came slinking in from a side street. The large V8 rumbled low and quiet as the tires—complete with four-inch-wide whitewalls—prowled the back of the building. The car passed by his table, drove to the end of the lot, then circled back behind him and parked four spaces down. The windows were jet-black, way beyond legal limits, Caleb surmised, stopping him from seeing the driver inside. Not that it mattered. The vanity tag—*peekaboo*—told him everything he needed to know. He was already drying the condensation from the can off his hands when the driver's door was pushed open with exaggerated slowness.

A tall, thin, aged to the point of being antique, Black man slowly stood. His hair resembled unruly cotton, thick and wooly. He wore gold aviator glasses that matched his car and an expertly tailored three-piece suit. He glanced Caleb's way and saluted.

Caleb smiled and returned the salute.

The man made his way slowly around the nose of his Buick, right hand trailing along the hood, left hand firmly planted on an ornate cane. He shuffled Caleb's way, the shoes making soft scuffing noises, the cane tapping the asphalt. Retrieving a monogrammed handkerchief from an inside coat pocket, the man wiped his forehead and bowed slightly.

"Joseph Abraham, as I live and breathe," Caleb said, his smile growing to a full-fledged grin, his eyes squinting in delight. "Bad pennies always show up when you're not looking for them!"

"In the flesh, young man, in the flesh." Joseph smiled and offered his hand.

Caleb shook it warmly. "I thought you'd be retired by now, living the good life in some old-folks home in Florida, causing trouble and pinching the butt of some nurse!"

"I was, sure enough. But I got tired of all those achy, moaning old men. Old farts can't do nothing but complain and play cards. That, and fall asleep in the middle of a sentence. I ain't got time for all that. I'm a rolling stone, and I ain't gathering no moss."

"You still using that PI badge to spy on folks, get the dirt on cheating husbands?"

Joseph nodded. "Gotta pay the bills somehow, young man. Plus, the more old men I run off, the better the pickings are for me." He grinned and waggled his busy white eyebrows.

Caleb laughed, gave the man a fist bump and inclined his head toward the classic Buick. "I see you're still driving Lucille."

"You know it! They don't make cars like her no more. Plus, when I'm prowling, I can shoot to my heart's content and not gather so much as a second glance." Joseph stared lovingly over at his two-ton hunk of Detroit iron. "Yessir, she's, old, creaky, and out of date. But so am I!"

Both men laughed hard.

"So, what brings you back to town?"

"My nephew said he needed help on a case—wanted me to do some surveillance work, watch a couple of guys, and see what they're up to."

Shaking his head, Caleb took a deep breath and glanced coolly at Joseph. "How did you come out so laid back and calm, and your nephew turned into such a—"

"Prick?" Joseph added for him

Caleb choked, surprised by the candor of his old friend. "I was going to say, 'hard ass', but your phrase is pretty accurate."

Joseph sighed and shook his head. "Boy's been wound tight as a tick since the day he entered this world. But we get along well enough, I suppose." He nodded as if in agreement with himself and leaned heavily on his cane.

"Well, Joseph, my breaks over, gotta get back to it. If you don't mind me asking, who does he have you watching?" Caleb pushed off the picnic table.

A twinkle came to Joseph's eyes and a wide grin split his face.

"You've got to be kidding!"

"Nope, 'fraid not. Whatever you done, it's gotten under my nephew's skin something fierce."

Caleb slumped back down on the table as Joseph cackled and patted his back. "Just funning with you, boy." He laughed again, having to use his cane and Caleb's shoulder to keep from toppling over. Joseph cut the laugh off, straightened his tie, and leaned on his ornately carved staff with both hands, his long fingers wrapped around the lion head topping it. "But he did ask me to take a look at some pictures he has and to see if I could help."

"Joseph, I know enough about your reputation, that if you sniff a good story building, you would insert yourself in the middle of it somehow." Caleb finished with a knowing grin. "So, were you really invited to help or decided to thrust yourself into the middle of it?"

Shaking his head, then nodding, Joseph said, "I hear stuff, weird things a-going on. I see my nephew the other day in the store and ask him what's up. You know Timmy, likes to keep everything close, thinks only he can see all the angles. After a few minutes of jawing he gives me the skinny, and I mean Ethiopian skinny." He laughs his thin, old man cackle again. "As in not a whole lot. But I listen to what he has to say and don't comment." Joseph's eyes take on a distant gaze as he recalls the conversation. "I tell him I'd come down today and we can hash it out. I take it he's in his office?"

Caleb nodded. "Yes, sir." Standing, he took the elderly man's arm and guided him across the parking lot.

"You still hanging around with that scrawny redhead fellow?" Joseph asked.

"Yep, see him almost daily." They took a couple of more steps before Caleb pulled the man to a stop. "How do you know Andrew?" he asked.

Joseph smiled his "boy, I've got lots of secrets" smile. "Just do. I keep tabs on folks—who's friends with who, who hates who, who's sleeping with—well you know where I was going."

"I actually don't," Caleb said evenly while still holding on to the other man's arm. "You and Andrew run in completely different orbits. You couldn't be more different."

"True, true," Joseph said. "But our local storyteller and me have a connection—one that goes back a long, long time."

The air no longer felt hot and stifling. The heat rising off the asphalt no longer baked his feet. Caleb felt his skin draw up, a cold ripple in his body. "Explain yourself, Joseph."

The old man's eyes narrowed on Caleb, then softened and he glanced away. "Take me inside and get me out of this heat. I'm an old man and don't feel like dropping dead just yet. I'll tell you what I can as soon as you get me out of this infernal outdoor toaster oven."

The door to the station opened as they approached. Barnes waited for them. "Did you have a nice break, Deputy?"

"Yes, I did, very refreshing," Caleb said and moved around his boss. He stepped through the door and paused just inside. He turned to face the elderly man now being gently assisted by his nephew. "Joseph, I want to finish our conversation—if possible, by the end of my shift today."

"I'll catch up with you, Deputy. If not today, then soon."

Barnes stood between the men, his back to Caleb, stopping Joseph from progressing further into the building. Caleb was going to push the issue when an officer manning the information kiosk called over to him, advising he had a call holding regarding a weekend burglary.

Shit. "Thanks, Judy. Tell them I'll pick up at my desk."

"Joseph," Caleb said as he backed away. "I really need to finish this conversation."

Joseph saluted. "Aye, aye, captain. We'll be in touch."

Barnes never turned around or acknowledged his withdrawal.

Caleb flipped the page on the small spiral notebook he always kept with him. It was as much a part of his daily routine as putting his service weapon into its holster on his belt. The next page was blank. It had taken two hours to transpose all his notes on the investigations he was working into his computer data log. *Thank God*, he breathed, rolled his head, and leaned back hard. His spine released a series of satisfying pops. He felt an instant release of pressure, not realizing how tense he was. The small cigarette pack-sized clock on the edge of his desk flashed eight minutes after seven. He should've been out of the building over thirty minutes ago, but the non-stop flood of reports kept him tied to his workstation. A shadow crashed down hard on the edge of his desk.

"Long day, Saunders?"

A small, wry smile creased Caleb's lip. "You could say that, sir." He sagged in his chair. "Judge Satterfield okayed a search warrant for Eugene Castle's storage unit. I believe we're going to find everything we need to connect him to the Speedway Gas-n-Go robbery."

"That's good, that's real good. I've been catching some heat on that one. Senator's son gets capped in the ass in a late-night robbery gone wrong and everyone gets excited." Barnes managed a smile.

"He's lucky the round hit his wallet. Bet he won't play hero again," Caleb said.

"True, very true." Barnes dropped his hands to his belt, resting his thumbs on the inside of the leather.

"Sir, I was about to log off the system. Is there something I can help you with before I do?"

Barnes continued to stare at the ceiling, took a deep breath, and let it out slowly. "Son, I know you think I'm giving your boy the bum rush, but we've got two missing people to locate."

Caleb pushed back in his chair so that he was no longer looking straight up at Barnes. He put his palms flat on the armrests and leaned back. "You've identified the girl in the picture?" His pulse quickened.

Staring out across the emptying precinct, Barnes nodded slowly. "We did. Amber Collins, age twenty-four, of Millstone, South Carolina. Reported missing five days ago."

"Five days ago," Caleb mused. "Before the Hanover kid."

"That's correct."

"Any connection between the two?" Caleb asked, his detective instincts ramping up.

"Between the kid and the woman? No, not a one."

Knowing he was being forced down a path he didn't want to go, Caleb steeled himself for his next question. "How about between Andrew and the woman?"

Barns' eyes brightened. "Between those two we do have a connection. She's the daughter of Michelle Collins."

"And Michelle is . . . ?" Caleb asked, his gut tightening.

"His current agent."

"You have got to be kidding!" Caleb sat up. "That's one I didn't see." He ran a hand over his short-cropped hair. "From what Andrew has told me, he has only met the agent in person a couple of times. The last being—" He paused and shook his head slightly. "A couple of weeks ago. Andrew said they were working out the details to option one of his books." Caleb leaned back in his chair, slouching and staring at the ceiling.

"And Amber disappears not long after." Barnes finished.

"I wonder if Andrew knows," Caleb said mostly to himself.

Barnes opened a single-serve pack of peanuts he pulled from his pocket, tore the top off with his teeth, then emptied the contents into his hand. He poured most of them into his mouth while keeping his eyes on Caleb. "We could ask him to stop by, show him the pictures, and judge his reactions, though I can't believe they will be genuine. I have the feeling he's already seen the photos," the sheriff said as he chewed.

Caleb closed his eyes and inwardly shuddered. He rocked slightly back and forth contemplating his next words. Opening his eyes and casting his gaze beyond Barnes, he said, "Yes. I shared the pictures with Andrew."

"Against my direct orders not to divulge information to Mr. Alewine."

"Yes, sir."

Barnes shook his head and sucked the peanut crumbs out of his teeth, making small whistling noises. "I damn sure hope you have a very good reason for doing this."

"It's more 'theory' than reason, sir."

"Theory?" Barnes sniffed and repeated Caleb's word with a hint of derision. He crossed his arms and stared down at his deputy. "Is it a solid, good enough take-to-court kind of theory? One that you would risk your badge, career, and freedom over?"

Frustrated and fighting the urge to bray like an exasperated donkey, Caleb shook his head, cupped his face in his hands, and this time he laughed. He pulled his hands down and stared up at a very unamused sheriff. "Oh, man, it's nowhere near that good a theory!" Even if he wanted to, Caleb couldn't stop the laughter. After a few moments, he gathered himself up. "Sorry, sir. Just been a long, trying day."

"Care to share your theory with me?" Barnes asked, his eyes down to slits, hands now planted firmly on the desk, fingers flexing hard as if trying to do pushups.

"Sir, give me a little more time to flesh out a few leads. If it doesn't blow your mind, you can have my badge."

"Son, if it doesn't make me levitate, you won't have to turn in your badge. I'll rip it off your belt myself." Barnes pushed off the desk, stalked across the room, and slammed the door to his office hard enough to make the blinds swing back and forth.

Caleb fought to keep back the giggles when he started humming, *Zip-a-dee-doo-dah zip-a-dee-a. My oh my what a wonderful day, plenty of sunshine headed my way, zip-a-dee-doo-dah zip-a-dee-a.*

Chapter Twenty-Eight

Andrew sat at his kitchen table with a steadily warming glass of iced tea and an untouched sandwich in front of him when the front door opened and shut. Vanessa entered and walked across the den calling his name. He raised an arm and waved.

"You still feeling under the weather?" She turned his way.

"I think I'm still hungover," he smiled sheepishly.

"Well, if the Amazing Andrew hadn't decided to drink a year's worth of alcohol yesterday, he'd be feeling better." She brushed his hair with her hand and kissed the small balding spot. "Have you taken anything?"

Andrew nodded, his head still pointed at his food, elbows on the table, chin resting in his palms. "Nothing works. Caleb said I should drink more." His words were muffled by the pressure on his cheeks.

"He did, did he?" Vanessa didn't hide her disdain for the advice given by Andrew's best friend.

"Well, he would have if I'd asked," Andrew murmured.

"I take it that you didn't?"

"Nope. Head hurts too much to talk." Andrew slumped forward until his nose was almost on top of his sandwich.

Vanessa ran her fingers through his hair and across his brow. "You're not hot."

"Yes, I am," Andrew countered with child-like petulance. "You just haven't noticed lately."

"Oh, you're hot, all right—a hot mess." Vanessa kissed him again on his balding spot. "Now, why don't you go lie down before you go night-night in your food? I'd hate to explain to your adolescent buddy that you drowned in a PB&J sandwich."

Andrew let himself droop until his nose was embedded in the bread. "Nope, not possible," he said, words now muffled by the flattened snack. "Can't inhale peanut butter. So, you'll have to find a better way to snuff me."

Vanessa sighed. "Okay, one attempt down, nine hundred more to go."

"You love me enough to try that many times?" Andrew rolled his head to the side and off his food.

"Honey, I love you enough to try *every* night!"

"That's sweet," he murmured.

Vanessa gently pulled him by his shoulders until he was sitting up. She put a hand on his forehead again. "You don't feel hot, but you don't look all that great. C'mon." She tugged his arm. "Go lie down and I'll wake you up for dinner."

"Do you plan on smothering me with another sandwich?"

"First chance I get." She guided him across the den and toward the bedroom.

"I love you." Andrew flopped onto the bed.

Andrew woke to his head pounding, his sinuses on fire. He climbed out of bed, grabbed his phone, and used the screen to see across the room. Even though his phone barely broadcast light, the blue glow hurt his head, his eyes. He squinted and staggered to the bathroom, reached for the light switch, then quickly reconsidered. Andrew turned on the water, bent, and drank from the faucet. The water was cool to his parched throat.

The carpet dulled the sound of his shuffling feet as he made his way back to the bed. He collapsed face down, stretched, and rolled over. Taking his hands off his eyes, he glanced around the room. The clock's weak amber display was barely visible. The room felt gloomy, cold. The clock's numbers winked out and a voice whispered, "Hello, brother. Have you missed me?"

Andrew shrieked and sat bolt-upright in bed, the covers flying off. The room brightened immediately; the depressive midnight air was replaced by pale early morning radiance. The door flew open and Vanessa ran in, coffee cup in her left hand.

"Andrew!" Vanessa shouted. "Are you okay?" She set the coffee cup on the dresser, dropped on the bed, and ran a hand through his hair. "What happened?"

"It—" Andrew's voice broke off. He shook his head and held a hand up to cut off any additional questions. "Was nothing. Had a really bad leg cramp." Noticing the sunshine pushing against the blinds, he turned to Vanessa. "What time is it?"

"Almost seven in the morning."

"Is dinner ready?"

Vanessa laughed and pushed him back down on the bed. "Sorry, that was over twelve hours ago. I can make you breakfast, if you like."

"Thanks, I'm starving." Andrew slid off the bed and staggered a bit. "I can't believe I slept so long."

"I tried to wake you, but you were out, and I mean *out*. I kept checking on you to make sure you were alive." Vanessa slipped an arm around his waist. "Did you sleep well?"

"I suppose so. I slept nearly twelve hours and never woke up." He shrugged.

"No dreams?" she asked, looking at him out of the corner of her eye.

Andrew pursed his lips as he thought for a moment, then shook his head. "Nope, not that I can remember." He followed her from the bedroom toward the kitchen. When he passed his small office, he noticed his computer was on, the cursor blinking. He stopped and leaned against the door frame, staring at the small desk. A document was on the monitor. Andrew leaned out of the office. "Did you work on the computer last night?"

"Me? No. I took advantage of you being comatose to watch my shows." Vanessa poked her head out of the kitchen nook. "Why?"

"The computer's on and there's a document on the screen. I haven't done any writing in a while." Andrew glanced back at the display. It was now in screen-saver mode, color bars flashing and flying around the monitor. "You sure?"

"Uh, I think I would remember giving up a night of solitude to work on a case. Yes, I'm certain. Plus, you know how much I dislike that chair. I would've used my laptop." Vanessa ducked back toward the stove. "How do you want your eggs?"

"Scrambled," Andrew said after a moment. *The same way I like my brain,* he murmured to himself. "Well, if it wasn't you, guess I just forgot to shut it down."

"You have been pretty rattled," Vanessa said after a few minutes, raising her voice to be heard over the sound of bacon popping and sizzling.

Tentatively, Andrew stepped into his office, casting his gaze around the small room. Everything looked to be in its place. The files he had spread out a few nights back were now all stacked on a corner table, just where he left them. His desk was still scattered with an assortment of notepads, pens, and the ever-present empty tea glass. He slid the mouse around until the screensaver abated. A blank word document was open, the cursor blinking, waiting for input from the operator. Andrew scrolled down. The file was blank. He turned the chair around to sit. He froze. "Vanessa, are you a closet baseball fan?"

"Baseball?" she repeated from the kitchen. "Uh, no. Not even the least bit. Why?"

"So, you've never been to Minnesota?"

There was silence from the kitchen, then the sound of feet shuffling across the carpet. "Minnesota? Pretty sure I never have. Kinda cold for my Southern roots. Besides, isn't that the land of igloos and Eskimos?" She laughed and moved to stand beside him.

"That would be Alaska," Andrew replied, glancing her way. "But still very cold."

"I know that! You sound so serious and tense, I was trying to make you laugh." Vanessa ran up to him, practically dancing on her toes. "Are you planning on taking me there, maybe to the Mall of America?" Her eyes brightened.

Andrew slowly shook his head, placed a hand on the back of the chair, and spun it around so she could see the quarter-dollar size Minnesota Twins button stuck to the armrest on the chair. The button had a pair of Minnesota twins shaking hands. Someone had written, 'me, you' over the batters. On the player listed 'you', red slashes had been drawn across it, the lines forming a red puddle at the feet.

"No, I was thinking about calling Caleb." Andrew pulled out his phone, brought up the camera, and took a close-up pic of the button.

Chapter Twenty-Nine

Caleb didn't knock, just pushed through the front door calling Andrew's name. "Sorry, man. Got here as soon as I could."

"You're good," Andrew replied from the couch. "Is the button a match for the one on the kid's cap? I can't remember what it looked like; I was kinda unconscious."

"I think it is," Caleb answered as he took a chair across from Andrew. "Hat's locked up in evidence and Barnes is in a mood. Didn't get a chance to ask to see it. The forensics boys took a bazillion photographs around the house and his bike. Unfortunately, they didn't get a clear pic of the hat's bill. But it does look similar."

"So, what do we do?" Vanessa asked. "Should we report this to Barnes?"

Caleb cringed, and his face tightened. He took a deep breath and let out a long, slow hiss. "Man, I'm not sure at all what to do. We call it in, and that's all Barnes needs to bring you into town and throw you into an interrogation room."

"Dude's been in my house, Caleb," Andrew said quietly. "He sat at my desk."

"Any idea when he snuck in or how?"

Both Andrew and Vanessa slowly shook their heads. Their normally vibrant countenance was now gone. Andrew seemed especially withdrawn. "I have no idea. I checked every window, every door. I didn't see any scratches or pry marks."

"Maybe you left the house unlocked."

Andrew shrugged. "Doubtful, but anything's possible. Best we can figure is that he came in while I was in the hospital. That's about the only time the house has been unoccupied for more than a few hours."

Caleb stood. "You two take a seat. I'm going make a quick search of the house. Then I'm going to take another look at the button on your chair."

"Why?" Andrew and Vanessa said simultaneously.

"To make sure no boogey men are hiding under a bed or in a closet."

"Do you really think someone could be in the house?" Vanessa asked, now pulling tight against Andrew.

Shaking his head, Caleb smiled reassuringly. "I sincerely doubt it. But I won't rest until I do my job. It's a cop thing."

"Gotcha," Andrew said. "Do you want me to come with you?"

Caleb shook his head. "No, sit tight.

Five minutes later Caleb returned shaking his head. "All clear, but Andrew, I gotta say, man, the dust bunnies under your beds. Now that's creepy!"

Andrew shrugged and sighed. "Sorry about that, they slip out of my brain when I dream at night."

"In that case, let me recommend some ear plugs." He pulled a pair of purple latex gloves out of his pocket and stretched them onto his hands. "Now, let's take a look at that button. And when we're done I want you to change your locks, get a gun, make sure your alarm is set, and change that code as well."

Caleb stood in the door to Andrew's Office. The air in the house had stagnated and chilled. The eclectic vibe that was always so prevalent was non-existent. The chair was turned with its back to the computer, the button still stuck to the air. He used a pen to nudge it. The souvenir was firmly secured, the pin pushing through the fabric, locking back in place. Crouching close, Caleb pulled a toothpick out of his wallet and touched the red ink below the batter. It was tacky, thick. *Oh, man, that's not ink.*

The computer monitor was still in screensaver mode. Careful not to smear any fingerprints, Caleb touched the mouse lightly with the end of a pen, pushing it around the rubber mat. The screen cleared immediately, showing a blank document. Caleb closed the file and stumbled back. The Windows desktop was changed to that of the missing boy sitting in the van, bound and gagged, his eyes closed and blood dripping from the corner of his mouth. A lot of blood.

"Andrew!" Caleb shouted. "We've got a problem—and I mean a huge, fucking problem!"

Caleb heard a muttered string of curses and felt certain they came from Vanessa and not Andrew. Seconds later, a pair of shadows darkened the door.

Andrew cleared his throat. "What kinda problem—"

"Dear God," Vanessa whispered.

"Like I said," Caleb replied in a quiet voice. "You, we, have a huge problem." He stood, held his arms spread waist-high, and shooed them out of the room. "C'mon, guys, let's not contaminate the office any more than we have already."

Andrew backed out of the room with his hands in front of his face, fingertips on his forehead, chin resting in the palms of his hands. "What in the hell is going on?" he asked angrily, his voice deep in his throat.

Vanessa placed a soft, gentle hand on his elbow and pulled his hands down. Andrew resisted momentarily, then let his arms fall. He stared absently over her shoulder. "Sweetheart, I have no idea. But we'll figure out."

"Yeah, man." Caleb placed an arm around Andrew's shoulder and gave him a supportive squeeze. "Shit's pissing me off too. Let's take a seat at the table and hash this out."

Andrew nodded, took a deep breath, let it out slowly, and nodded toward the dinette. Caleb took a seat by the French doors, and Andrew and Vanessa sat across from him.

"If I don't tell your boss what we found, he's going to haul my ass into jail for withholding information. If I do tell him what we found, he's going to haul my ass into jail for being the abductor," Andrew said in a voice near a whisper. "Like you said, I've got a fucking problem."

Caleb leaned forward with his elbows on the table, fist clenched in a knot, chin resting on his knuckles. He nodded slowly and measured his words very carefully. "Andrew, you're my best friend," he said with a wan smile. "But I have to ask—"

Andrew held up a hand, then leaned back in his chair, pushing it back on two legs, and stared at the ceiling, a lopsided grin splitting his lips. "It's okay, man. I've been waiting on this." He dropped forward and met Caleb's gaze straight on. "No, I had nothing to do with any of this. I don't know how that button ended up on my chair, nor where in the hell that picture came from. Bastard had to have done this while I was in the hospital."

"Good enough. I know you didn't. But Barnes is going to ask me if I asked you. And that anal jackass can smell a lie from a mile away." Caleb crossed his arms over his chest and leaned back. "Counselor, what happens after we call Barnes?"

"Oh, Lord," Vanessa said, biting her lip and shaking her head. "It's not going to be pleasant. I'm sure they are going to take Andrew and his computer in. Barnes will try to get Andrew in front of a judge as soon as possible and argue for a high bond. Hopefully, the bond will be manageable."

"And then there's the chance Barnes will be reasonable, hear us out, and just take statements." Caleb offered.

"Like that's going to happen," Andrew muttered.

"You never know," Caleb countered. "Barnes is an ass, a jerk, and everything else you want to call him—which he roundly deserves. But as much as I hate to admit it, he's a damn good cop."

"I hope so." Vanessa slid closer to Andrew. She wrapped an arm around his shoulder, hugging him to her.

Caleb unlocked his phone and held a finger above the dial button.

"Do it," Andrew said quietly, now slumped in his chair and staring out the French doors. "Nobody lives forever."

Rolling his eyes and shaking his head, Caleb dialed.

So far, the Spanish Inquisition—that was the way Andrew thought of the questioning—hadn't been too painful. Barnes and been mostly civil, asked where his office was and left him with a deputy for a detailed account of the day. The forensics officer he met earlier—Sweeneyhoffer—was picking through his office, carefully and painstakingly dusting for prints. Caleb lingered by the office and occasionally leaned around the corner to give Andrew a thumbs-up.

Andrew was biting his fingernails when he felt eyes upon him. He glanced up to find the young female deputy, her notepad open, pen hovering just above it.

"I'm sorry, I zoned out for a bit. What was your question?"

The woman smiled. Her fresh face and honest wide brown eyes once again relaxed him. "I was just asking if you guys noticed anything else amiss—windows cracked open, scratches on the door frames. Any indication that someone had been in your home."

Andrew and Vanessa shook their heads. "Nope, nothing," Andrew said. "We took a quick look, checked the window latches, y'know, the basic stuff." He slouched against the couch, dropped his hands in his lap, and stared blankly across the room. "Caleb asked us to not mess with the windows too much, that you guys would want to dust for prints."

The deputy nodded. "He is correct. We wouldn't want you guys to accidentally taint the evidence or mess up a print." She closed her notebook, placed the pen she was writing in a top shirt pocket, and stood. Andrew and Vanessa followed.

"Is that all you need?" Vanessa asked.

"Yes, ma'am. Just wanted to write down everywhere you guys moved around the house and everything you touched while it's still fresh in your mind."

The woman crossed the floor and stood with Caleb and Barnes. The investigators huddled and talked quietly, glancing in the small office on occasion. Caleb nodded several times. Barnes was clearly directing the conversation and not allowing even the briefest of body language to give his thoughts away. He clapped his hands once and nodded toward Andrew's office. Caleb broke the huddle and strolled over to his friend.

"So, do I need to pack a toothbrush and come with you?" Andrew asked.

"Nope, Barnes is—surprisingly—not that wigged out. I'm not sure if he's playing it close to the vest and not letting me know his true thoughts. But my gut feeling is that he's taking everything at face value."

"Why?" Vanessa asking stepping into the conversation. "He's hammered Andrew on everything else."

Caleb shrugged and shook his head slowly. "Don't know. We had an old private eye stop by today and they held a closed-door meeting. Maybe he has new info I'm not privy to. On the flip side—" He grinned when Andrew appeared to shrink into the background. "Relax, son, this will just be a minor annoyance. Forensic dudes want to take your chair to see if they can find any fibers, blood, etcetera."

Vanessa barked a quick laugh. "Thank God. I've always hated that chair!" She leaned forward and clasped her hands. "Tell them that if it gets lost or destroyed, that's completely fine."

"You hate my grandpappy's chair?" Caleb feigned disappointment, then turned back to Andrew and took a breath before continuing. "And they're taking everything on your desk, including your computer."

"They're taking my computer?" Andrew said, alarmed. "For how long?"

Caleb held his hands out, palms up, and took another slow tentative breath. "Don't know. They'll have computer geeks analyze everything on it trying to figure out how the picture got on your desktop. You don't have any porn or anything you wouldn't want found on it, do you?"

"No! Of course not!" Andrew blurted.

"I can't believe you just asked that!" Vanessa yelled, her eyes narrow and angry.

"None?" Caleb pressed.

Andrew licked his lips and glanced at the floor. He glanced up but failed to make eye contact with Caleb. "Well, just depends on your definition of porn. There was this video with a midget and a—"

Vanessa rounded on him, eyes glaring, fingers biting into her palms.

"Just kidding! Sheesh, thought I'd just make a little joke—"

"A little people joke?" Caleb asked, smiling.

"Enough!" snapped Vanessa. "You two morons need to take this seriously."

Andrew cringed when he noticed Barnes and company staring intently. "As I've previously stated, I am taking this seriously," he said in a low, forced voice. "But I feel that if I don't get some relief from all this—" He waved his arms around as if fending off invisible foes. "I might go nuts."

Caleb nodded. "Hang in there, buddy. We'll get this figured out soon enough." Placing a hand on Andrew's shoulder, he gave it a firm squeeze. "Barnes is giving me the stink-eye again. Need to see what else has put a bug up his ass."

Vanessa kept an eye on Caleb as he retreated across the house. "I wonder why they brought in a private detective."

Shaking his head, Andrew said nothing.

Chapter Thirty

Caleb sat at the kitchen table with his best friend as the activity began to wane. Barnes had spent most of the morning huddled with Sweeneyhoffer and a lieutenant talking in hushed tones, usually hiding their mouths behind clipboards to prevent lipreading. Thirty minutes later, he stepped over to the table, thanked Andrew and Vanessa for being so cooperative, and left. The techs hung around Andrew's house for another hour before packing up. They turned the office inside out, poking and prying through all his folders, desk drawers, and even sifting through the carpet fibers. They scraped, tweezed, and swabbed almost every square inch of the room. Lastly, they checked the doors and windows one more time, took additional swabs, and made notes. Andrew's chair and computer were bagged, tagged, and carefully placed in the back of a waiting van.

When the door shut behind the last forensics tech, Caleb leaned forward, put both hands flat on the table, and stood. "Well, that went better than expected."

"Yes, it did," Vanessa agreed, getting to her feet. "I was expecting to have to get my claws out."

"Let's all be glad it didn't come to that," Caleb said, grinning.

"Caleb, why'd I get a pass?" Andrew asked, still sitting. "He asked me to recap the day's events and that was it. He was actually—" he paused, took a breath, then leaned back in his chair. "Civilized."

Caleb shrugged. "Don't know. Cat's a strange dude. Maybe someone slipped him a valium before he came over."

Andrew snorted. "I'd have slipped him something a bit stronger—possibly mushrooms."

"Now, now let's have none of that talk." Caleb winked. "You never know if they left a listening device behind."

"Wouldn't surprise me." Andrew sat back in his chair, arms crossed over his chest.

Clasping his hands and cracking his knuckles, Caleb backed away from the chair he was leaning on. "Alrighty, guys, time to head back. I'm sure to get debriefed later today."

Vanessa walked around the table and gave him a warm, heartfelt embrace. "We can't thank you enough for all you've done."

"Hey, girl, not in front of you-know-who!" Caleb said in a low, conspiratorial whisper as he nodded toward Andrew. He fully embraced her, then let go, straightened his shirt, and pulled his sunglasses from the top pocket. "It'll be okay, guys. Now I gotta git before Tall, Dark, and Very Scary sends a unit out looking for me."

"Take it easy, man." Andrew stood.

"You too, amigo." Caleb's phone vibrated. He glanced down and shook his head. "Speak of the devil." He held the phone so they could see the caller ID indicated a call from the sheriff's department. "Later, gators." He broke into a fast walk as he answered the phone.

"Deputy Saunders," Caleb said as he pulled Andrew's front door closed.

"Caleb, it's Marianne. Are you on your way back to the station?"

An image of the long-time dispatcher flashed behind his eyes. Marianne was in her late fifties and was fair-skinned with sharp green eyes. Her once jet-black hair was now streaked with iron-gray. For a woman approaching retirement, she was still fit and even led a new-recruit strength-training class in the morning. At no more than five-foot-two and a hundred twenty-five pounds, she was the only person who could make Barnes back down.

"Hey, girl, what's going on?" Caleb replied as he backed out of Andrew's drive. He glanced over his shoulder, dropped his truck in drive, and pulled out onto the highway fronting his buddy's home.

"You have an older gentleman waiting for you here. Said he needs to talk with you. He's kind of impatient and wanted to know your ETA."

"Tall, Black man? Acts like he's worth a million bucks?"

There was a soft chuckle from the caller. "That's him to a tee."

"Tell him to hang tight. I should be there in about twenty minutes. And, just so you know, he's Barnes' uncle, so don't say anything you don't want to get in trouble for."

"Seriously? They're related? The uncle seems so—nice. Was Barnes adopted?"

Caleb laughed. "No, but it makes you wonder." He ended the call and was about to turn his music on but stopped. Joseph saying he knew about Andrew surprised him. *Never in a million years would I think they have anything in common.* He sighed and pressed the accelerator harder, his truck jumped forward, traveling faster than the posted speed limit. *More and more curious.*

When he circled through the station's parking lot, Joseph Abraham's vintage Buick was parked in the rear of the building, near Barnes' county-issue Tahoe. *Interesting.* Caleb parked two spaces down from the Buick

Joseph was sitting in the breakroom, sipping a cup of coffee when Caleb walked past. "Hey, there, young man!" Joseph called out. "You said you wanted to talk to me, and I can't agree more." The older man slowly stood, leaning heavily on his cane. "Want a cup of coffee? Your barista is pretty good. Doc says I need to lay off the caffeine, but what does he know?" Joseph cackled.

Caleb smiled. "'Barista' is a bit of a stretch. Ms. Earline Waters is the brew master around here. She's got adding coffee and water in a coffee maker down to a science. But I'm good," Caleb said, entering the breakroom. He nodded to a table in the back. "You said the other day that you knew Andrew."

Joseph allowed Caleb to pull a chair out for him, then lowered himself into it. Caleb sat opposite of him. "That's right. I'm not buddy-buddy like you are, but I remember when he was born, sure do."

Caleb leaned forward, eyes directly on the older man. "You remember when he was born?"

Joseph nodded. "That I do, or at least I believe I do." He said nodding.

"Well, which is it? You said the other day you've been keeping tabs on him, and now you don't seem so sure." Caleb sat back and crossed his arms over his chest.

"Poor choice of words on my part, Caleb." Joseph leaned forward and clasped his thin, aged hands together. "Thirty years ago, I was working with the Warrenton Daily News covering local events. The crime blotter was my baby." He grinned and rocked in his chair for a moment. "Back in those days, the worst crimes were car thefts—mostly joyrides—and the occasional pot bust. This ain't no big city, and back then, it was even smaller. So, my crime blotter piece was mainly about trying to run down who stole the hubcaps off the mayor's car and who smashed the windows of the Sak-and-Save and stole a case of beer.

"But every now and then, something a bit more unsavory would drift in on the winds. And I'm sure you've heard the media axiom, 'if it bleeds, it leads'."

Caleb nodded but didn't say anything.

"Well, one day, I'm down at the old hospital—now torn down a good twenty years ago—and hear about some lady stumbling into the emergency room in full labor. Clothes were all tattered, no shoes, looked like she'd been sleeping in the woods."

"And this piqued your interest? A pregnant drifter?" Caleb asked, an eyebrow raising.

Joseph patted the table with his left hand and laughed his old-man cackle. "Nope, not in the least bit." He leaned forward again and made direct eye contact with Caleb. "No, sir, I've seen lots of pregnant ladies in my life, even made a few of 'em that way many a year ago." He winked. "But this one was having what we used to call back then 'Siamese' twins."

The ambient sounds of the station faded as Caleb's heart rate increased. "And this was newsworthy?"

"Son, when you have a pregnant woman suddenly, out of the blue, burst into the emergency room doors of a rural hospital, folks get excited. When they figure out she's having twins, the excitement increases ten-fold. When the staff found out these poor kids are conjoined, the place went into overdrive." Joseph smiled as he recalled the story. "Yes, sir, it was very newsworthy."

"How did you get involved?" Caleb asked. "Did you know the girl?"

"Know her?" Joseph said leaning forward, brow-raising, his hands wrapped over the top of his ornate cane. "Heavens, no! I was there chatting up Miss Doreen Foster. She was the head nurse and a lovely woman who kept me in the loop—as long as I brought her the occasional Krispy Kreme donut."

"In the loop?" Caleb interrupted.

Joseph stared at Caleb for a moment, then snorted lightly and shook his head. "You know, gave me tips of folks being brought into the ER—gunshot victims, car wrecks. It's how I kept tabs on city officials or newsmakers."

"And that's how you found out about the twins?"

"Precisely!" Joseph replied emphatically. "She came racing by and paused just long enough to fill me in. I had to jog along with her to get the full story."

"And you think one of these kids was Andrew?"

"Think? Son, I saw them babies. Doc had to deliver by caesarian. Doreen let me follow the nurse into the labor and delivery section of the hospital and snap a few pics. Both babies had fiery red hair."

"Did you get a good look as to where they were attached?" Caleb was breathing rapidly, heart racing.

"Sure did." Abraham nodded. "Babies were hooked together at the skull." Leaning forward far enough to give Caleb a clean view of his head, Abraham drew a circle in his curly white hair. "Looked to be just past the crown of the head. Poor kids had to spend nine months back to back!"

Chapter Thirty-One

"Joseph, red-headed kids are born every day, not as much as blondes or brunettes, but it's not that rare. How do you know for certain in was Andrew?"

"Oh, it's your redheaded buddy, that I'm sure of." Joseph countered, quieted for a moment, and slumped slightly in his chair.

Caleb leaned back and studied the white-haired man. "I'm still not clear why you would have followed Andrew's life. If what you say is accurate—"

"It is," Joseph said quickly, cutting Caleb off.

"I still don't get your interest in my buddy's life. Sure, conjoined twins are rare, and it's wild how this woman shows up out of the blue. But—" Caleb shrugged, letting his words drift off.

"Son, when you live long enough and see everything I've seen, there's events that pull you in whether you want to or not."

"And this was one of those events?"

"Damn straight." Joseph leaned forward again, his elbows on the table, hands clasped tight. "It was big news around here. I later learned they flew them all to Atlanta to have the kids separated. A few weeks or so after the surgery the mom vanished from the hospital—just walked out into the ether, taking the kids with her."

"Now how in the world could she just gather up her kids and leave? They have security procedures in place." Caleb scoffed.

"Not back then they didn't. Hell, I even knew a few doctors that still smoked in the hospital! But that was then, and this is now."

Caleb ran a hand over his head and rocked slightly in his chair, mulling over Joseph's words. "Joseph, she probably decided to head back to wherever she came from to raise the babies by herself."

"The hell she did!" Joseph scowled. "She sold them babies. That's what she done."

"How in the hell could you know that?"

"Because, Caleb, I was there. I seen it all go down!" Joseph's nostrils flared, his brown skin drawing tight around his mouth. "I followed up on a tip I had gotten about a woman with two kids that were once connected at the head. Tip said a woman was trying to sell them, that one of the kids was evil."

"Evil?" Caleb half-barked, half-laughed. "That's nuts! I've heard some of your kook-ass conspiracy theories, but this one takes the cake."

"Nuttier than that hoodoo-voodoo your boy does? Finding a body no one knew was missing? Knowing the location of a submerged van? Like I said, I've followed this story for a long time."

Caleb crossed his arms, leaned back in his chair, and stared at the old man.

"How do you explain the parlor tricks he's been pulling off since y'all was kids?"

Caleb shrugged. "I can't."

"Not to mention them scary-ass books he writes! Damn things scared the bejeezus out of me when I tried to read them. Never finished one or got past the first few chapters." Joseph relaxed, straightened his shirt, and rested his cane between his gnarled fingers. "Son, that boy's birth mamma was strange—weird beyond description."

Taking a deep breath, Caleb leveled his eyes on Joseph. "So why did you follow Andrew, keep up with him?"

Joseph shrugged and waggled his cane between his boney knees. "Call it instinct. Year after year, I thought something would happen. When the story broke about the old depot and him finding the dog, I knew something was up. Just had to wait long enough."

Caleb glanced at his watch, then out of the breakroom. He was pushing it with Barnes. They'd already wasted twenty minutes talking, and he didn't feel like anything had been accomplished. The old man was just spinning more of his wild, unsubstantiated stories.

As if reading Caleb's mind, Joseph chuckled and pushed unsteadily out of his chair, using his cane to support himself. "That's all right, son, you ain't got to believe me. Just old Joseph Abraham spreading his wild tales for all that would listen." He straightened his tie, pushing the knot tight against his throat. "Barnes didn't believe me and doesn't believe your buddy. But that's fine, no harm, no foul, in listening to an old man gabble on and on. When you have a bit more time to talk, you give me a call." Joseph offered a brief, lopsided salute, patted Caleb on the shoulder, and shuffled from the breakroom.

Caleb watched the old man make his way through the maze of desks and cubicles. Joseph stopped by the dispatch desk, said something he couldn't hear, and made the lady manning dispatch laugh hard enough to cup her mouth and pound on the desk. Drumming his fingers on the table, Caleb thought about the old investigator's words. Surely there would be some record of a conjoined birth twenty-plus years ago. That should be easy enough to research. How many of the nurses and doctors might still be around? The hospital was now a Wal-Mart Supercenter, bulldozed decades ago after years of abandonment.

Caleb picked at a piece of apple stuck in his teeth and let his mind freewheel.

"Not enough breakfast, Saunders?"

Caleb's eyes flew up to find Barnes lingering in the door, his hands behind his back, legs apart, back ramrod straight. *Man needs to give up the soldier-boy posture.* He smiled at the sheriff. "Naw. I think better with a finger in my mouth."

"Is that so? What do your teeth have to say?"

Caleb sighed. "Unfortunately, not a lot. I was hoping Joseph might have something salient to add, but he's still as crazy as always."

"Son, I could have told you that and kept you from wasting thirty minutes of your day."

"Yes, sir. I feel the same way." Caleb pushed from the table. "So, any news from the tech boys?"

Barnes relaxed a millimeter and leaned against the doorframe to the breakroom. "Not yet. They are just now starting their work on the drives. Medical examiner is certain the red fluid on the button is blood, but not sure if it's human or if it's from the boy."

"What's your take? Your gut feeling?"

Barnes' eyes, which moments earlier had taken on a neutral, almost reflective softening, hardened again. "Mr. Alewine is elbow deep in this."

"Sir, how you can still think Andrew is involved? The man can account for almost every minute of every day for the past week."

"It's the minutes he can't account for that has drawn my interest."

"For Christ's sake, Sheriff. What will it take to convince you Andrew's not your guy?"

Instead of answering, Barnes stared through him. "I believe you have several people to find."

"Yes, sir," Caleb answered curtly and stepped around Barnes.

Caleb was sitting at his desk writing down as much as he could remember of his conversation with Joseph Abraham when his phone rang. It was Andrew. *Dang, son, gonna be a while before I know more.* "'Sup, Copper-Top?"

"Not much. Just doing the same ol', same ol'. Sitting at the kitchen table wondering when the proverbial black-and-white is going to pull up and haul me off."

Andrew was his best friend—ever. But sometimes the "woe is me" attitude wore him out. Caleb took a breath and tried to put himself in his friend's shoes. "Just try and relax, Copper-Top. Everything is mostly cool."

"Mostly, huh?"

"Yep, for the most part, nothing has changed. Techies are digging through your computer and forensics hasn't released anything. Hey, Barnes hasn't dragged you down to sit kneecap-to-kneecap, so I'd call that a good sign."

For several moments, there was no sound except for Andrew breathing on the other end.

Caleb finally broke the silence. "Okay, spill it. I've known you long enough to tell when there's something else going on."

Andrew paused before speaking. "Shadow boy is back."

The statement surprised Caleb, but not completely. Andrew always became nuttier than normal when he started a new novel, and after the revelation in the ambulance, he felt the tension in Andrew building. "Shadow boy, as in *the* shadow boy?"

"Yep, the one and only," Andrew replied in a hushed tone.

"So—what happened?"

"Not much—so far. He visited in my dream last night. This time it felt closer to reality than ever before, almost tangible. I think if I had reacted sooner, I could have touched him."

Caleb leaned back hard and laced his fingers. His old desk chair creaked in protest. "Wow, Andrew. He's never been that close before, has he?"

"No, never. I think he's here, somewhere . . . lurking. I think he's the one that messed with my computer and left the bloody button on my chair."

Caleb mulled over Andrew's words. "Y'all need to leave. Grab a few day's clothes and stay with me. Maybe we can have a few units roll past your house, see if anything's up."

"I appreciate the offer, man. But, you know, this is my home. He got the first punch in, but I'm going to finish this fight."

"Andrew, I've seen you fight. It ain't pretty. You get all flustered and red-faced. Then you attack like a karate-master having a seizure—arms and legs going every which-a-way." Caleb chuckled but didn't hear laughter on the other end. "Naw, man, stay with me."

For several moments, the phone was silent.

"Yo, man, you still there?" Caleb asked, wondering if the call had dropped.

"I'm here, Kemosabe."

"And?"

"I'm staying put. I might have Vanessa crash at your place. I'd feel better if she was staying with you. But this is my nightmare, my tar-baby to deal with."

"Alrighty then, I completely understand. I don't like it, not a damn bit. But I do understand where you're coming from."

"Thanks. Thought you might fight me on it."

Caleb smiled, knowing if he pushed hard enough, Andrew would relent. But he also knew it was time for Andrew to buck up and stand his ground. Not that he wouldn't be checking on the boy hourly. "I hear you. Is there anything you need? I've got that old twenty-two I keep around the house. If you promise not to shoot your eye out, I'll bring it over."

Andrew laughed. "Thanks, but I was hoping for something with a bit more firepower."

"Such as?"

"Still got that rocket launcher in the evidence room?"

Caleb laughed hard and shook his head. "Man, 'fraid not. Barnes is kinda funny about lending out weapons of mass destruction. But I might be able to toss in a nicely dented Louisville slugger."

"That'll work. See you soon."

I sure hope so, buddy. I really do.

Chapter Thirty-Two

Caleb let out a long-held breath and slumped in his chair. The sun was getting low on the horizon, the rays pushing through the tops of the trees and barely penetrating the tinted glass of the sheriff's department. He rolled his head on his shoulders, trying to work out the kinks. Most of the day was spent following up on possible sightings of the missing woman and boy. None were considered viable after a few minutes with the caller, but all had to be worked. The callers all said essentially the same thing, that they *think* they *might* have seen them at the airport, Wal-Mart, walking down the street, and so on. Caleb had an officer drive out and meet the person if they couldn't make it to the station. Each time the officer returned shaking his head and dropping off his notes.

Caleb drummed his fingers on his desk, working out the last of the day's exhaustion when his cell phone rang.

"Deputy Saunders," he said into the phone while staring across the room but focusing on nothing.

"Caleb, it's Vanessa."

"Hey, girl, what's up?" Caleb sat up quickly, thankful it wasn't another false lead.

"I spoke to Andrew earlier, and he said you advised him to stay with you or get a motel room or some such idea until this mess has straightened up."

Caleb's brief excitement waned. "That's correct. This guy— whoever it is—has managed to get into Andrew's house without anyone knowing and without leaving a mark or trace. I don't like it, not a bit. I think it would be better if you guys stayed with me or some of my folk, but Andrew won't hear anything of it."

"And since you offered him a twenty-two for protection, he's strutting around like he's Wyatt Earp, talking out of the side of his mouth and fast drawing with a banana." Vanessa's voice rose slightly. "Caleb, you should know better than to give that boy anything that might increase his imagination. Now you're going to have to walk back that offer."

Caleb sighed, the brief enthusiasm he felt when she called now exhausted. "If it makes you feel any better, he wanted to upgrade to a rocket launcher we confiscated several years ago. Obviously, I said 'no,' but I did offer him a battered aluminum Louisville Slugger."

"Well, thank you for your restraint," Vanessa said.

"In my defense, I only offered the use of the twenty-two, but made no mention of bullets." Caleb laughed, soon realizing he was the only one. "Anyhoo, and back to my original thought, I think you guys should stay somewhere safe."

"I'm staying at my mom's apartment. The building's secure and the guards have been looking for something more meaningful to do besides rousting teenagers out of the pool."

"I'll agree with that." Caleb pictured the high-end complex. Pass-cards were needed to access the courtyards and elevators. Even local law enforcement had to be buzzed in. "Governors Terrace is extremely nice—several city officials live there. See if your pal will join you."

"I'll try, but that boy's stubborn. And several days with my mom and Andrew in the same apartment would be brutal—for all of us." Vanessa released a quick laugh. "I was hoping he'd stay with you."

"Same here. I'll try again."

There was a moment of silence on the phone before Vanessa spoke up. "Well, I think I'll let you get back to it."

"Sounds good," Caleb said, then a thought hit him. "Hey, Vanessa, hang on a second." He swiveled around in his chair and flipped his notebook open, reviewing his conversation with Abraham. "Do you ever review property titles, old tax maps?"

"Me? No, wouldn't really know where to start. Why?"

"I'm following up a really strange lead from a known crackpot dude."

"Is this in regard to Andrew's mysterious visitor?"

"Yeah, and the missing kids. Can you, though your recourses, dig up any information on the old Spring Street Hospital—"

"You mean the *old* hospital, the one that was sitting where Wal-Mart is now?"

"Yep."

"Sure, I'm certain I can find some information. What are you looking for?"

Thumbing through his notes, he found the page he was looking for. "I'm looking for hospital records going back about 27 years. Birth records around mid-April, to be exact. That, and nurses who were employed there."

"Birth records and nurses? Mid-April thirty years ago?" Vanessa paused, and Caleb clearly heard the sudden intake of air. "About the time Andrew was born?"

"Correct. Can you do it?"

"Probably. I'll have to make some phone calls, might take a few days. As for former employees, not sure where to start on that. Can you give me any more information?" Vanessa asked.

"Let's leave it at that for now. Let me know what you find," Caleb said.

"Caleb, I get the sense you are nervous about upsetting an apple cart."

"Counselor, your instincts rarely fail you. I hope this time they do. Let me know what you find." Caleb ended the call. The sparkle of streets lights flickered to life as the last of the sun dropped down behind the trees lining the property. The last of the sun was melting into the gray of twilight. An ambulance passed by the station, partially hidden by the water oaks. The vehicle's safety lights were flashing, but it moved at pedestrian speed. *Poor bastard must not have made it.*

An idea bloomed to life. He opened his notebook and thumbed through his notes from his meeting with Abraham until he found the name he was looking for. Opening a web page on his computer, he typed the name of the nurse the old coot had mentioned in the search engine. *Doreen Foster.* Dozens of listings appeared. Caleb clicked on the links, methodically reviewing all the webpages and postings. Over an hour later he narrowed the focus—Doreen Foster Warrenton Hospital. This time only one listing. A cold-case murder from well over a decade ago.

Caleb logged back into the main server for the department, typed in his password, then searched the nurse's name. And there was the report. July 9, 2008. The city inspector was called in to perform a pre-demolition inspection. At first, he thought the abandoned, grocery freezer contained an old CPR dummy. It wasn't until he started to open it that the stench and flies come boiling out. He bolted from the hospital and dialed 9-1-1. Autopsy reports that the victim, a former nurse, had been bludgeoned to death, a hammer left impaled in the back of the skull. The medical examiner stated she'd been dead nearly a week. A link connected Caleb to crime-scene photos and an autopsy report.

The mouse hovered over the autopsy link for several seconds, the cursor blinking as if daring him to click the hyperlink. With two quick stabs of his right index finger, the M.E.'s report began to load. A generic ambiguous outline of a body formed on his monitor. The M.E.'s report was listed below the image. Caleb ignored the comments and scrolled down to the last silhouette, one showing the body outline from the rear. A hammer-impact area was circled in red. It was on the back of the skull, just where Andrew's hair was thinning.

Caleb X'ed out of the page without going through the formal process of logging out, as if the abrupt process would shut down the images in his mind. He opened his notebook and dialed the first number he came to.

The phone was answered slowly on the third ring, the sound of it being roughly pulled out of its cradle synched the feeling in his head. "I've been waiting on your call, Deputy," the old watery voice said.

"You knew about the nurse!" Caleb snapped. His hand gripped the phone tight, nearly cracking the handset.

"Ah, you found out about Doreen Foster," Abraham said slowly. "I wondered how long it would take you."

Chapter Thirty-Three

"I think she was one of his first," Joseph Abraham said to the silence on the phone. "He got much better as the years went on. Little bastard has been on a decade-long murder spree."

"We are talking about this supposed twin of Andrew's?"

"Of course we are, son!" Joseph said, his voice rising. "Who the hell else would be talking about?"

"I just wanted to make sure we're on the same page," Caleb replied.

"So, you starting to come around to the idea that Andrew might have some kind of evil twin, as cliché as that sounds?"

Caleb leaned back hard in his chair and stared out the front windows. The sun had surrendered completely, only lingering dark shadows from the oaks remained. He took a deep breath and slowly let it out. "How sure are you?"

"How in the hell do you explain these murders? Do you see the M.E.'s report on Ms. Foster? Blunt force trauma to the back of the skull, right about where Andrew and this demon were connected. 'Splain that to me, son."

"I can't, and you know it."

"Caleb, as the saying goes, I might be crazy, but sure as hell, I ain't insane. You can take that one to the bank."

Caleb took his eyes off the tree shadows and slumped into this chair. He laughed, holding his hands over his face and letting his fingers massage his eyes. "Okay, whatever. I'm hooked. Reel me in."

"What do you have planned for tonight?"

"Nothing in the hopper that I can think of." Caleb sat up in his chair. "Were you thinking dinner or drinks?"

"I was thinking both, if it does you fine," Joseph said. "I'm sure you know about Blake's Backwater Saloon?"

I know about Blake's. Caleb rolled his eyes. *As does every vice cop and DEA agent in the state.* The rustic old building with its gravel driveway was way out Highway 8 and down a long winding driveway. A rear deck listed out over the Socastee river; the shack nestled among centuries-old water oaks. A rickety dock allowed hunters to pull up bass boats for a quick beer or twelve. "Oh yeah, very familiar."

Joseph laughed his old man cackle. "Knew you would. See you there in about an hour?"

Glancing at his watch, the shorthand pointing nearly straight down, Caleb answered, "Sounds good. I was about to wrap up everything and leave. I should be there eight-ish."

"I'll have us a booth in the back so we'll have some privacy. See you then."

The call ended and Caleb stood. He retrieved his sidearm from a desk drawer and clipped it to his belt, opposite his badge. *Okay, old man, let's see what you got for me.*

Andrew sat on the couch watching television, absentmindedly doodling on a notepad. The itch to write was pulsating painfully in his head. He didn't have a novel planned out yet, not even sure he wanted to write one, but the antsy nature he was suffering through was always a precursor to writing one. Not that he actually could do anything productive—the good ol' sheriff had confiscated his PC and laptop. Vanessa was supposed to bring a spare laptop over for him to use, but until then, he was left to twiddle his thumbs.

Muting the TV, Andrew grabbed his six-shot banana, a beer from the fridge, and stepped out on the rear deck. The warm air caressed him immediately, practically holding him back as the night birds sang. He popped the beer, sat on the top of his outdoor table, and drank deeply. Drawing the banana, he took a couple of potshots at dancing bats. "Gotcha, you wascally wabbit!" he said in his best Elmer Fudd voice and laughed.

The pages of his notebook fluttered under the late summer breeze. Andrew was glad for the light winds; they helped keep the mosquitos at bay and stirred the gently swaying Spanish moss. The beer tasted especially good. He swished the remainder in the can and then downed it. Probably time for another one.

The wind caught several pages of his notebook, lifting them to reveal the page of doodles he'd scratched earlier. It took him a moment to make out what he'd drawn. It was a page of fire. Flames were engulfing a building and burning stick-people were strewn around the grounds. The next page was the building in ruins, the charred skeletal remains of the structure looming over corpses on the ground.

What in the hell? Andrew turned to the next page. This set of drawings showed a boat half-sunk in a river, bodies floating nearby. He rotated the image, finally noticing the dock and apparent fuel pump. Andrew scratched his head and licked his lips. The pictures didn't make sense. He hadn't been dreaming about buildings or rivers or burning bodies. Usually, the roughed-out images paralleled whatever he was writing.

He thumbed to another page of scribblings. Like the first two pages of random drawings, he didn't remember inking these or what they correlated to. This page completely mystified him. It was just so

. . . random. He lifted the pad and slowly rotated it, trying to make out the images from a black set of chicken scratches.

"If you want to fly, that propeller is going to have to spin much faster," said a voice behind him.

Andrew jumped up, sending the notepad tumbling, and jerked around.

Vanessa leaned against the French doors leading to the deck, a glass of wine in her hand.

"Hey, I thought you were going to stay in town, in that grossly over-priced fortress your mom lives in," Andrew said, trying to keep his heart from pounding out of his shirt. He strode over to Vanessa. She held her wine glass out to the side, and he gave her a quick kiss. "How long have you been here?"

"Long enough to watch you study your notebook." She kissed him back. "You're drawing again?"

Andrew shrugged. "Apparently so. I don't even remember drawing any of these—not sure when I've had time to, what with Barnes all up my butt."

"Can I look at them?" Vanessa asked.

"Are you sure? You've never been much of a fan of my artwork." Andrew picked up the notebook.

"Hand it over, old man, before I wrestle you down for it!"

"Take your best shot!" He clenched the notebook to his chest.

Vanessa poked him quickly in the side. "You'd like that, wouldn't you?"

Andrew nodded quickly like an eight-year-old being asked if he wanted more candy to increase his sugar rush.

"Maybe later, writer-boy. Let's see what you've got there." Vanessa extended her hand, flexing her fingers towards herself.

Sighing, Andrew held the tablet out to his fiancé. "They're not as bad as my previous drawings, but I don't know why I'm doodling these. Normally, they help a story solidify in my head. But these . . . ."

"So, no clandestine writing when I'm asleep?"

Andrew shook his head. "Nope. Not even any bad dreams. Things are pretty normal now."

Vanessa cocked an eye at him. "Normal for you is bizarre for everyone else." She laughed. "Let's take this inside. I think I'll need something stronger than wine after looking through your notebook." She waited for Andrew to step back inside before following and closing the French doors behind him. Vanessa took a seat at the table, put the tablet down, and held her hands on the cover. She took a deep breath and stared at Andrew. "Let's see what your little demon has made you draw."

Flipping the cover off the notepad, Vanessa hunched over the table, glanced down at the pages, gasped, and put a hand to her face.

Andrew stared at her, his face stricken. "I didn't think they were that bad, really. I mean, not children's book material, but probably okay for Harry Potter."

She swallowed hard before answering. "Andrew, these are—" She gulped, her throat moving up and down. "Terrible."

Cringing, Andrew sat at the table across from Vanessa. "They were disturbing, I agree. But I've drawn much worse."

Vanessa lifted her head, both hands covering her face. She lowered her palms until her eyes peeked above her fingertips. "Gallon of Neapolitan ice cream? Pizza rolls? Root beer? My God, Vienna sausages? What in the world has gotten into you? This is far worse than I ever imagined!"

Andrew blinked twice as his mouth tried to form words. "You were reading my grocery list?" He slumped against his chair. "Seriously? You scared the shit out of me!"

"Sweetie, this—" Vanessa tapped the first page of the writing tablet. "Is the most noxious collection of food I have ever seen. The Vienna sausages are enough to call an exorcist on their own!" Laughter and tears streamed down her face.

"So, you didn't look at the pictures?"

"Heaven's no! I love you, Andy-man, but I never sleep well after looking at your art. And after seeing your comfort-food list, I know why you have nightmares." Vanessa used her pinkies to wipe the last of her tears from her eyes. Without flipping any additional pages in the notepad, she slid it back across the table.

Silence dropped over the room as Andrew sat with his arms crossed staring at Vanessa.

"Are you mad at me?" she asked.

"I don't know if I'm mad as hell for that little prank, or blown away by how well you pulled it off." Andrew clapped slowly three times, shook his head, and laughed. "Well done. Really had me going." He leaned forward, put his elbows on the table, and clasped his fingers.

"Okay, what's going through that silly mind of yours?" Vanessa mirrored his posture.

"I think you owe me a wrestling match."

Vanessa pushed back from the table, squared her shoulders, and flexed her arms as if to show off her biceps. "You think you can take me?"

Andrew jumped from the chair and took a sumo wrestler pose. Then in his best Yoda voice said, "Take you, I can."

"Bring it on, writer boy!" Vanessa motioned toward him with her fingers, feigning a karate position, and backing toward the hallway.

Andrew brought it.

Chapter Thirty-Four

Flames lapped the building. The drapes roared like multicolored eight-foot candles and the furniture blazed. He stepped deeper into the structure. A red exit sign flickered and exploded, the plastic case raining down molten embers. One of Andrew's greatest fears was being realized: trapped in a burning building with no exit. As he ran, the structure continued to extend before him, rooms branching off exits just beyond his reach. His name was being called, but he couldn't tell from where. And in the middle of the maelstrom, laughter taunted him.

The smoke was suffocating, pressing him lower. The heat tore at his skin. Andrew back-peddled fast, the flames racing up the floor, along the walls, chasing him. Black, flame-riddled smoke billowed, reaching for him, offering to embrace. He slammed against a cold metal door. His hand searched for the push bar that would let him out of the conflagration and into the muggy night air. The push bar snapped back, but the door held fast.

The flames slowed their approach, but now stretched from floor to ceiling, tendrils of flame snaking horizontally across the ceiling. A stream of black clouds jetted forward as if thrown by a molten boxer. Andrew ducked, the smoke-fist smashing the door and shattering a thick glass window that allowed a narrow, vertical glance outside. He tried to scream, but his words were reduced to a muted gasp. A face appeared in the smoke, one he readily recognized. It was his own misshapen face.

The carpet at his feet melted and flowed toward his feet, the fabric shriveling and hissing.

Hello, brother, the flames seemed to whisper. *It's been a very long time since we've played together.*

The fear that had him paralyzed finally broke. Closing his eyes, he spun away from the broiling black clouds, slammed a shoulder into the metal surface, and braced for impact. He stumbled unopposed across the threshold and onto cold, wet sand, his momentum carrying him across a narrow shore and then into knee-deep water. When he turned around, the burning building was gone, as was the smoke. The firestorm was replaced by the buzz of crickets and the calls of a whippoorwill. He glanced up into a canopy of Spanish moss-laden, cypress trees; a black sky dotted with stars peeked through the gently swaying branches above. Turning away from the slow-moving river, he splashed from the water and back onto the beach. Barely visible, soft amber light filtered down from a house high up on a bluff.

Andrew instinctively patted his pocket, feeling for his phone or wallet. All he found was the panda pajama bottoms he wore when lounging around the house. "What in the hell?" he muttered as his head began to clear and the clouds of fear dissipated, giving way to shock and bewilderment. Rubbing his face, he glanced down at his hands. They had black smudges on the palms. His soaked pajama bottoms clung to his legs as he walked away from the sandy riverbank, angling toward the structure in the distance. After a moment he recognized the shape, the configuration of the windows. It was his house.

Picking his way over fallen logs, through muddy bogs, and over neck-high brambles, Andrew slowly pushed his way from the river and toward the bluff his house set on. The rough scrabble cut his feet and ripped his pajamas. He still had at least another mile of walking to make his way around the bluff to where the land sloped sharply up toward his house. It was a daunting climb, but at least the hillside had been timbered, and waist-high grass now covered the rise. He just hoped he didn't trip and roll back down to the river. Taking a deep breath, he reached forward, grabbed the first clump of vegetation, and crawl up the incline.

The moon had fully risen and was on a downward trajectory when he finally crossed over his property line. He collapsed on the picnic table outside his backyard and took a deep breath.

Lights flared on inside the house. The French doors leading inside were thrown open. He sat up. An intense flashlight blinded him.

"Copper-top, that you?" his best friend asked.

"Yeah," Andrew managed in a low voice, shielding his eyes with his hand. "Caleb?" he asked and fell back on the table.

The light was extinguished, and the soft glow of the porch light replaced it. "Yeah, man, it's me. Where the hell have you been?"

Before Andrew could answer, Vanessa shouted, "Andy!"

"Out here," Caleb called.

The table rocked slightly as Vanessa dropped down onto it, then her soft, cool hands were holding his face, stroking his hair. "Where have you been?"

Andrew lay down on the bench and stretched out. "What time is it?

"It's four in the morning, man. You've been missing since around midnight."

Vanessa sat down at the other end of the bench, lifted Andrews legs and pulled at the tattered remains of his pajamas. "Something woke me up, a sound, I think, and when I rolled over, you were gone. I checked the house and couldn't find you. The house was still locked up and the alarm set." Vanessa gently rubbed the mud off his feet. Andrew winced at her touch. "Did you go outside to get something?"

Andrew shook his head, then glanced at Caleb. "Why are you here?"

"Why am I here?" Caleb repeated, eyes wide, a slight laugh escaping him. "Your fiancé was in a dead panic. She didn't know what in the hell was going on. She called me to come look for you."

"She panics easily," Andrew deadpanned.

"Yeah, well, I think she had a good reason," Caleb said evenly. "Andrew, we've been looking for you like crazy. I even put in a call to Barnes to see if we could get some dogs out here. And let me tell you something, son. You think he didn't like you before? That crazy-ass sonofabitch *really* has it out for you now!"

"So, not so keen on being woken up in the middle of the night to hunt for his least favorite civilian?" Andrew's voice grew stronger. He took a deep breath, rolled to his side, and sat up. "Do you want me to run off into the woods so he can find me? I've always wanted to ride in a chopper."

"Fuck, no!" Caleb barked at Andrew, a vein pulsing in his temple. "He isn't sending anyone out yet anyway." Pulling out his phone, he unlocked it with a swipe of his finger and dialed. "And this shit is serious, man. You need to take a break with the smart-ass attitude."

Andrew was about to speak when Caleb waved him off. "Sir, we found him. We're good." He walked a small circle while holding the phone to his ear, nodding vigorously. "Yes, sir, first thing in the morning. A full report." Ending the call and shaking the phone at the sky, Caleb screamed until he was hoarse.

Andrew stared at his best friend. Caleb had never cussed him that harshly before. He glanced at Vanessa. She, too, gawked at him, her eyes wide. He looked back at Caleb.

"Was that the missus?" Vanessa asked, a smirk sliding across her face and breaking into a wide grin.

Andrew held his palm up to her, and she high-fived him. "She sounded irritated."

Caleb's eyes flashed murder as he stomped up to her. "Give me one damn good reason not to lock the both of you up! I'll do it in a heartbeat!" He stood with his hands on his hips as if going for a weapon. Then his stony expression cracked into a thousand pieces. He doubled over laughing with his hands on his thighs. He stood and wiped his eyes. "If you can get your lame-ass boyfriend off the table, we need to go inside and talk this out."

Vanessa reached over to Andrew. "C'mon, lame-ass boyfriend. Let's go inside. I'm exhausted and want to hear all about your night."

Gingerly, Andrew climbed from the table and limped inside.

"Sit down and put your feet on a chair," Vanessa directed. "I want to get a look at your tootsies to see what all you've done to them."

Andrew sat at the end of the table, pulled a chair out, and rested his feet on it.

Vanessa returned with a wet rag and a tube of Neosporin. She kneeled and gently wiped the accumulated muck and debris away, then washed the bottom of his feet. She tenderly spread a thin film of the healing gel and blew lightly on the cuts, taking some of the sting out of them.

"Are you hurt anywhere else?" Vanessa looked up at him.

"Not that I know of," he said and stretched his arms out. Andrew rotated his wrists, turning his elbows over, and examined his palms and forearms.

"What's this?" Vanessa asked, then took one of his hands and gently turned his arm to look at his elbows. "Looks like grease." Using a fingertip, she wiped the smudge from the back of his arm and studied the remains on her finger. She then leaned down and smelled Andrew's head. "Have you been smoking?"

"Smoking? You know better than that," Andrew replied.

Caleb walked over and took a sniff. "That's not cigarette smoke, that's wood and—" He took another breath. "Chemicals. Like house-fire smoke." Caleb grabbed a chair and dragged it by Vanessa's, his back to the kitchen. "Andrew, you didn't wander off and burn down some old shack, did you?"

Andrew shook his head, slumped in his chair, and smiled. "I knew it felt real."

Vanessa and Caleb stared at each other.

"Sweetie, what felt real?"

Scratching at the back of his head, then staring at the ceiling, Andrew said, "The dream I just had." He leaned forward and rested his palms on his knees. "Y 'all want to hear some freaky shit?"

Caleb nodded. "Absolutely. You know I'm always down for some freaky shit. And your shit's usually the freakiest."

Andrew smiled, drew in a deep breath, said, "Hold on to your asses," and told them about his dream.

Chapter Thirty-Five

When Andrew finished, Caleb leaned back in his chair and rocked it up on two legs. He tilted his head and glanced at Vanessa. "Well, counselor, is that not some freaky shit?"

Vanessa had been holding her hands over her face as if trying to keep her breath from escaping. "That was positively disturbing."

Caleb set all four legs of his chair on the floor and cupped his chin. "Man, I don't even know where to begin." He looked over to Andrew, who shrugged.

"I guess we could see if any buildings burnt down around here last night," Vanessa said. "Maybe he sleep-walked through a burning building and didn't wake up until he was in the river."

"Maybe." Andrew's eyebrow dipped up. "But I can't imagine walking through a burning building barefoot. That would've woken me up, for sure."

"You could have been wearing shoes but lost them in the river," Vanessa offered.

Andrew shrugged, then twisted to look toward the hall leading to the bedroom. "Man, I seriously don't want to check and find I'm missing a pair of shoes."

"I'll check," Vanessa said rising. "The bottom of your feet makes me cringe." She tussled his hair as she walked past.

"You should be attached to them," Andrew replied, rubbing the soles of his feet. He turned to Caleb, realizing that his friend had been unusually quiet the last few minutes. "What are you doing?"

Caleb held up a finger as his other hand made rapid swipes down his phone. After a moment, he took a deep breath, set the phone down, and faced Andrew. "Tell me what you remember about tonight, starting with the evening. Go into as much detail as possible."

Andrew settled back in his chair and rocked slightly while glancing at the television. The screen was blank, the glass reflecting the ceiling fan spinning nearby. "Well," he began, "Vanessa and I had dinner, watched a movie—"

"What did you watch?"

"What did we watch?" Andrew asked, repeating the question. He closed one eye and thought about it. "Some chick-flic that bored me to tears. I fell asleep on the couch. Why?"

"Humor me," Caleb said. "What was the name of the movie?"

"It was *The Lake House*," Vanessa said, reentering the room. "I love that movie," she said enthusiastically. "Mr. Snore-snore was out halfway through." She took a seat opposite Andrew, lifted his legs, and placed them across her knees. "Do you think this might have incited Andrew to take a midnight march through the weeds?"

"No, not really. But if he watched a movie where buildings were burning, it might have influenced him somewhat." He stood and walked toward the kitchen. "It was his basic description of the dream that got me going." He pulled the fridge open, grabbed a bottle of water, and returned.

"How so?" Vanessa asked.

Caleb held a hand up to Vanessa, motioning her to hold on a minute. "What did you say about the building, Andrew? Long hallways splitting off each other, lots of doors that were all locked, old tile floors, flicking fluorescent lights hanging from the ceiling. Then the back door opens into a river. Is there anything else you can remember?"

Taking a deep, full breath, Andrew squinted, and then he rocked slowly back and forth. "Man, it was a dream, a weird one, really intense and not that long. The details are really murky now—almost faded away."

Jumping from his chair, Caleb darted over to the couch by the television and grabbed one of the multiple notepads Andrew kept stashed around the house to jot down ideas when they erupted in his brain. He stood beside his friend and dropped the tablet and a pen on the table. "Andrew, close your eyes and imagine the best description you can, and then scratch out what you think the floorplan was and what the building looked like."

"Are you serious? This was just a—"

"Andy-man, just draw, please."

Vanessa looked around Andrew to Caleb. The detective caught her eye and shook his head quickly.

Andrew closed his eyes and tilted his head toward the ceiling. After a moment, he opened his eyes, leaned close over the table, grabbed the pad, and began to scratch at the paper, his right hand a blur. He spun the paper, made a few more shadings with the blue pen he was holding, then slid the tablet over to Caleb, who was now sitting across the table from him.

Catching the tablet before it slid off the table, Caleb glanced down and nodded. His eyebrows lifted and he nodded. "Thank you, Andrew. I knew you had it in you."

"Had what?" Vanessa and Andrew asked at the same time.

"Hang on, I'll be right back. Just need to get my laptop." Caleb pushed out of the chair and ran out the front door. Several moments later, he returned with his ever-present shoulder bag. He sat back at his spot at the table and removed the county-issued laptop from his bag. Caleb whistled softly as he waited for the laptop to boot. Once the Sheriff's Department logo faded away, he bought up a webpage and typed quickly on the small keyboard.

"Caleb, what are you doing?" Vanessa asked.

The detective held up one finger to her. "Hang on, almost there." He leaned forward, typed furiously again, stopped, then leaned back with his hands beside the computer.

"Do you need the notepad?" Andrew asked.

Caleb shook his head, stared at the ceiling for a moment before turning his gaze to his friends. "Okay, hand me the pad." Andrew slid it over. "Per our prior conversation of Andrew and his freaky shit, tell me what you make of this," he said, placing the drawing on the laptop's keyboard, and then spinning it around so his friends could see it.

The couple leaned forward, their eyes flitting from the rough, scratched-out drawing to the computer display, then back to the drawing.

As if controlled by the same puppeteer, the pair glanced at each other, shook their heads, then slumped back in their seats simultaneously.

"That is indeed freaky shit," Andrew concluded. "What did I just draw?"

Caleb closed the lid to the laptop and leaned forward with his elbows on the table, chin resting on his laced brown fingers. "That, my friend, is the Crushwood Creek Rehabilitation Center in all its former glory."

"Crushwood Creek?" Vanessa asked. "I've never heard of it."

Caleb nodded. "I'm not surprised. It originally opened in 1952 as a psyche ward for the mentally insane. Later, in the mid-seventies, it became a private facility catering to the well-to-do. County picked it up about a decade later at a tax sale, and it was once again used as a psyche ward, but for county inmates. It burned to the ground in 2002 with the loss of eleven patients. The fire was arson and started in the women's wing. Someone chained the exterior doors and put glue in the locks to slow down first responders."

"And no survivors?" Vanessa asked quietly.

Caleb reached across the table, retrieved his drink, and licked his lips. "There was one, a female patient. She was able to escape at the last minute as the building exploded. From reports I've seen, she was on fire as she ran from the building, but her body was never recovered. Some doubt anyone escaped, and some say that she drowned."

"Drowned?" Andrew and Vanessa said together.

Caleb tilted his head slightly in confirmation. He opened the laptop, brought up the location of the now-destroyed building using Google maps, then spun it around. "Yes, drowned."

The icon on the map was on the edge of Lake Sinclair on a small tributary river that spilled dark water into the cypress-lined lake.

Andrew touched the screen with his finger, then dragged it across, stopping at an aerial view of a park and landing. He glanced at Caleb. "Is this the landing at Fisherman's Cove?"

Caleb nodded. "Yep."

"And this is the area where they caught the pics on the trail cams?"

"Correct again."

"Wow," Andrew said and sat in his chair. "More freaky shit."

"Yes, it is."

Chapter Thirty-Six

"Caleb, who was the woman that escaped?" Vanessa asked.

Inhaling deeply, Caleb held his breath for a moment before letting it out slowly. "Now, before you react to what I'm about to tell you, the information I have is suspect, at best. I haven't fleshed it out yet."

"Doesn't matter. What do you have?" Andrew asked.

Caleb stared straight at Andrew. "It's possible that the woman was your birth mom."

Vanessa and Andrew sat back, their eyes wide, mouths hanging open.

"My birth mom?" Andrew whispered. His hands began to tremble. "Could she be alive?"

Caleb shook his head, then shrugged. "Andy-man, I have no idea. I'm not even sure this woman was your mom."

"Why would you think she was there?" Vanessa asked.

"It's all circumstantial, at best. But, with the weirdness we've been dealing with, it just fits in with the bizarre set of unbelievable connections."

"Let's hear it, detective," Vanessa said, slipping into attorney mode.

"Like I said, this is from a less-than-reliable source, but some of the things he told me left me wondering if this guy was a crackpot or—"

"Or what?" Vanessa pressed.

"Gifted with incredible foresight."

"So, what are these incredible connections?" Andrew asked.

Caleb glanced at his watch. It was now near five a.m. "Best to hear it from the man himself. I've got to get home and cleaned up, then head on in. Barnes is probably going to be in riot mode. I want to be at my desk when he storms in." Caleb picked up his laptop bag and thumbed through it until he found what he was looking for. He handed Andrew a small white card. "Call this guy, he'll explain everything."

Andrew took the card, flipped it over, and read the title. "Joseph Abraham, Private Investigations."

"Oh, hell, no!" Vanessa shouted. "Not that charlatan! Man is nuttier than a jar of dry roasted peanuts."

Caleb snapped around to face Vanessa, unable to speak for a moment. "You know him?"

"Know him?" Vanessa said exasperated. "I'm the one that had him banned from the courthouse for tampering with witnesses. He's damn lucky not to be in jail."

"Tampering with witnesses?" Caleb sputtered. "Are you serious? Why the hell isn't he in jail?"

Vanessa waved a hand in the air. "Well, *tampering* is a bit of a stretch."

"How much of a stretch?" Andrew asked

"Old man kept trying to bring in a psychic on a malpractice case. Said the psychic could channel the spirit of a patient who died on the table, proving that the surgeon wasn't at fault. And that is just one of the many shenanigans he has tried to pull."

"And these didn't go over well?" Andrew asked with a smirk.

Vanessa's frosty glare was all the answer Andrew needed.

"My, he sounds peachy to me." Andrew said.

Caleb stood and stretched. "Well, y'all meet with Mr. Peachy and make your own decision. Just be careful, he's very convincing. Later, gators. I gotta get."

Vanessa followed him to the door and gave him a big hug. "Thanks for coming over. Hope Barnes doesn't go too hard on you."

"You and me both, girl. I'll be fine. Don't you worry." He gave Vanessa another quick hug. "Keep an eye on sleep-walking beauty over there." Caleb waved to Andrew, who gave him a thumbs up.

Vanessa shut the door behind Caleb, turned the deadbolt, and set the alarm. Yawning widely, she shuffled over to Andrew. "Sweetheart, I'm going to bed. It's been a long night. Why don't you and your ruined pajamas join me?"

Smiling, Andrew pushed from the table and hobbled over to Vanessa. He took her by the hand, pulled her in close, and kissed her lightly on the lips. "I'll be to bed soon. For some odd reason, I'm a bit wired. I think I'm going to watch TV, then I'll join you."

"Okay, just no unauthorized midnight strolls." She kissed him back.

Andrew shook his head emphatically. "That, I promise. My tootsies still hurt."

Once Vanessa had shut the door to the bedroom, Andrew hunted down the notebook he'd been drawing in. He found it by the couch. He sat, turned on the TV, and thumbed through the notepad. A dozen or so pages in he found the crude sketches he had drawn. The building depicted in his drawings looked nothing like the one he'd sketched earlier. Even through the rough scratching, he could tell the building was older, rustic—abandoned. How he knew it to be vacant, he didn't know. He just *felt* it deep in his core. The building was abandoned and malignant. If it existed, which he felt like it did, it was consumed with death, and the charred bodies surrounding it confirmed that fact.

Noticing black smudges on the edge of the pad, he flipped several more pages and found a new set of drawings, these of a woman in motion—running maybe? One crude sketch was just a set of fear-lined eyes, the skin around them wrinkled in terror.

A subtle odor caught his attention. He stood and walked around the house, trying to determine the smell and location. After a moment, he decided it was that of oily smoke, wood, and burnt plastic. Andrew ran to the kitchen and checked the stove, toaster, and refrigerator. All seem to be fine, but the faint essence remained, trailed him. Fighting panic, he darted through the house, checking the spare rooms, then checking electrical outlets and lamps. He disarmed the alarm system and checked the garage. No smoke or flames, but the smell continued to follow.

"What the hell," he growled and ran a finger through his hair. The odor of burnt wood and plastic intensified. Glancing at the notebook, Andrew raised it to his nose and took a deep breath. The smell emanated from his hands. He put his hand under his nose. It wasn't his flesh; it was the notebook.

Andrew carried the book by the edges to the kitchen table, afraid to take a solid hold of it in case it burst into flames. Looking at the book from the side, he could see signs of charring he hadn't noticed before. Taking a pen, he inserted it in the middle of the charring and opened the book. There was another set of eyes, but these were drawn to near perfection, a talent he didn't possess. He stared intently at the pupils. In the center of each orb was a drowning woman. The notebook was out of his hand and flying across the room before he realized he'd thrown it.

Caleb was sorting through a night's worth of incidence reports and starting on his third cup of coffee when a presence fell across his desk. He glanced up to see Barnes looming nearby, staring down at him. "Morning, Sheriff."

"Mr. Saunders, how is your friend?"

"Andrew?" Caleb asked, realizing a moment too late that was precisely who he was asking about. "He's fine, sir. Muddy, scratched up, and tired, but seems to be okay. And a bit confused."

Barnes's expression was neutral, giving away nothing. "I would suppose so. Getting lost in the swamp late at night would be very traumatizing."

Inwardly, Caleb tightened and clenched his jaw. Barnes was being condescending to him. "Yes, sir, it was. Andrew had no idea how he ended up in the woods. He's never sleepwalked before."

"I see. In the future, give the missing person a few more hours before calling out a search team. Helicopters and dogs—not to mention officers—are an expensive commodity to use for a person out for a midnight stroll."

"Agreed, sir. Normally, I would have waited until morning, but with recent events, I thought it might be prudent to at least get additional assets in place."

Barnes nodded and worked his jaw as if he was thinking over Caleb's words. Apparently in uncharacteristic agreement with Caleb, he changed the subject. "Forensics has determined that the red fluid on the pin stuck to Mr. Alewine's chair is human blood."

"Really? Have they had a chance to compare it to the boys' family? See if there's a DNA match?" Caleb asked.

"No confirmation yet. The lab said they will have a definite answer later today, maybe tomorrow." Barnes took a deep breath and let it out slowly. "You probably know this already, but the van was clean, not so much as a hair. It was as if the vehicle had just rolled off the assembly line. Not even dried boogers under the seat." The sheriff chuffed out a weak laugh.

"Yeah, I heard it was clean. How are the boy's parents holding up?"

Shrugging, Barnes glanced over Caleb's head and across the building. He let out a sigh and slumped a bit. "As best as could be expected with their boy missing and us at a stand-still. I had high hopes on the van, but so far it's a complete dead-end. It's like the boy stepped into a black hole and disappeared."

"I take it the previous owner was of no help?"

Barnes snorted and crossed his thick arms over his broad chest. "You could say that. Owner's in a dementia ward, and his children said the van was stolen years ago." He pulled a toothpick out of a shirt pocket and rolled it between his fingers before propping it in the corner of his mouth. "Here's a kicker. According to the odometer, the van only has around a hundred miles more on it than when it was reported stolen."

"Seriously? How did you figure that out?" Caleb leaned back and mirrored his superior's posture.

"Owner's son said the car had just been serviced. He still had the paperwork from the dealership updating the vehicle's status. Said his father kept everything."

"So, where has it been all these years?"

Barnes shrugged and repositioned his toothpick to the other side of his mouth. "Dunno."

Chapter Thirty-Seven

Joseph Abraham opened the door to his small wooden house and ushered Andrew and Vanessa in through the door. "Welcome!" he said. "Can I get you anything? Water? Tea? Really stiff drink?"

Andrew shook his head. "No, thank you, Mr. Abraham. We don't want to trouble you, since we won't be here long."

Joseph raised a wiry white eyebrow at the young redheaded man before him. "You sure?"

Andrew smiled. "Yes, sir. We have plans later today and didn't want to take up too much of your time."

"Well, son, whether you have time or not, I suggest you have at minimum a stiff drink." Joseph backed further into the small clapboard home. A tidy kitchen sat off to his right; a cozy den adorned with old, faded furniture swept off to their left. The vintage couch and loveseat were covered with an equally old and faded blanket.

Vanessa leaned forward. "We'd love to be able to stay longer, Mr. Abraham—"

"Joseph!" the elderly man said. "Call me 'Joseph.' It's my God-given name. Plus 'Mr. Abraham' makes me sound so *old.*" He winked at Vanessa, who rolled her eyes, then blushed just a bit.

"Okay, maybe a glass of water if it isn't too much."

"Of course, it's not too much!" Joseph said amiably. He turned to Andrew. "Are you sure you don't want something? It's no bother to open a bottle of whiskey." The elderly man cocked his head and glanced at Andrew out of the corner of his eye. "Though you look like a tequila man, now that I take a good look at you."

Vanessa laughed. "If you only knew!"

Andrew smiled sheepishly. "Me on tequila equals bad decisions." He laughed. "But a beer, if you have one, would be great."

"Yes, sir. One beer coming up." Joseph walked over to the fridge without the use of his cane, rocking back and forth as he moved. "Hope you're not a light-beer drinker," he said, pulling the old, avocado green cooler open. "That's girly beer. Never could understand why a man would want to drink something so weak." He held up a long-neck Budweiser. "Will this do?"

"Perfect, sir." Andrew smiled.

"Excellent, then." Joseph grabbed a second beer for himself, closed the door, and shuffled across the kitchen toward the den.

Andrew met him halfway, took the beer from his old, thin hands, and tipped it up.

"There's more if you want 'em. But if you do, you'll have to fetch them yourself. My hospitality only goes one beer." Joseph cackled and twisted the top off his beer. "Plus, my legs hurt. Been doing way too much runnin' around lately."

Andrew twisted the cap off the beer, took a deep pull, and sighed. "Man, sometimes a cold beer just hits the spot."

"Well, there's more in there if you want them. Just gotta fetch them yourself." Grabbing his cane by the front door, Joseph carefully stepped past Andrew and Vanessa, then took a seat perpendicular to the couch.

"One's good," Andrew said. "We've still got a few things to do."

"I understand, surely I do, but the beer's there nonetheless." Joseph leaned forward, both hands grasping the top of his ornate stick. "So, my detective buddy sent you my way?"

Vanessa said, "He did. Said you have some information we might find of interest."

"Of interest, you say?" Joseph's eyebrows went up and looked from one of his guests to the other. He leaned back in his chair, cane still clutched in his old, thin fingers, and laughed. "Oh, that Deputy Saunders. He's a man of very few words."

Andrew and Vanessa glanced at each other, then back to the older man. "Caleb said you might have some info on the fire and a lady possibly drowning at the old Crushwood Creek Rehab Center."

Joseph stared at her silently, his dark rheumy eyes not moving off her gaze.

"He, uh," Vanessa said after a moment. "He also said you might have some knowledge of the woman rumored to have drowned being Andrew's birth mother."

The elderly man's bushy white eyebrow ticked up a bit. "He did, did he?"

Andrew leaned around Vanessa. "Yes, he did. Said you would know more."

"Mayhap I do, but my question to you is, why do you want to know?"

Andrew told him about the dream.

Joseph sagged in his chair and shook his head. "Son, if you don't mind, shelf above that God-awful ugly fridge is a pint of Wild Turkey. Would you bring it to me with a glass from the cupboard?"

"Mr. Abraham, did my dream scare you to the point you need a drink?"

Joseph shook his head very slowly. "No, son. The drink's for you. When I get through telling you what I know, that little pint of Wild Turkey is going to be the alcoholic appetizer for your brain."

Chapter Thirty-Eight

"I met your birth mom once, sure did," Joseph said nodding. "Showed up at the hospital out of nowhere, as if she blew in on a devil wind." The elderly man paused to glance at Vanessa and Andrew. Neither moved, completely raptured by the start of his tale. "Yep, just showed up in full labor, ready to pop like an over-stuffed turkey."

"Did you work at the hospital, Mr. Abraham?" Vanessa asked in a hushed tone.

"Me? No, ma'am!" He chuckled. "The sight of blood or brains is more than I can handle. I was just a small freelance reporter working a crime blotter. I liked to hang out at the hospital with the nurses. If I treated them well, they tipped me off when someone interesting was brought in." He smiled and took a deep breath, releasing it slowly, relishing the memory. "Them were the good days before the hospitals started cracking down.

"Anyhoo, I was visiting with the head nurse when doctors came rushing by, grabbing everyone they could get a hand on and dragging them to the emergency room, then the OB ward. Doreen Foster—she was the head nurse at the time—pulled me aside and said they had a woman—your birth mom—in labor with twins." Abraham paused to add more impact to his words. "Conjoined twins."

Abraham smiled when his words hit pay dirt like a sledgehammer on a concrete floor. He could see factures of disbelief in their eyes.

"Conjoined twins?" Andrew whispered. "Are you sure?" His hand slid to the back of his head.

"Oh, I'm sure. Yes, sir. They called in all kinds of medical staff, dang near emptied the hospital." He took a sip from his beer. "Anyway, the babies were born, and they stayed in the hospital with their mother for a couple more days before being taken to Atlanta. Our little ol' building full of country saw-bones just wasn't equipped to handle something like that." Joseph took a long pull off his beer.

"It didn't take long for all the excitement to end, for the news folks to back up their vans, and for Warrenton to go back to being just a sleepy little town."

"I guess things didn't stay that way?" Andrew asked.

Joseph Abraham laughed his old man cackle. "Son, you have a way of understating the obvious!" He pulled hard on his beer, spilled a little around his mouth, wiped it with the back of his hand, and burped. "Must have been about a year later I heard whispers of a pair of twin boys living in a mobile home out in the woods with their mom, and that their mom was trying to sell them."

Andrew's eyes flicked to his finance, then back to the old man. "Sounds familiar, don't it, son?"

Speaking haltingly and in a quiet voice, Andrew nodded. "Yes, it does."

"Very few people knew about it. I think the number of folks around here that were privy to that knowledge is less than a handful now," Joseph added quietly.

Vanessa glanced up, brow pinching slightly. "What do you mean by that?"

Here we go, Joseph thought. *The slipperiest slope of all slippery slopes. Shit's about to get real, as the kids say.* He restrained a chuckle, leaned back in his chair, and cracked his knuckles. "Because folks keep dying. Have been for a while now."

"Dying?" Vanessa asked as if she didn't understand the statement. "From old age?" Her question was more than an inquiry, it was almost a plea.

Andrew turned away from her as if Joseph's statement were crystal clear. "If it were from old age, I don't think Mr. Abraham would be having us over, isn't that right? Mr. Abraham is hinting at something a bit more nefarious."

The old man bobbed his head several times. "'Fraid so, counselor. Not a one has died of natural causes. And there's been a number of them, too, sure enough."

"Caleb said you think I have a so-called 'evil twin,'" Andrew said with smirk. "Evil twins are just villains from cheap horror stories."

"Son, are you sure about that?" Joseph adjusted his position in the chair so he faced Andrew. "I've some information that might change your mind."

"Look, Joseph, if I had an evil twin brother, I think I would know about it."

Remaining calm, Joseph smiled softly and nodded. "You might not want to accept the possibility of such a cliché villain, but all the victims were killed by the same person. All the murders were by a psychopath that looks very much like you." Joseph finished his statement leaning forward, all his weight now resting on the golden knob atop his walking stick. "Plus, I think you believe it too."

Andrew's face was neutral. He stared directly at Joseph's watery, red-rimmed eyes. He was quiet for several minutes. "How did you know about me having a twin?" Andrew said. "I didn't even know until the last very recently."

Joseph put his weight fully on his cane. "Son, I know lots of stuff folks around here have never, ever in their life heard about. Warrenton has its ghosts—it's demons—if you like. And if you stay to the shadows like I have most my entire life, you hear things, see things." His eyes took on a faraway gaze before fixing on Andrew again. He pulled a long, ebony finger off the lionhead on his cane and pointed toward Andrew. "And I heard lots about you, son. Yes, sirree, bobcat." He pushed up off the cane, got his legs under him, then reached back for his near-empty beer. "Sweetheart," he said motioning to Vanessa. "Would you be a dear and put this dead soldier in the recycle bin and fetch me a new one?"

"Really, 'sweetheart'?" Vanessa rolled her eyes. "You do know this is the year twenty-twenty-two. I know a lot of women who would be offended by your comment."

"Oh, but not so offended if I picked up their tab at the diner, now, would they?" Joseph countered, holding the bottle out. "Despite the year being two thousand and twenty-two of the Lord." He winked.

"Fork the bottle over, old man, before I knock that cane out of your hands!" Vanessa made a feeble swipe at the walking stick with her foot.

"Ooh, feisty *and* beautiful!" Joseph cackled. "I might just hold a door for you at the courthouse next time I see you." He said with a raise of his bushy white eyebrows. "Come." He motioned with a tip of his cane town a dim hallway. "Our conversations were just the appetizer. I'm about to serve you the entrée." He then tottered unsteadily on his feet, his cane acting like a counterbalance as he shuffled down the hall.

Andrew caught Vanessa's eye. She raised her shoulders slightly and held her hands out, palms up. "After you, *dear*." She opened the refrigerator and grabbed a beer. "Do you want me to grab that liquor bottle? Somehow, I think our day's not quite over."

"Keep it in reserve. I'm going to see if I can take it like a man," Andrew said with a nervous grin and waited for Vanessa to catch up. "Any idea what this old dude is up to?"

Vanessa shook her head. "But from what I know of him, and if Caleb is correct, it won't be boring."

They walked down a hallway lined with vintage paneled walls and thick carpet. An old, yellowing fixture scattered meager light from the ceiling, casting muted shadows on the dark walls.

"Charming." Andrew glanced at the closed doors they passed. "In a slasher-movie kind of way." He reached out to open one when Vanessa smacked his hand away.

"Don't be so nosy!" she chided him. "You wouldn't want strangers opening closed doors in your house, would you?"

Andrew shrugged. "Wouldn't bother me. I don't have an old woman skeleton wearing a tattered nightgown sitting in a rocking chair by herself, now, do I?"

Vanessa shivered. "Let's not go there. I'm sure there's a reason all these doors are shut."

"Cause he got a bunch of dead people propped up in corners that he reads too late at night."

Vanessa elbowed him but didn't comment.

At the end of the hall, Joseph waited, smiling. "In here," he said, flipping a light switch that illuminated a well-appointed den. Compared to the small, tidy kitchen and den, this room was practically futuristic. Recessed lighting cast a soft glow on a leather couch, a seventy-inch television, and a computer station with a trio of fifty-inch monitors that would have made the execs at Google envious. Multicolored lights flickered and danced from the array of assorted computer paraphernalia.

"Wow," Andrew said, walking through the door. "Not what I was expecting."

Joseph smiled, showing off a few gaps between his stained teeth. "I do have a few indulgences, son. And one of them is a nice workstation, a comfy couch, and a big ol' television where I can watch King James shoot the ball. When you're as old as I am, you need a big screen."

Andrew circled the desk. It was three times the size of his own and ergonomically designed. He sat in the chair and rolled it up to the wireless keyboard. He bumped the mouse and the screens warmed to life. "Are you serious?" He swiveled around to glance at the old private eye. On the computer desktop was a larger-than-life image of Marvin Martian.

Joseph shrugged. "Kind of my alter ego—always one of my favorite characters. But hop up, this isn't what I wanted to show you." Using his cane, he shuffled over to a darkened alcove and held his hand on the wall. "*This* is what I wanted you to see."

Andrew and Vanessa exchanged glances.

Flipping a switch, a fifteen-by-ten section of the wall was illuminated by ceiling-mounted spotlights. On the wall were dozens of pictures with a red string running from photo to photo. Notes and newspaper clippings were tacked to the spiderweb-like timeline.

"What the hell?" Andrew said quietly and walked over to the wall.

"Nope, not 'what the hell,' son. More like 'welcome to hell.'"

Chapter Thirty-Nine

Behind the mass of pictures, notes, and string was a map of the United States. The strings started in Warrenton and extended to Oregon, then back across the county, sometimes doubling back and across themselves. Andrew fingered several pictures of himself, then perused the news clippings. Joseph walked over and stood beside him. "My wife used to collect spoons from everywhere we went. Most were ornamental with engravings and pictures and whatnot. Some were just plain-Jane generic spoons from IHOP or Waffle House—just depended on where we were when she decided she needed a spoon.

"I, on the other hand, collect true horror stories, murder clippings. Walls used to be full of strings and pictures. I used to start at the nexus of their evil intent and work my way out. Once I felt I knew who/what/where/why, I'd catalog everything, take down my timeline, and start a new one."

"That is macabre as hell," Andrew said in a rush, his breath rapidly escaping him. "Why did you do it?"

Joseph Abraham sighed. "My wife asked me that for more than forty years. Best answer I could give is that I had an obsession to understand how/why a man—it's always a man, you know?—never a woman—goes completely batshit and starts killing people." Joseph touched a string and let his finger run up and down it. "Just one of the things that always fascinated me and still does." He rubbed the sparse white stubble on his chin and cheeks. "And it gives me a non-scientific view into the inner workings of psychopaths. I even helped your friend's boss on several occasions. Barnes is too thick necked to see around the corner."

Vanessa unclipped a picture of an attractive woman who appeared to be in her mid-thirties. She studied the caption. *Doreen Foster, November 9, 2008.* Stapled to the picture was a news article. *Local nurse found dead at the site of the closed Warrenton Hospital. Authorities have no suspects.* The string the story was on was only a few inches long, running from a pin in the middle of Warrenton to just outside of the city limits.

From the same center-pin, a second, longer thread trailed out, this one due north of the city toward a large tract of land. Vanessa tapped her finger on the map. Another article and a grainy black-and-white picture of an old man were attached. *Phillip Mills, January 29, 1998,* was neatly printed on the picture. The corresponding print said he was the *facility director of the Sunrise Children's home and was found bound and gagged with his throat slashed.*

"Mr. Abraham, do you remember when the Sunrise Orphanage closed?" she asked.

"Not positive. Maybe around nineteen-ninety-nine. There was a fire in one of the dorms. Three children died and a dozen more were sent to the hospital. Also caught up in the flames were several orderlies. Two died at the scene."

"What caused it?" Vanessa continued.

Joseph shrugged and shook his head slowly. "Don't think we'll ever know. Fire Marshal said nothing was conclusive. Might have been wiring, a gas leak, static electricity. Said no accelerants were used, but there were multiple ignition spots. Ol' Layton Pope, he was the investigator at the time, said it appeared the carpet and drapes just suddenly went up in flames. No spark, no smoke, just Whoosh!—fire everywhere." Joseph threw his hands in the air. "Only clue they have is a grainy video showing someone short, either a young teen or a woman, walking down the hall. After the shadow passed, the walls burst into flames. By the time the first engines rolled on the scene, the place was fully engulfed. By the time they left, it was leveled." The old man hobbled over to his desk, sifted through several drawers, and then returned with a think manila folder.

"That is weird as hell," Andrew said in a subdued tone.

"Damn skippy, it is," the old man agreed. "Here, check out these pictures."

Andrew took the folder and opened it flat for him and Vanessa to view. "When you say 'leveled,' you weren't kidding. There's nothing left but ash and some metal supports."

Andrew closed the folder and followed a long red string that stretched across the map, ending in Portland, Oregon. He flipped up a picture and read the small information tag attached. "Bart Carmichael. Who was he?"

Joseph hobbled over. "He's the one that provided me with my 'aha! moment.'"

"Your 'aha moment'?" Andrew asked as he flipped up the pictures and information attached to each one.

"Yes, sir, my 'aha moment.'" Joseph pulled a desk chair over by Andrew and sat facing the board. "Y'all excuse me while I take a load off my feet. This story might take a few minutes, and my dogs are tired." The old man slowly lowered himself into the chair, sighed, and stretched out his legs. "What happened is this," he said, settling deeper in the chair and resting his cane across the chair's arms.

"When them young folks were bludgeoned to death out there in Oregon, the news was headline-stuff here." He nodded at the surprise in his guest's eyes. "Now, any brutal killing is going to hit all the newswires from coast to coast. What sparked interest here is that young man's picture you were holding. Bart Carmichael was the son of Wallace Carmichael. Y'all won't know his name, but folks around here would. He was the hospital photographer who took all the pictures of the new babies and their mamas for decades. So, when young Bart was murdered, it made news here."

"Was his father also murdered?" Vanessa asked.

Shaking his head, Joseph said, "No, ma'am. Wallace passed away years before his son of a heart attack."

"So . . . ." Andrew began. "What brought on your epiphany?"

"I was getting to it, son, I was getting to it. Indulge an old man in his storytelling!" Joseph laughed lightly. "The killings in Oregon were a few years after the hospital closed. I was in the Oaken Tavern one night, imbibing in an adult beverage or three, rehashing the latest scuttlebutt around town." He paused when he noticed Andrew and Vanessa glancing back and forth quizzically. "Tavern's long gone— that's why you never heard of it. But I digress. Anyhoo, there's talk of the Carmichael boy being killed, and someone—still can't quite remember who says something about that old hospital being cursed—that folk associated with it have been dying out the last few years. And not just old folks. Some relatively young—late forties, early fifties. Some were murdered, some simply vanished."

Taking his cane, Joseph pointed at the first picture in the string. "Bang!" he said, then followed up with several more "bangs" as he worked his cane down the string. "Every last one of them was in some way associated with the hospital where you and your devil twin was born."

"What about the birth mom?" Vanessa asked.

Joseph shrugged. "Dunno. Just vanished after giving up her babies. No one around here ever saw her again."

"Cops never find anything?" Andrew slumped against a wall.

"Son, cops don't spend no time looking for hippy-dippy drifters. Especially if no one asks them to." As if reading Andrew's mind, Joseph continued, "I made some inquiries, asked around town. Even checked with the hospital in Atlanta." He shook his head and shrugged. "Sorry, son. Sometimes folks just disappear."

Vanessa walked along the wall, tracing the string with her fingers, occasionally flipping up the pictures and reading the captions. She shook her head slowly. "Why would anyone do this?"

Joseph shrugged. "Why does any nutjob do what they do?"

"But you have a theory?" Andrew asked, turning his back on the wall.

"I do, that's right. But so far, no one wants to cotton to what I think."

Without turning to face Joseph, Vanessa said, "He's erasing his past."

"He's erasing everyone that had a part in his coming into the world," Joseph corrected.

"Why in the hell would he do that?" Andrew asked.

"Dunno," Joseph said with a shrug. "Crazy-ass people do crazy-ass things."

Andrew crossed his arms and stared at the thin old man. "I think you do know," he said directly and stepped from the wall

Joseph took a long, deep breath and let it out slowly, the exhalation coming as a soft whistle from his nose. He nodded and glanced up. Clasping his hands together, he gripped his fingers tight and leaned on his cane. "What I know is this: I am one hundred percent certain you were born a conjoined twin. I'm also one hundred percent certain that days after your birth, you were taken to Atlanta for separation. I'm ninety-nine percent certain your birth-mom sold you to Mary Beth Alewine. And I'm about ninety-five percent certain that a copy of you has been on a decades-long murder spree, removing from the earth all who were involved with your birth. And, by my recollection, there's only a handful of folks remaining."

"Mom and I," Andrew said in a whisper.

"And a few more, I suspect," Joseph said still leaning on his cane.

"You," Vanessa added, "were there from the beginning as well—at the hospital, the adoption."

Nodding and smiling wistfully, Joseph said, "Yes, counselor, that is correct."

"You can't stay here," Andrew said. "Caleb can arrange protection for you. Maybe stay with me."

"Son, it don't matter a wit of beans where I stay. When that twin of yours is ready to take me, there's nothing I can do."

"That's nonsense!" Andrew replied. "Stay with me. I have a top-of-the-line alarm system, and Caleb has a friend watching out. Plus, I have a mean Louisville Slugger for protection." Andrew smiled and mocked swinging the bat.

"Andrew, I appreciate that, I do. But none of that's gonna help. Not no alarm, not no guarded house. Nope, I'll stay here in my ratty old easy chair."

"At least let me give you the bat," Andrew begged.

"For what, son?"

"Protection! Maybe you can get in the first strike, knock him out, or something."

Joseph struggled out of the old recliner and patted Andrew on the shoulder as he hobbled across the floor turning off lights. "C'mon, you two. I'm an old man, and I'm getting tired. Seriously doubt I could swing a bat to much effect. Plus, *Wheel of Fortune* is coming on, and I think I'll set a spell and watch some TV."

"I could stay with you if you like," Andrew said, following the old man.

"To protect me from your brother?" He raised a wiry white eyebrow.

"Yeah. Maybe with me here, he won't hurt you."

Joseph flipped a wall switch and the overhead lights dimmed. "I appreciate that, son. I do. But there's really nothing you can do to stop your brother."

"What do you mean, I can't stop him?"

Joseph took another long, nasally breath, then let it slowly seep out between tightly held lips. "Andrew, your brother is dangerous. Might be the most dangerous person any of us will ever confront in our lifetime. I've been around a lot longer than the two of you, and I've been inside the Showanne Prison Complex—helped with a journalism class there once in the SuperMax wing. These predators were only given one hour of natural light each day and were confined the other twenty-three hours. Sometimes even chained up, except when they slept." He leaned heavily on his cane.

"But your brother . . . ." Joseph shook his head. "Now, he scares me. Bad. I firmly believe with all my heart, lungs, and soul that he's worse, much worse, than anyone I ever met in SuperMax."

Andrew swallowed hard; his throat dry. "Why do you say that?"

"Whilst those other men were reported to be evil, I believe your brother is the embodiment of it."

Vanessa took Andrew's right arm in her hands and pulled up against him tightly. "So, where does this leave us?"

"Right where we were, young lady." Joseph shuffled toward the light switch. "I'm going to retire back to me old easy-chair, prop my feet up, and watch something that don't take too much brainpower. Then I'll turn in, and if the good Lord is willing, see the sunrise in the morning."

"What if he comes for you?" Vanessa asked.

"Well, if that should happen, don't suppose there's anything I can do about it." Joseph patted her on the shoulder. "I'm an old man. I've done a lot and seen a lot and ain't got no real complaints. Now, if he interrupts my TV time, we gonna have a little go at it. But if he comes in my sleep . . . . " He shrugged and smiled wanly.

Vanessa hugged Joseph before the man could take another step. "Take care of yourself, Joseph."

"I'll do what I can, pretty lady."

Withdrawing from the embrace, the old man hobbled over to the wall and swiped at the light switch. The room darkened immediately.

Chapter Forty

Andrew started the car but had yet to put it in reverse. He sat with his hands on the wheel, staring straight at the old investigator's house. "What the hell do you think?"

Matching his gaze, Vanessa slowly shook her head and spoke in a halting voice, "I have absolutely no idea. This is the scariest thing I've ever been through."

"So, what do we do next?" Andrew's hand was now on the gearshift, but he hadn't made any motions toward shifting the car out of park.

"Consult a Ouija board?" Vanessa asked with a grin.

"Not just no, but hell no. I don't want any part of that." This time Andrew moved the transmission into reverse, and then backed out of the driveway and onto the lonely blacktop. "I've already got a possessed piece of furniture in my house. I think we'd be playing with fire if we brought a possessed game home as well."

Andrew drove slowly down the road, drumming his fingers on the steering wheel. "I think I should have taken Joseph up on that hard liquor." He lowered the driver's-side window and held his arm out, letting the warm summer air flow through the car. His hand rose and fell like the wing of a plane.

Vanessa glanced his way and put a hand on his shoulder. She gently massaged the base of his neck, teasing the hair that grew over his collar. "Maybe he's wrong," she offered.

"I'm not so sure he is. There's something evil here. I've felt it my entire life, especially since I touched that damn collar. I knew this day was gonna happen." Andrew chuckled. "I always thought I'd be a bit more prepared." Putting his arm back inside the car, he rolled the window up and pressed on the accelerator. "Guess not."

"Where are we heading?"

Andrew rocked slightly in the driver's seat and scrunched up his shoulders, relaxed again, and shook his head. "Not sure. Home, I guess." He was about to say more when his phone vibrated. He glanced down, then unlocked the phone with a swipe of a finger. He fumbled until he managed to get the device to his ear. "Hello?"

Andrew listened for a while, nodded several times, and agreed to questions only he could hear. "Nope, haven't eaten," he said after a prolonged silence. "Sure, Compton's Chop House is fine. Definitely give us some privacy. We'll see you there in about an hour." Andrew ended the call and set the phone back on the center console, eyes on the road ahead.

"Anything you want to tell me?" Vanessa asked.

"Not really. Wasn't Caleb. Just a guy from India trying to save me money on my credit cards," Andrew replied, staring straight down the highway.

"And we're meeting this scammer at Compton's Chop House? I thought cows were sacred in India?"

"They are. He's having soup." Andrew barely glanced at Vanessa.

"And having dinner with us?" Vanessa asked, leaning away and staring over her shoulder at him.

"That's right, having dinner, talking credit card rates—you know, basic financial stuff."

Vanessa held her hands in front of her as if strangling an invisible assailant. She half laughed; half groaned. "I swear you drive me nuts, Mr. Alewine!" She shook her head. "Now, what's really going on?"

Andrew rocked back and forth behind the wheel, his hands resting at the ten-and-two o'clock position. "Oh, nothing much." He sighed. "Caleb thought it would be nice if we could have dinner together."

"And . . . ?" Vanessa prompted.

"Barnes is coming."

"Well—that takes the joy out of dinner."

Andrew glanced her way, smiled, and nodded. "Yes, it does." He turned back to the road.

"Okay, Copper-Top, what the hell aren't you telling me?" Vanessa's eyes focused hard on him, then softened before turning worried.

"Oh, nothing much." Andrew brightened and shifted her way. "Did I tell you Caleb got a fax today with the missing boy's picture on it? Sure did. Nice fax, great detail. Has the boy holding my last book—if you can believe that. The fax number it was sent from hasn't been in service for several years. They think the number was spoofed and haven't been able to track it down yet. Apparently, this has Barnes in a tizzy, and we're to meet and have a long, cordial talk."

Vanessa stared at Andrew. "When did this happen?"

Andrew squinted his left eye as he thought about it. "Caleb thinks about an hour ago, maybe ninety minutes. It didn't hit his desk fax, but one in an empty office. The only way they knew it was there is that someone heard the fax printing—and printing. It appears my brother—if that's who is truly doing this—faxed the picture hundreds of times."

"I have no words for this," she said quietly.

"Neither do the cops." Andrew continued to drive toward town.

"Any idea what Barnes wants to talk about?"

Andrew shook his head. "Well, it's a given he wants to rehash things about the kid."

"What else can you tell him?" Vanessa asked, anger creeping up in her tone.

Driving with his knees and holding his hands out, Andrew shook his head. "Not much."

"And…." Vanessa persisted.

"And, 'what'? Andrew said not looking her way.

"What aren't you telling me, Andrew?"

Andrew took a long breath and held it before releasing it in a rush. "And…they might want me to twinge on something."

"I don't want you doing this, Andrew." Vanessa said shaking her head.

Swallowing hard, Andrew nodded. "I'm not real thrilled about it either. But they have no leads on the boy or the woman." He drove for a few minutes more. "And the woman, I almost feel indebted to her."

Vanessa turned his way. "Indebted? Why?"

Andrew almost smiled. "It's Amber Collins, my editor's daughter. If I hadn't written the books, she wouldn't been abducted."

Compton's Chop House was a rustic, former mill set back in a cospe of towering oak trees. Gray stones made up the walls; weathered, faded timbers dressed the front as if the building had been appropriated from an old western movie. Heavy lead-glass windows cast yellowy flickers of light out the windowsills. The gravel parking lot was mostly empty when they arrived, but that would soon change as the early-dining discount would end within the hour. Andrew circled the gravel lot until he spotted Caleb's truck. Next to it was Barnes' SUV.

They parked a few spaces down from Caleb and exited the vehicle. Vanessa took Andrew's hand. "I'm really nervous."

"Me, too." Andrew squeezed her hand and pulled the thick wooden doors open.

The interior of the building was made of rough-hewn lumber, and artificial oil-burning lights hung from chandeliers made from old wagon wheels. The waitstaff looked as if they'd just left the set of Bonanza. The restaurant was mostly empty, except for a few tables. The hostess was just turning their way when Caleb waved to them from the back of the restaurant.

Vanessa's hand gripped Andrew's tighter as they made their way around the tables. Barnes and Caleb had sequestered a small, private alcove in the rear of the restaurant. The room might have been a horse stall generations ago—the twelve-by-ten space had dark walls and wrapped partially around in front of them. An array of old livestock equipment clung to the walls and hung from the ceiling. Barnes stood and motioned for them to sit.

Caleb caught Andrew's eye and gave him a subtle nod. Barnes sat at one corner of the long table with Caleb to his right; Vanessa sat at the other end facing Barnes; Andrew took a seat across from Caleb.

"I've taken upon myself to order an appetizer for all of us. I hope you like deep-fried mozzarella sticks," Barnes announced.

"Uh, sure," Andrew said, focusing on Caleb, whose only reaction was to tip up a beer that was already half-empty and stare across the restaurant. "I like them just fine."

"Excellent, I thought you would," Barnes said with a smile. "Have you ever eaten here before? Their steaks are out of the world."

"We have, several times," Andrew answered. "And you are correct, steaks are phenomenal."

Barnes leaned forward; his massive arms braced on the table's edge. "What's your favorite?"

Andrew leaned back slowly as he glanced at the menu. "Hard to say, but the Ponderosa is divine!" He closed his eyes as if reliving the flavor.

"It is, isn't it?" Barnes agreed, tipping his water glass in Andrew's direction. "Personally, I'm partial to the Wild Saloon bourbon topped—"

"What the hell is this?" Vanessa demanded.

Barnes' expression didn't change while Andrew shrank back from the table.

"For the better part of a week, Sheriff, you've been harassing Andrew and even put him in the hospital!" She slapped the table, making all the utensils clatter. "And, Andrew, what gives? He's treated you like shit, and now you're talking steaks like you're long-lost buddies?" Vanessa turned her fire to Caleb. "Want to enlighten me, Deputy?"

"Vanessa." Caleb turned up the wattage of his smile. "Just wanted to find a way to reboot this investigation—stat over, if you will. Try to put some of the ugliness out to pasture."

"I'll reboot my foot up your ass if you don't wipe that donkey grin off your face!" Vanessa shouted, leaning toward Caleb, lips pulled back tight against her teeth in a contained snarl. "Now someone tell me why in the hell Andrew and I are here."

"I like you, counselor," Barnes said with just a hint of a grin. "Never liked being across the table from you in the courtroom, but you don't mince your words." The sheriff glanced over Vanessa's shoulder to a young waitress standing nervously with her order pad in one hand. "Miss, I don't think we're ready to order yet. Can you come back in a few minutes?" The server spun on her heels and practically sprinted across the restaurant.

Barnes watched her go, then turned back to Vanessa and Andrew. He picked up his water, swirled the ice with a flick of his wrist, making small waves in the glass, then took a sip and put it back down on the exact moisture ring it had previously sat on. After a moment, he glanced at Caleb, then back to Andrew. "Since I have been given additional insight into the case by both Deputy Saunders and my uncle Joseph Abraham, I'd like to apologize, if I may, to you, Mr. Alewine. Though I have a hard time wrapping my head around recent events, the evidence seems to speak for itself."

"Sir, you now believe me that Andrew has an—evil twin—for lack of a better word?"

"I'm still not set on that theory, Deputy. But I no longer feel Mr. Alewine is entirely involved in the recent disappearances."

"*Entirely* involved?" Vanessa parroted. "How about not involved in any way, shape, fashion, or form?"

Barnes held a hand up to ward off another onslaught from the attorney. "Let me rephrase." While still holding his hand up, he took a deep breath and let it out in a slow, measured release. "I do not believe Mr. Alewine had any *physical* connection to the events of the past week or years. And—" Barnes continued to hold his arm out, palm up. "I am coming around to the concept that there are forces involved that can't be explained, coincidences that defy logic." The sheriff lowered his arm and invited Vanessa to speak.

"So, what *are* you saying? That you now believe in Andrew's twinge-thingy?"

"I'm saying—" Barnes paused, his face strained and jaw muscles flexing. He put his hands against the edge of the table as if he were going to shove it away. "That I *want* to believe. That my intractable position might have hurt this investigation." Barnes took a long breath and calmed. "I now realize how much value Mr. Alewine's information has been."

"As a highly valued CI—" Andrew began. "I can only assume this meal is being comped?" Andrew asked.

A slight crack of a smile split Barnes's lips, and he nodded almost imperceptibly.

"Good." Andrew stood, whistled, caught the waitress's attention, and motioned to her that they were ready to order. "Chop, chop! Let's not dilly-dally," he sang across the restaurant. "The 'Amazing Andrew' is about to perform, and he needs to be totally wasted for this one."

Chapter Forty-One

The server cleared the last of the dinner plates and Andrew's empty beer bottles. "Can I interest you in a dessert? We have a collection of wonderful pies and cakes that are made fresh daily."

Caleb and Barnes shook their heads while Vanessa pushed back in her chair. "Thank you, no. I have to fit in my clothes tomorrow."

"And you, sir?" the server asked Andrew.

"Cake? No, ma'am. But if I could trouble you for one more beer, that would be excellent."

The waitress hesitated and bit slightly on her lower lip. She drew in a deep breath, held the dessert menu tight against her chest, and began apologetically, "I'm afraid our policy on alcohol is to not over-serve a guest; I am so sorry."

Barnes stood slightly so that he towered over the table. He smiled the best he could to take some of the menace off his appearance. "Let me commend the management on an excellent policy. As the Sheriff of Warrenton County, I can promise you that Mr. Alewine will neither be driving nor will he get out of hand. I will personally take responsibility for him."

Andrew smiled broadly as he glanced between the ebony mountain looming over the table and the waitress whose eyes were a mixture of fear and indecision. "What he said! Two more of your finest local craft beers, my lady!"

Vanessa cringed while Caleb leaned back and laughed.

"I, uh, will have to ask my manager." She backed up, pivoted, and fast-walked away.

"Mr. Alewine," Barnes asked, keeping an eye on the young waitress as she disappeared into an office near the entrance. "How many more beers will it take for you to become desensitized?"

"Oh, I'm there," Andrew slurred a bit. "I don't want to just get the ball across the goal line; I want to punt it into the stands."

"And two more beers will accomplish this for you?" Barnes asked, now sitting back.

"Yes, indeedy, nice and speedy!" Andrew sang. "What'cha got for me?"

Barnes rolled his eyes, stared at the ceiling, and shook his head slowly. "What I *have* for you," he began, overly emphasizing the correct grammar, "is an item I hope will help bring this case to a swift conclusion." He reached down and placed a simple, brown paper bag on the table. Stenciled across the top of the bag in block letters were a date, a number, and "EVIDENCE."

"Sheriff, can I take a look at what you have in the bag?" The hairs on the back of Andrew's neck and arms stood up.

"In time, Mr. Alewine. I want to make sure you are as prepared as you say you need to be."

As if on cue, the waitress walked up with a pair of dark-bottle beers. She worked up a nervous smile. "Manager says we can go ahead and serve a few more beers." Her smile faltered and struggled to reform. "But only while he is with you, Sheriff."

"Perfect. Thank you for accommodating us," Barnes said.

The server sat the beers beside Andrew and hurried over to another table.

"Me thinks I intimidate her." Andrew's slur increased.

"Drink up, funny man," Vanessa told him. "I'm curious as to what we have here."

"That makes two of us," Caleb added.

Andrew held up three wavering fingers and pulled hard on the beer. Within minutes, he had drained the first beer and was working on the second.

"Good God," Vanessa said, staring at him and shaking her head. "Your eyes are so bloodshot that when you wake up tomorrow, you are going to hate today."

"We shall sheee," Andrew replied, now struggling to finish the second beer. Gathering a second wind, he tipped the beer higher and slugged down the last of the brew. He dropped the empty bottle down hard on the table, grimaced, then let loose with a lusty burp. "That was really goosh," he managed to say. "Now if you will be so kind, show me wat'cha got."

Caleb pointed toward the tri-fold doors at the corner of the stall. Each could be closed to increase privacy. "Vanessa, if you don't mind, let's close up this room—just in case Andrew has another— uh, event."

"Yes!" Vanessa said and pushed from the table. The mostly glass partitions slid silently on their tracks, then locked together with a click. She returned to the table and smiled nervously at Andrew, then Caleb. "I guess now is as good a time as any."

"How do you feel, Mr. Alewine? Are you prepared for this?" Barnes asked.

"I feel peachy and right as rain!" Andrew responded more enthusiastically than necessary. "Let's see what goodies you have for me." He leaned forward over the table, his elbows on the polished dark wood, and rubbed his hands together in anticipation.

Barnes reached into the bag and pulled out a generic-looking track-phone. He set it on the table and slid it Andrew's way.

Without hesitating, Andrew reached out and slapped his palm onto the phone. He took a breath and let it out. "Sorry, no winner. Is this the kid's phone?"

"Yes," Caleb answered. "His parents said he didn't like it much."

"Well, that explains why I didn't get anything," Andrew said evenly. His eyes were beginning to droop.

Next out of the bag was the faded orange ballcap that had been on the handlebars of the boy's bike. The same one that shot him down the rabbit's hole. Andrew recoiled slightly, withdrawing his hands to his lap. "Uh, what else do you have for me?"

"Mr. Alewine, I suspect you will be fine with the hat as you were with the phone," Barnes said.

"You 'suspect'?" Andrew laughed softly. "Excuse me for not feeling all that confident. I've been your suspect for a week now, and it hasn't been pretty." His words were clearer, but the volume was dropping.

Sighing, Barnes folded his massive hands in front of him and nodded. "Just procedure. We have to eliminate everyone before we can focus on just one person. I'm sorry if you feel we were a bit over-aggressive. But when a child goes missing, we have to move quickly and apologize later."

"Whatever," Andrew muttered and reached for the hat before he realized he was doing so. He clenched the hat in his fist—and nothing happened. "Huh," Andrew said when he realized the room hadn't slipped out from under him. "I thought for sure I was going to wake up in the hospital."

"It wasn't the hat that set you off," Caleb said. "Joseph was right."

"Then what in the hell put him in the hospital?" Vanessa asked, glancing between Caleb and Barnes.

"We believe he touched this, and not the hat." Barnes carefully set the Minnesota Twins pin on the table; the button protected in a clear plastic sleeve.

"After talking with Joseph—and, I admit, his theories sounded crazy at first—we think this pin is the 'twin', if you will, of the one in your house. We also think it's a direct link to your brother."

"Do you think he knew that me touching it would rock my world?"

Caleb shrugged. "I have no idea. Could just be his sadistic mind at work."

"But if it linked you to him once, it might work again," Barnes said. "Mr. Alewine, I can see in your eyes that you don't want to touch it. After the incident with the bicycle, I can sympathize with you. But time is of the essence. If touching it gives us a direction to travel—"

Andrew grabbed the plastic sleeve covering the button, broke the seal, and dropped it into his palm. He closed his fist around it. And his mind exploded.

Chapter Forty-Two

The ceiling fan spun lazily above him, way above him. Miles in the air, it seemed, the rotations leaving colorful streamers behind. He tried to focus on the fan, but his vision was watery at best. The saliva in his mouth tasted coppery. His chest compressed as if his lungs were frozen. His ears hurt. A crushing, pounding hush of noise pulsed in his head. And then the room tilted forward, threatening to pitch him off the planet. He fought against the movement, then heard his name being called from somewhere. And then Vanessa's face hovered just above him.

"Andrew, talk to me!" she was saying, her words slightly louder than the roar in his ears. She looked behind him, talking to someone, her words muffled. Then hands grabbed him by the shoulders and lifted him back into his chair. Vanessa knelt beside him, face fear-stricken. A cold cloth appeared over his head and brow. He glanced up and saw Caleb with a dripping wet towel. Finally able to gulp in a lung-full of air, his vision focused enough for him to see Barnes marching back and forth with a phone to his ear, barking orders he couldn't understand.

Another rain of cold water ran down his brow, the ice-cold fluid shocking his senses. The rushing in his ears diminished as his eyesight sharpened. The first really clear words he heard were Barnes bellowing, "Two-twenty-seven Oakmont Terrace! Run code-three all the way." *227 Oakmont Terrace*, wavered through his mind. *Run code* tripped something internal. Two-twenty-seven Oakmont Terrace was—Joseph's house. Run Code was lights, sirens, everything.

He saw it now, the dissipating cloud. The sight of the twinge snapped him back against the chair and took his breath away again, but the adrenaline charge cleared his head and supercharged his senses.

Caleb was ducking a towel in another water glass and was about to baste him with it when he grabbed Caleb's arm and shook his head. "I'm back—I think," he whispered. "How long?"

Dropping the linen napkin to the floor, Caleb nearly fell to the floor in relief. "A while. Maybe ten minutes."

Vanessa threw her body against Andrew, almost toppling them over. "Dear God, I thought you were dead! Your eyes rolled up in your head and you quit breathing." She kissed his face and head, tears spilling from her eyes.

Andrew gently pushed her off him. "Joseph," he wheezed, trying to stand. "Is in trouble."

"We know," Caleb replied. "You screamed his name before flatlining. Barnes has a cruiser hauling ass there now."

"C'mon," Andrew said, starting to rise. "He's not done, he's moving." He staggered from the table and toward the folding doors. It was the first time he noticed everyone in the restaurant staring their way.

Vanessa reached out and took him by the arm. "No, Andrew, you're staying here. An ambulance is en route."

"I'm fine—mostly." He leaned against the partition doors. "I think I know where my brother is heading. I need someone to drive."

"Andrew, I'm not driving you anywhere!" Vanessa cried. "You practically died back there! If Barnes hadn't given you CPR, it would be the morgue coming to get you, not an ambulance."

"Yeah, buddy, you're still about three shades paler than death," Caleb said. "If the EMTs say you can travel, then we'll boogie." He stood beside Andrew, glancing through the folding door's windows. "Tell me where he's going, and I can send someone."

The wail of a siren sounded outside the building.

"We don't have time for this," Andrew growled, digging his keys out of a pocket in his jeans. He shoved the doors open and stumbled through.

Caleb reached for his friend's arm, but only managed to get his fingers on Andrew's shirt sleeve. "Hey, man, you can barely walk. You're in no condition to drive!"

"Then drive me, damn it!" Andrew fired back and pushed past the first row of tables. "If I don't catch up with him now, he'll be gone again, and we'll never find him."

"Caleb, don't you dare!" Vanessa cried out. "He needs to go to the hospital. Have Barnes drive wherever Andrew tells him."

"The Sheriff is too busy dealing with Joseph to run out on an unsubstantiated tip." Caleb said quickly.

Andrew staggered and put a hand down on a table, ignoring the people eating. He sagged and now held onto Caleb to keep from falling. "The woman who gave birth to me is there—and my brother," Andrew gasped. "I know where they are, we've got to go! And only me and you, Caleb. No sirens or he's gone."

"How do you know?" Vanessa asked.

Shrugging and struggling to talk, Andrew threw his hands in the air. "I don't know how I know! I just do. Maybe my evil twin planted this shit in my head."

"I thought she was dead," Caleb said, his voice shaky.

"She might be, I don't know." Andrew let go of Caleb and nearly fell.

"And go where, Andrew? Where are you heading?" Vanessa asked and helped Andrew stand.

"I . . . I'm not sure. Caleb, did someone get to Joseph's in time?"

Caleb brought his eyes up to Andrew, then slowly shook his head. "We were too late. He was long gone by the time officers got on scene."

"How?"

"Don't know. I just overheard Barnes on the phone telling the responding officers to secure the scene."

Andrew pushed his keys into Caleb's hand. "Drive!" he barked.

"You don't even know where you're going!" Vanessa argued. "Please, Andrew, you look terrible. You're in no condition to go anywhere." She put a hand on his arm and pulled him toward her.

Andrew calmed himself and stepped from Vanessa. "Look, you have to trust me. I know why that pin knocked my ass out. It wasn't the kid's or my brother's. It was my birth-mom's."

Before Andrew could continue, the doors to the restaurant opened and a pair of EMTs rushed toward them. Caleb stepped forward, grabbed the lead medic, and broadcast his best smile. "Sorry, guys, but someone jumped the gun. Andrew is a narcoleptic and fell out during lunch. He's fine now."

Andrew stood and tried to look sheepish. "Yeah, I'm fine. My fiancé was just being cautious." He playfully nudged Vanessa.

"You don't look okay," the first paramedic, a middle-aged man with a half-day's beard and sharp eyes, said. "You look like you've had a rough go of it." He pulled a penlight out of his pocket and shined it in each of Andrew's eyes. "Have you been drinking or taking any prescription drugs?"

"No, nothing like that. Probably just allergies," Andrew responded, trying to step around the man.

The EMT took Andrew's wrist, put two fingers on it, and cocked his head slightly. "Well, your pulse is very rapid."

"I'm just in a hurry. I have an appointment I'm late for."

"Alrighty," the man said with a nod. "If you feel short of breath, don't hesitate. Call nine-one-one or head immediately to the hospital."

"Will do," Andrew said genially and shook the EMT's hand. "Caleb, let's go."

Andrew glanced over his shoulder and saw Barnes walking their way, his hand waving. "Caleb, we've gotta go—now."

Caleb held a finger up and backed away. "Two minutes, Andrew. Barnes looks like he's about to go into hyperdrive. Let me brief him, then we'll go."

Caleb engaged in a very animated conversation Andrew couldn't hear, but it didn't look like Caleb was faring very well. Eventually, Barnes threw his arms up in the air, pointed toward the door, and then pointed repeatedly to the watch on his wrist. Caleb nodded turned towards Andrew.

"Are we good?" Andrew asked.

"Oh, yeah," Caleb said, forcing a grin. "Me and Barnes are good."

"Didn't look that way," Andrew said, now pushing himself to a staggering jog across the room.

"Well, looks can be deceiving." Caleb rushed ahead and held the doors for Andrew and Vanessa.

Vanessa paused outside the restaurant while Andrew tossed his car keys to Caleb. "You sure about this?"

Andrew shook his head. "No, not in the least bit. But that feeling of shit about to hit the fan is damn near tangible."

Caleb slid in the driver's seat as Andrew took up the passenger-side front. Vanessa jumped in the rear and they buckled up. "Okay, Kemosabe, which way?"

"Do you have the button?"

Caleb nodded and pulled a small plastic bag containing a quarter-sized white metal circle with a Minnesota Twins mascot on it from his shirt pocket.

"Hand it over, please." Andrew extended his arm, left hand out, palm up.

"Andrew," Vanessa said slowly. "The last two times you touched this button, you've almost ended up in a coma. Are you sure you want to do this again?"

"Am I sure?" Andrew glanced over his shoulder. "Hell, no, I don't want to do it. But sometimes you gotta do the things you least want to do."

Removing the plastic seal and dropping the button onto his pants leg, Andrew shook his head and chuckled. "We are about to find out." He lowered his hand beside the button, made a few passes over it as if trying to grab it, then made contact on the fourth attempt.

Chapter Forty-Three

The twinge exploded out of Andrew. Every fiber in his body seemed to be electrified and arcing. A fireball of pain blinded him, turning the world into a white cloud of superheated air. The air seemed to scorch his lungs when he inhaled; his body was being cooked from the inside out.

Then the cloud began to fade, and blue sky peeked in through the top of the windshield. Someone was screaming his name, the voice echoing from a million miles away. Sensation returned to his hands and he pushed himself upright in the seat.

"I'm good," Andrew croaked and licked his lips, they tasted coppery again as if his mouth was bleeding. He turned back to Vanessa and tried to smile.

Vanessa sat back with her arms crossed, tear stains on her face. "Remind me to kill you when all this is over."

"Roger that." He said weakly, reached back, squeezed her knee, then turned to face the highway. "Caleb, drive toward Mount Valley. It's off Highway Seventy-Nine."

"I know where it is," Caleb said, cranking the steering wheel and pulling out onto the highway. "Not much out that direction. Going to take about thirty-five minutes to get there."

"Need to hurry. He's out there, somewhere, waiting." Andrew slumped against the seat.

"Do you know exactly where?" Caleb asked as he pressed harder on the accelerator.

Shaking his head, Andrew closed his eyes. "When we get closer, I should. The twinge is nearly gone, but when we get close, it'll strengthen."

"Wish I could tell Barnes where we're heading. He could have assets there to help."

"No, we absolutely can't do that. It has to be me and only me. You and Vanessa are going to drop me off. I have to handle this myself. If he sees or senses either one of you, he'll be gone into the wind and that kid and lady will be dead."

Caleb let off the gas, the car slowing suddenly.

"What the hell are you doing?" Andrew gasped.

Caleb slowed the car even further and turned to Andrew. "Let me put this plainly. There is no way in hell I'm letting you meet up with that lunatic bastard without backup. Vanessa is not getting out of this car—"

"I'm going!" she snapped back.

"No, you're not!" Andrew and Caleb shouted.

"When we get close and Andrew has an idea of where we are going, I'm going to park. You will call Barnes and tell him where we are. Then you are going to turn around and haul ass back to town." The car coasted down to under forty miles per hour. A string of cars lined up behind them. One risked passing on a double-yellow line and sat on their horn as they did.

"Caleb, speed up. I'm losing touch with the twinge." Andrew leaned forward.

"Fine, but she's not coming with us." Caleb mashed the accelerator to the floor and the car leaped forward.

"Agreed," Andrew said, pulling down the passenger visor and mirror. He angled it so he could have a direct look at his girlfriend. "Vanessa, I don't want you anywhere near this. I have no idea what I'm walking into."

"What *we're* walking into," Caleb corrected.

Vanessa wouldn't look forward. She kept her attention on the window, watching as the tall brush alongside the highway flew past.

No one spoke as the miles rolled by. Twenty minutes passed in silence. Caleb drove with the radio off, Vanessa sat back with her eyes closed, and Andrew reclined the seat with his hands in his lap, chin resting on his chest.

Andrew sat up quickly. "Slow down, we've got a turn coming up." He glanced right and left. "Slower. We're close." A brown, rusted sign, partially obscured by a thicket, peeked out of the pines. "Hold up." He patted the air over the dash. He knew what the name was going to be before he was close enough to read it.

"Portugal Landing, three miles," he said as Caleb drove past it slowly. "Ever heard of it?"

Caleb pursed his lips slightly and shook his head. "Never. I've never been out here before. We are in the middle of nowhere. Could be an old landing on Lake Sinclair."

Andrew glanced at his phone and snorted.

"What?" Caleb asked.

Andrew laughed without humor. "No signal." He turned his phone toward Caleb. "Guess we're on our own."

Caleb nodded and pointed toward another rusting brown sign. *Portugal* was barely legible; nearly all the paint had peeled off. But the direction arrow indicating where to turn had been recently cleaned. "Subtle, huh?"

"Yeah, real subtle." Andrew closed his eyes and inhaled deeply. "We are close."

Caleb steered unto an old, clay road.

"Do you have any idea of what's waiting for us?"

Andrew shook his head.

"Any idea how much farther?"

"Nope, but can't be far. The twinge mist is heavy here."

"Okay," Caleb said, holding onto the steering wheel and rocking slightly. "You tell me when it's time for Vanessa to leave, and we'll go on foot." He twisted in the driver's seat to see Vanessa better. "Are you okay with that?"

She shook her head.

Taking his foot off the brake, Caleb let the car idle forward. The road narrowed, going from almost two lanes to barely one. The limbs from pine trees brushed up along the side of the car. The roadbed was worn down, the car bottoming over storm-carved ruts. Andrew held a hand up. "This is good," he said in a near whisper. "See if you can turn the car around for Vanessa."

Caleb nodded, put the car in reverse, and backed up until he found a relatively flat area to maneuver the car around. After making a ten-point turn, he had the Taurus pointing back the way they came. He put the car in park, and he and Andrew climbed out.

Vanessa met Andrew halfway around the car and wrapped him in a hug. "You don't have to do this," she whispered, hugging him tighter.

"I do," he said quietly. "He's been tormenting me all my life. It's time for it to end. I'm not taking it anymore."

Vanessa pushed back, but held Andrew by his shirt, the fabric knotted up in her fist. Her mouth twitched as her eyes clouded with emotion. "Let Caleb handle this," she begged. "He's trained for it."

"But he'll never get close, never find my brother. He's hiding . . . somewhere close by." Andrew gently unfolded Vanessa's fingers from his shirt. "I'll be fine, I promise." He leaned forward and kissed her softly. "Now I, we, need you to head back toward town. As soon as you have a signal, call Barnes and tell him where we are."

Vanessa nodded, but wouldn't make eye contact.

"I love you." He hugged her again.

"I love you, too," Vanessa repeated in a nearly inaudible voice.

Andrew put a hand on Vanessa's back and walked her toward the car.

"Let's do this while I still have the nerve," Andrew said and started down the road.

Caleb nodded, pulled his service weapon off his hip, chambered a round, then placed it back in its holster. "She'll be all right," he said as they watched the brake-lights wink out on Andrew's Ford as the vehicle rolled along the old clay road.

The road narrowed and penetrated deeper into the woods. Century-old cedar trees approached the roadside as the brush thickened. The trees eventually crowded out the sun, which was beginning its late afternoon descent. Shadows stretched across the road like misty gray fingers.

Andrew took a deep breath and fought back a shudder. "Air smells like the depot when we were kids."

"Yeah, same time of year. The depot was in thick woods like this." Caleb ran a finger along the horizon, pointing out the heavy foliage.

They walked in silence.

The sun was now balancing on the tallest treetops, casting diffused shafts of orange and yellow light their way.

"Y'know," Caleb started, "it never occurred to me to bring a flashlight."

"We can use our phones," Andrew said. "Though my battery is pretty low—only about thirty percent."

"Yeah, mine's not much more." Caleb shrugged. "Just awkward to hold my phone and gun."

"I'm sure," Andrew agreed. They fist-bumped without breaking stride or glancing at each other. He let his fingers fly open as if his fist had exploded. "What do you think? We have about another hour of good light?"

Caleb nodded. "Maybe an hour and a half."

Five minutes later they reached the end of the old clay road. A heavily rusted fence was secured by an equally rusted chain and padlock. The fence, topped with dull-looking barbwire, extended deep into the woods. An old drive resembling a forgotten hunting road traveled from the gate and turned left, disappearing down a slight hill. Beside the entrance was a weathered, rotted sign: Welcome to Portugal Landing. Andrew could just make out the faded picture of an old wooden building and several small structures positioned nearby.

"You think it's an old fishing lodge?" Andrew asked.

Caleb shrugged. "No idea. Never heard of this place. But we are near the Onatabe river, and it flows into Lake Sinclair." He reached out and gave the padlock a quick shake. Dust particles floated down from the lock, but it didn't release. "Huh. Thought that lock would dissolve if I gave it a hard tug."

"You could shoot it off," Andrew suggested.

"Shoot it off?" Caleb laughed. "That only works on TV." He walked to the edge of the gate, jumped into the air, and gave it a quick kick. The rotten metal shattered, and the gate toppled inward.

"Or you could do that," Andrew said, smiling, slightly in awe. "But shooting off the lock would have been cool too."

Caleb led the way through the fence. Andrew stopped and tugged at his friends' shirt. "Isn't this breaking and entering or something?"

Glancing over his shoulder toward the fallen gate, Caleb closed an eye as if he were thinking over the question. "Well, to be honest, it's not really breaking and entering if the gate has already collapsed. At this point, we're just investigating."

"Ah, gotcha. When did the fence collapse?"

"Right before we walked through," Caleb answered.

"Excellent timing, if you ask me," Andrew said, catching back up.

The clay road turned into a brick-lined drive, now supporting a thick coating of moss and dirt, continued to descend, turning as it did. Andrew pointed out gray, chipped, and broken statues. An ornate iron fence joined the drive, its once black paint pocked with rust decay. The drive made one final sweep to the left before straightening out. At the end of the old brick pavers stood a weathered two-story building. A wide porch, now sagging and in danger of collapse, ran the front of the building. The brick steps leading up to the porch were covered with leaves.

The ground-floor windows were boarded over; the second-floor windows were shattered, leaving teeth-like glass shards in the panes. Many of the shingles were gone, leaving large patches of exposed roofing timbers. A large stone chimney was partially collapsed, the open maw now holding a large birds' nest.

"Wow, must have been something around the time electricity was invented," Andrew said.

"Yeah, I bet. Looks like it hasn't been touched in fifty years."

"So, what do you think we should do now?" Andrew asked.

Caleb stood with his hands on his hips and slowly turned left and right, examining the broken windows. "Dunno," he murmured with a partially closed jaw. "Do you hear anything, feel anything?"

"Like my twinge?"

Caleb shrugged, then nodded slowly. "Yes, precisely. What's your twinge tell you?"

"It says we're at the right place. I can still feel it." Andrew closed his eyes and drew in a deep breath. "I can smell it, too."

"You can smell your twinges?" Caleb asked with eyebrows raised.

"Sort of—leaves an essence surrounding it. Maybe not a true odor or scent, but I can definitely detect *something*."

"Good enough." Caleb walked toward the drooping porch. "Stay behind me." He unsnapped his holster and rested his hand on the gun's butt. They ascended the steps carefully, testing their footing with each movement. The cantilevered porch was slick with algae and decay. Caleb crossed and stood before the two twelve-foot doors with a finger to his lips, then put an ear to the surface of the door. After a moment, he stepped back and put a hand on the green-tarnished knob. He rotated the once-brass, now green doorknob in his hand. There was a slight click. "It's unlocked," he said in a near whisper as the door swung inward.

The stench hit them immediately.

"Oh, God, what is that?" Andrew gasped and held a hand over his mouth.

Caleb had an arm over his face, forearm blocking his nose. "Dead body—or bodies."

With his weapon now drawn and ready, Caleb shoved the door open with his foot, letting it swing wide and low in the fading afternoon light. "Try the other door," he said to Andrew, pointing with his shoulder.

Keeping one hand over his face, Andrew searched the door until he found the clasps that held it closed and released them. He nudged the door until it swung slowly open on balking, rusted hinges. The extra light illuminated a thirty-by-thirty-foot section of warped wooden flooring.

Staying against the far-left door jamb, Caleb used hand signals to usher Andrew behind him and out of sight of the door. He raised his weapon and sighted into the gloom where the sun failed to penetrate. "Warrenton Sheriff's Department!" Caleb shouted. "I am armed and prepared to fire! Identify yourself immediately!"

Andrew turned on his phone flashlight and helped illuminate the room, pivoting with Caleb as if part of him. The bright floodlight beam of the phone shined down on a sea of cracked, rotting flooring.

Caleb turned left. Andrew revolved with him, keeping him in the small cone of white light. A brick fireplace and exquisitely carved mantle came into view. The tall, boarded-over windows let in a minuscule amount of light, the deteriorated drapes partially blocking what light slipped past. They made their way past what had been a smoking lounge and traveled deeper into the building. The odor of decaying flesh intensified.

A massive chandelier crushed the remains of a ten-foot dining table. The lavish table lay in splinters, the elegant chairs shattered. Stepping over the tangle of wires, Caleb took a moment to remove his hand from his face and point toward to doors with glass panes behind a bar. "I think that's the kitchen," he said in a muffled voice, his mouth partially covered by his arm. "And I think that's where the smell is coming from."

Andrew nodded, the light from his phone flashing light on a blackened, moldy ceiling.

"You ready for this?" Caleb asked, his words barely audible.

Andrew motioned toward the double kitchen door.

"Here we go." Grabbing a splintered section of crown molding, Caleb pushed the door to the right open. The buzz of flies and the intensity of the stench were almost overpowering. He fell back, pushing Andrew as he did.

"Andrew, do not go in there. I'm serious. You do not need to see beyond this door!"

"Okay, no problem," Andrew replied in a whisper, his free arm now draped over his face.

Caleb used a splintered chair to push the door open and step through. The door swung shut behind him.

Chapter Forty-Four

The light from Caleb's phone splashed about the room, the sound of his steps echoing as he cautiously moved. The footsteps and light slowly faded. Andrew fought the urge to whisper his best friend's name and ask him how he was doing. Instead, he backed away from the door, turned, and walked quickly out of the house and back to the drive. Once away from the building, the stench lessened. He took a couple of deep, clean breaths, and contemplated the will it would take to stay inside the house.

How long had it been since Vanessa had driven off in his car—fifteen minutes? Maybe twenty? How much longer would it be until Barnes came flying up the road with sirens blaring and lights flashing? He unlocked his phone. NO SERVICE. "Crap," he muttered. Standing outside made him feel useless. This was *his* problem, *his* brother, *his* albatross to deal with, dammit. The sun seemed to be falling from the sky, the shadows lengthening and beginning to melt into the encroaching dusk. He paced, trying to keep himself from going crazy.

Walking up the path and back along the side of the building didn't help. The hairs on his neck stood straight up. He was being watched. He had no doubt. But from where? *Barnes, get your ass out here!*

A muffled thud stopped his pacing. He remained motionless, ears straining to detect additional sounds from the old mansion. "Caleb, you okay?" he called out to the dark building and waited for a response. Andrew cupped his hands and shouted, "Caleb, what's going on?" When there was no answer, he yelled, "Caleb, I'm coming in! Don't shoot me."

Andrew ran back to the front of the old house, his nerves vibrating. He loathed the thought of going back inside, but something was wrong. He took the steps two at a time, ignoring his feet slipping on the slimy brick risers. He ran across the wide porch and skid to a stop. Both massive entry doors were shut.

"Caleb?" Andrew asked in a fear-choked voice. "Why did you shut the doors?" He put his hand on the knob and twisted. This time the brass orb refused to budge. Pounding on the door with his fist, he shouted, "Caleb, who locked the doors? Let me in!"

From deep inside the house came a large crash followed by a call of pain. Andrew sprinted around the house, looking for another entrance. Gunshots sounded. Once. Twice. Three times. Four. The muzzle flashed on the second floor.

Then silence.

"Caleb!" Andrew screamed and ran looking for another way in. There were no doors on the side, but in the back was a rusty metal door lacking a window he could smash to gain entrance. The knob was stuck and refused to turn.

Frustrated, Andrew turned a fast circle, looking for anything he could use to pry the door open. A small building stood partially hidden by a thicket of bushes about a hundred feet away. He ran toward it, his breath rasping in his chest, his adrenaline spiking

It was an old garage with wide, wooden doors. Andrew yanked the doors free. They flew open and he stopped.

A coroner's van was parked inside the garage. "Oh, shit," he whispered and took a cautious step forward. The musty odor of a long-closed garage gave way to the smell of death. The odor wasn't as strong as in the house, but it was present. Stepping on the rear bumper, he cupped his eyes and peered inside the van. The dark tint and gloom of the garage prevented him from seeing anything. He tried the rear doors: locked. He walked around to the driver's door. Andrew was forced to put a hand over his nose. The front window tint was as dark as the rear windows. Putting his hand on the door handle, he pressed the latch button with his thumb and pulled the door open.

The scream blew out of him before he could stop it. His nerves reacted so fast he was unable to prevent himself from leaping back and against the wall of the garage. Old tools fell in a clatter and dust drifted down lazily from the ceiling. "Oh fucking shit."

It was an old woman, stringy gray hair hung down over her shoulders, the skin was stretched thin over her near-skeletal frame. A pair of Minnesota Twins buttons impaled her eye sockets. Dried rivulets of blood ran down her face from where her eyes had been. Andrew dropped to his knees and dry-heaved. He staggered to his feet, kept a hand over his face and his eyes on the ground as he walked toward the van. Ignoring the body, he concentrated on the vehicle lock button on the open driver's door.

Swallowing hard, Andrew pressed the button and the van responded with a series of ch-chunks. He jogged to the rear of the van and pulled the doors open. A canvas painter's tarp covered two forms in a prone position. Taking the tarp by the corner, Andrew grimaced, turned away from the van, and hauled back hard, running as he did. The cover went airborne and over his head.

He returned his focus to the back of the van. Before him, bound and gagged, were the missing boy and editor's daughter. Both were on their stomachs, arms tied behind them with red cords. Thick, tacky blood pooled around them.

Andrew sagged and bit into his lip to prevent the tears he knew were an instant away from exposing themselves. He staggered toward the vehicle, struggling as if the air now had a tangible viscosity. Shaking so severely it took both his hands to hold his phone, he unlocked the display, hoping he might finally have at least a single bar on his phone that he could use to send a text. NO SERVICE filled the screen.

A weak moan snapped his eyes up. Andrew rushed over to the van as the young woman's foot twitched. "You're alive!" he sang and leapt over to the van.

"The boy," the woman said in a faint whisper. "How is he?" She didn't move.

Andrew, not sure of what to do, put two fingers on the child's neck. The flesh was warm, but he didn't stir. "Alive. Are you hurt? Where is all the blood coming from?"

"It's coming from their bodies, dear brother."

Andrew spun around to see a mirror image of himself exiting the rear of the house and walking toward him. They wore matching faded jeans and basic tan tee-shirt with their hair parted on the same side. The man carried a long, bloody knife. He wiped it clean as he approached. "But not for much longer. The body can only lose so much blood, you know."

"What did you do?" Andrew snapped and backed away.

"Oh, a little of this, a little of that." His twin sighed dramatically. "I had to occupy myself. I was rather bored. You were quite dense in finding me. I left you clues *everywhere*."

Andrew drifted further back, keeping his hands up, eyes darting left and right.

The man smiled. "Oh, brother, I have no intention of hurting you. We are of the same skin, same blood." He pulled a car key out of his pocket. "Now, Wynoma, our *mother*—" He sneered.

"I'm not your brother, and never have been!"

"But you are." His twin said smiling, then turned to the corpse in the driver's seat. "She abandoned me. Just tossed me away like a used tissue." He opened the driver's door, grabbed the dead woman by the hair, dragged her out, and dumped her on the ground.

"What are you doing?" Andrew asked, paralyzed to react.

The man waved goodbye and dangled car keys out for Andrew to see. "Until we meet again, brother." He climbed into the driver's seat.

"Wait…" Andrew stammered as the engine coughed to life. "Wait, Goddammit!" he shouted, the paralysis abating.

The van began to back out of the garage. Running, Andrew grabbed the driver's door and wrenched it open.

His brother glanced down at him and slowly shook his head. "You have a major decision to make."

"What are you talking about?" Andrew asked.

"Who are you going to save?" His brother nodded toward the bound individuals in the back of the van. "Or your best friend?"

Almost on cue, a muffled *whump* echoed from the old mansion.

Andrew turned away from the van to see smoke rising from the upper windows of the building. Red and orange flickered on the remaining glass. "Why are you doing this?" he asked, feeling the urge to rush into the building.

His brother smiled but didn't answer. "Parting is such sweet sorrow, my brother." The van continued to back out of the garage.

"You can't do this!" Andrew shouted. Heavier smoke seeped from the attic windows. "I'll find you!"

Andrew's brother leaned out the window as he shifted gears into drive. "It's all I've ever wanted. Until we meet again." He waved, closed the window, and drove up the drive.

Andrew crashed through the rear door to the mansion. "Caleb!" Light wisps of smoke clouded the first floor. He ignored the smell of burning wood and decay. Holding his breath and steeling himself for what he might find, he kicked the kitchen door open and looked inside. Several partially dismembered bodies lay on the floor, their blood flowed across the vintage tile flooring in a sea of red. Backing out, he turned and ran through several small rooms on the bottom floor. Fallen plaster and moldy furniture littered each room. But no sign of Caleb.

Smoke slid down the stairway, seductively intertwining with the spindles that held up a sagging railing and rolled maliciously toward him. "Caleb!" Andrew shouted again and took the steps two at a time, the boards creaking and cracking as he did. He reached the second-floor landing.

The smoke made him crouch, the toxic cloud now drifting down to eye level. Andrew draped an arm over his nose to block the noxious fumes and darted from room to room. Most were vacant, the contents long removed. One held a small bed and dresser. *So, this is where you've been hiding.* On the bed were several pants and shirts that matched his clothing. *Bastard has been watching me.*

A set of steps rose near the far edge of the floor. Andrew raced toward them. The steps climbed three risers and turned left. At the top, a solid door blocked his path. A deadbolt lock replaced the doorknob. Andrew pushed the door. It refused to move

"Caleb!"

There was no response to his call, but the popping sounds of wood heating, the smoke intensified under the door.

He slammed against the door, retreated, and tried kicking. The old wood held fast. Remembering the tools in the shed, Andrew ran down the steps, leaping halfway down in one stride and running out the door.

Grabbing a dull ax, Andrew sprinted back to the house and up the stairs. The smoke on the ground floor was growing heavy. On the second floor, he had to crawl to remain in breathable air. The small landing facing the attic door barely gave him room to maneuver the ax. After a few swings that mostly dented the wood, he turned the ax around to the flat hammer side and used it as a battering ram, aiming at the lockset. On the fourth attempt, the wood around the lock splintered and the door crashed inward.

With the influx of fresh air, the fire, which had been set in the middle of the floor, erupted, the burning furniture and debris exploding in new flames. Andrew pulled his shirt up and over his mouth and dropped down to his knees to breathe. The air too hot to inhale, he struggled to keep the dizziness at bay.

"Caleb!" Andrew croaked, his lungs searing and eyes burning. He crawled halfway around the room, stumbling over a century of discarded furniture. Then he saw it. A blood trail leading toward a corner. He followed it, heart pounding fiercely from lack of oxygen. The trail ended at a toppled dresser. A jean-clad leg extending out from under it. Andrew grabbed the leg and called his friend's name in a hoarse whisper.

No response.

Finding a pocket of relatively fresh air under the dresser, Andrew greedily gulped in the air. *Now or never.* He got his knees under him and muscled the furniture off his best friend. He rolled Caleb onto his back, grabbed him under the arms, and dragged him across the room.

The smoke was burning his eyes, the heat blistering his hands and face. His lungs were getting ruined by the toxic fumes making breathing nearly impossible. The rafters were now burning, hot embers falling on him, burning his clothing, singeing his hair. He was becoming oxygen deprived, disoriented. His vision narrowing to pinpricks of light. Panic raced through him when he could no longer find the exit through the flames and wall of billow black smoke.

A section of roof collapsed and he saw a square of light off to his left. He crawled for the door, dragging Caleb with the last of his strength. His muscles were quivering and he was almost blind. With a final effort he pushed Caleb through the door, then himself. They tumbled down the small set of stairs just as the ceiling in the attic collapsed in a deafening roar of smoke and flame.

Chapter Forty-Five

Andrew rolled to his knees, the black smoke now just feet off the ground. Fighting the inferno burning a dozen feet away, he climbed the steps and jammed the ax against the door to the attic. There was an immediate drop in heat.

Before Andrew could exhale, timbers crashed above him. *Which will we die from? Flames, smoke inhalation, or crushed by falling timbers?*

He scrambled back from the door and lay on his back panting, sweat pouring profusely from his body. Caleb was not moving, his face and clothing smeared with ash, his breathing shallow. Andrew crawled over to him, put a hand on Caleb's shoulder, and shook him gently. "Caleb, hey, man. Need you back with me. There's no way I can get you down the stairs to the first floor."

Caleb's eyes remained closed.

The door to the attic exploded open and a wall of fire burst through, carrying with it burning timbers and new waves of volcanic heat. The remaining old curtains ignited instantly. The walls sizzled and popped.

Andrew grabbed Caleb around the shoulders and dragged him to the foot of the stairs, sat down on the ground, and cradled him from behind. He nudged Caleb's legs forward and over the first step. Holding his friend tight, they descended the steps on their butts, one at a time. When they reached the bottom, the entire second floor was ablaze.

Staggering to the front doors, Andrew grabbed them by the handles and pulled. Neither moved--both were both wedged shut. "Shit!" He staggered over to where Caleb lay on the stairs.

"One more time, Kemosabe," Andrew hissed, his strength failing, lungs cooked, and exposed skin scorched by the heat. He gritted his teeth. knelt beside his buddy and lifted Caleb as best he could. "I am not going to let you die!" He screamed as lances of white-hot pain shot through every pore in his body.

Andrew partially carried, mostly dragged Caleb's unconscious body through the house. As he approached the rear door, his legs buckled and they both went down. Andrew tried to rise, but his arms

232

wouldn't comply. The smoke on the first floor choked out the light. "We will not die this way!" he growled and pushed to his knees, but toppled over again. He tried to get his feet back under him, but his body wouldn't respond. The light in the room began to dim, the fire fading away.

Then he was moving, being dragged. Someone was coughing, gagging. Was it Caleb? Or was it him? Or someone else? He didn't know.

Cold, fresh air slapped his face. His eyes wouldn't open. Then the darkness descended on him.

When Andrew's eyes opened, the red flashes in the air momentarily made his heart race. *We're still in the house!* But he wasn't. He and Caleb rested on soft, cool grass. A breeze drifted in off the river. The building was fully engulfed, black smoke spiraling up against a darkening evening sky. He and Caleb were a hundred feet away from the fire, near the garage. Sirens grew louder, clashing with the crackling of wood being consumed by a voracious fire.

"Caleb," Andrew croaked. "Are you okay?" He gave his friend a tentative nudge.

Caleb groaned, his eyes flickering, then closing. "Not sure," he grunted.

"Where'd he cut you?"

"Stomach."

Swallowing hard, Andrew gently put his hand on Caleb's stomach . "I'm going to pull your shirt up and take a look. Let me know if anything hurts."

Caleb nodded but didn't speak.

Andrew slowly, gingerly rolled Caleb's shirt up revealing his friends tone abs and a deep red gash running horizontally across his gut, blood flowed freely from the wound.

"How bad is it?" his friend whispered.

Andrew held a hand to his mouth and shook his head but didn't talk.

"Bad?"

"I think I can see your intestines," Andrew said nearly inaudibly.

"Seriously?" Caleb gasped.

"Nah, not really." Andrew managed a weak smile. "But he got you pretty good. You're probably going to need stitches or staples, whatever they do now. You're also gonna have a helluva scar. Just lie still. Sounds like help's around the corner."

"Did that psychotic bastard got away?" Caleb asked, his voice growing weaker.

Andrew nodded but didn't speak as he watched fire trucks, followed by an ambulance, race down the narrow drive. The first responders slid to a stop and bolted from the truck, prepared to attack the conflagration. He pushed to his knees and waved to the ambulance. It circled past the fire trucks and drove his way. The EMTs jumped from the vehicle, equipment at the ready.

Andrew coughed spastically but pointed at Caleb. "Him first," he coughed.

The house roared defiantly as the fire department unleashed torrents of water at the flames; smoke and ash billowing skyward. Andrew noticed a pair of familiar headlights now entering the grounds. "I'm sorry, I need to talk to my fiancé."

"Are you sure?" the EMT asked waving a light in front of Andrew's face. "You look a bit singed."

Andrew brushed the light away, motioning toward Caleb. "He's in worse shape than I am. I'm fine." He turned and hobbled toward his car, his back and arms aching from carrying Caleb through the burning house.

Vanessa climbed from the car. "Are you okay? You look terrible!"

"I'm fine," he said, trying to take deep breaths.

"No, you're not. Let the medics check you out." Vanessa tried to turn him back toward the paramedics.

A dozen steps later Andrew crashed to the ground gasping for air.

"Help!" Vanessa screamed. "Someone!"

An EMT ran back to Andrew, rolled him over and put an oxygen mask on his face. "Hang on there, sir," the medic calmly said as he took Andrew's pulse, "just breath in, breath out. We've gotta clear some smoke from your lungs."

Andrews tried to pull the mask off, but one glance into Vanessa's eyes made him give up the effort. He lay flat on the ground taking measured breaths, fighting the desire to chase after his brother. The impulse grew too strong.

"I'm good," Andrew said, his voice muffled. He pulled the mask off, tossed it to the medic and staggered to his feet.

"Are you sure?" Vanessa asked. "We can let the sheriff's department take care of this."

"No time. Toss me the keys," he said quickly.

"They're in the ignition," Vanessa responded hesitantly.

"Good. Did you contact Barnes?" he asked, stepping around her.

"Yeah, he said he knew what was going on and was trying to intercept your brother. Barnes is the one who sent the fire and EMS."

Andrew paused and leaned against the roof of his Ford Taurus. "How in the hell did he know to do that?"

Vanessa shrugged. "Just said he was aware of the situation and then hung up."

"Intercept my brother? Where in the hell . . . ." Andrew turned to Vanessa. "Get in. You have to drive—and fast." He staggered around the car and climbed into the passenger seat. "Vanessa, let's *go*!"

"Where?"

"Just head back towards town. I'll know soon enough."

Vanessa started the car, stared out the rear glass, and backed out of the driveway. "What about Caleb?"

"He's gonna get a free ride back to town on the county's dime." Andrew leaned out the window as they backed away, helping her navigate the narrow entrance. When they reached the clay road, she executed a three-point turn. Andrew slapped the side of the car. "C'mon, you're gonna have to drive faster."

Vanessa snapped her eyes at him. "If you want to drive fast, you take the wheel! I'm having a hard enough time avoiding the washouts."

"I can't. The moment we get back on the highway, I want you to punch it, stomp it to the floor."

"Toward town?"

"Yes. Don't worry about cops or getting pulled. If I'm correct, and I think I am, Barnes will find a way to get the ticket voided."

Vanessa bit her bottom lip, grimacing slightly. "If you say so."

"I do, but we've gotta fly." Andrew grabbed a pair of nearly black sunglasses out of the glove box, slipped them on, then leaned his seat back and pulled his seatbelt tight.

"What are you doing?" Vanessa asked glancing sideways at him, as the car rocked and dipped over a series of small washouts.

Andrew reached down and grabbed the small sleeve of plastic that contained the Minnesota Twins button. He opened the seal and held the bottom gingerly, insulated by the plastic cover. "I'm reaching out to dear brother. But this time, I'm hanging on."

Chapter Forty-Six

Vanessa pulled onto the highway leading to town and pressed the accelerator as instructed. When the car sped past seventy miles per hour, she glanced nervously at Andrew. "You sure about his?"

"Mostly." He held the button just above his palm. "Keep your phone ready. I might scream, yell, or go silent. But I'm hoping I might be able to tell you where to direct Barnes. At least, that's my plan."

Andrew relaxed in his seat, took several deep breaths, then dropped the pin in his palm. *Probably should have worn a mouthguard.* Then the twinge slammed him hard, and he bit his tongue.

Andrew felt the familiar drawing of energy, his essence, as he thought of it, out of his body. Electricity surged through every fiber of his core. The breath in his lungs expelled, replaced with a cold vacuum. Tensing himself against the wall of blackness that rushed toward him like a mountain preparing to erase his existence, he reversed course and let himself mentally fade, allowing the pain and horror to wash over him like a highway mirage. And then it was gone.

He could sense heavy breathing, but not his own; he felt a swaying motion that was not of his making. A new, almost euphoric, energy swirled around him.

Welcome, brother. I didn't think you had it in you.

Andrew forced a wall around the terror that welled up at his brother's touch, a border to hold back the rabid insanity. And with a heavy mental push, he extended the border, giving him room to think, to breathe.

Well done, brother! You have gotten so much stronger. Not the unwilling toy you used to be.

You have no idea how much stronger I am. Andrew didn't relay these words, just let them ferment inside him.

I have nothing to say to you, he sent.

Oh? And why is this, dear brother?

Andrew didn't respond, just probed into the swirling clouds of gray and black that permeated his vision. The imagery never changed: iron-gray clouds and mist, inundated by currents of cold and unease.

You are a coward, a murderer. Torturing dogs for enjoyment. Sick is a poor word to describe you. Andrew fought to keep his tone flat, but jagged edges of hatred escaped.

A writer unable to come up with a better word is so sad, dear brother.

Andrew didn't respond, just probed the mind he was linked to. He had the sensation the being was grinning.

Such fun, brother! I've missed this so much. And I have so much to share with you! Today will be the first time you get to experience firsthand what I do.

No, it won't. I'm going to stop you, dear brother, Andrew sent, the scorn in his thoughts increasing.

My, someone has just grown some teeth. I like this side of you.

Andrew concentrated on seeing through his brother's eyes and, for the first time, pierced the gray clouds. Red sparkles of light trickled in and coalesced into taillights. The view widened, and he could see other lights now, blue lights. Red and blue lights that strobed and flashed. A surge of hope flared inside Andrew. Gotcha now, you sick fuck.

As if sensing Andrew's thoughts, the view changed, climbed until he was looking back at himself in the rearview mirror. But it wasn't his face he was looking at but a child's plastic skeleton Halloween mask. *Now the fun is going to begin!*

The view moved from the rearview mirror to the passenger front seat. A black object protruded out from under a newspaper. Andrew could just make out the butt of a weapon as the sensation of moving slowed and came to a halt. An electric window lowered. The view was now straight ahead, focusing on a lone patrol car sitting just off the road, the officer standing beside it with an arm out in a "halt" position.

The image swung quickly from the patrol car to the weapon, then returned to the officer as the vehicle stopped short. The cop impatiently waved them forward, a flashlight now flickering up and down. One hand rested on the magazine, the other on the steering wheel. Adrenalin rushed through his brother's mind.

Oh, this is going to be sensational, dear brother! A rush like you have never experienced.

The van rolled slowly forward before stopping again. "Good evening," a male said. The vision focused on the speaker. *Barnes!* Emotions blurred. The weapon was grabbed, pointed out the window, and fired.

"*No!*" Andrew screamed, and was ejected from his brother's mind in an explosion of white light and pain. He doubled over and held his head in both hands. "He shot Barnes! He shot Barnes," he whispered and fell back against the seat, rolling toward the window.

"Andrew!" Vanessa shouted, startled, the car swerving in the lane. She regained control and glanced at Andrew. "What happened? What's going on?"

"It's Barnes," Andrew croaked, tears welling up in his eyes. "He's dead."

"How do you know?"

Andrew struggled to sit up in the passenger-side seat and ran a hand through his hair. His breath came in shallow gasps of air. "My brother shot him, point-blank range at a roadblock. There was nothing I could do to stop him."

"Are you sure? Maybe it wasn't Barnes. Or maybe that sick bastard is messing with you."

"It was Barnes. My brother stared right at him—focused on his face so I could see him clearly." Andrew slumped back in the seat. "He just shot him, point-blank range, never gave him a chance." Taking several deep breaths to compose himself, Andrew sat up. "Do you see my phone? I need to call Caleb."

Vanessa felt around on the console before seeing it on the floor by her feet. "Hang on, I can't reach it, I'm going to pull over just ahead." She pointed toward a well-lit gas station and convenience store. Vanessa braked hard, swerved into the parking lot, and stopped with the hood of the car pointing at the highway. She fished around with her foot and finally retrieved the phone. She swiped the unlock button and handed it to him. "Isn't he on the way to the hospital?"

Nodding, Andrew dialed. "I'm sure he is." He waited as the phone rang. Caleb answered on the fifth ring, his voice very rough and was in mid-sentence before Andrew could say anything.

"Did you hear," Caleb shouted, his words initially muffled. "Barnes has been shot. Was setting up a roadblock—"

"I know, I was there—sort of. In my brother's head. Saw it all go down. How is he?"

"He's lucky, real lucky. Your brother flinched when he pulled the trigger. Gave Barnes just enough time to step back and turn away from the barrel. The round creased his cheek and took a chunk of ear with it."

"But he's okay?" Andrew asked, the relief flowing off him in torrents.

"He's rattled, bloody and super pissed. He and his partner unloaded their service weapons on the van—an old Warrenton coroners' vehicle if you can believe it."

Andrew could hear someone, possibly an EMT trying to get Caleb to lie back down.

"Caleb, tell them to be careful, that kid and lady are in the back of the van!"

Additional muffled argument between Caleb and the EMTs. The sound cleared and Caleb was back, "Sorry, man, but the ambulance guys are trying to make me lie still. But I'll pass the word about the van. We're almost at the hospital, and to be honest, I'm starting to fade."

"Thanks Caleb, and do what the docs tell you."

"Be careful, Copper-top." Caleb wheezed before the line dropped.

"You know it," Andrew replied to a silent phone.

Vanessa reached over and squeezed his shoulder. "You okay?"

"I'm fine." Andrew pulled down the passenger vanity mirror. In the lighted reflection, his eyes were blood-shot and sweat peppered his brow. Andrew reached down on the floorboard and picked up Vanessa's handbag. "Do you still have that bottle of Benadryl?"

"Yeah, it's in there somewhere. Why?"

"I'm gonna find out just how connected my brother and me truly are."

"What do you have planned?"

Andrew forced a weak smile. "Hopefully, a way to slow him down." He dropped two small pink pills in his hand, then doubled the amount.

"Please don't tell me you are taking all of those. One makes you drowsy and two puts you out."

"And four should flatline me." He grabbed a bottle of water from the armrest and wiped Vanessa's lipstick from the rim. "Don't want to get myself sick, or anything." Andrew winked.

"If you're knocked out, how will I know where to go?"

"One step ahead of you, counselor." Andrew started the GPS on his phone. When the route appeared, he propped it up on the console and turned it where she could see. "We should find dear brother right here." He tapped the screen.

"You're sure about this?"

"Oh, yeah, definitely."

Andrew swallowed all four antihistamines, washed them down with a large gulp from the water bottle, then burped. "Okay, I'm about to go night-night again, but I'm taking my brother with me. As soon as I'm out, call the station, have dispatch tell Barnes where to go."

"As in the address?" Vanessa asked with a wry grin.

Andrew nodded and laughed slightly. "Yeah, give him the address as well. Time to catch up with my dear psychotic bro." He gingerly picked up the button off the floor with a gas receipt, careful to avoid touching it, and positioned it over his open palm. He turned to Vanessa. "Over the knee and into my palm, look out brother, here I come." He dropped the button into his palm, closed his fist, and life around him faded.

"That doesn't rhyme. You know that, don't you?"

Andrew never heard Vanessa's words as he slipped easily into his brother's mind, the closeness of their bodies and the recent contact making it easier. His heart rate relaxed and the clarity of his vision increased, the gray clouds of haze falling away. And as if someone had wiped the condensation off a window, he was there: seeing through his brother's eyes, feeling his brother's racing heart, and hearing the van's engine as it wove through dark streets. He was content to just be a passenger. When the time felt right, he would announce his presence.

Andrew exhaled and let himself *be*. He was absorbed into his brother, a sensation he soon realized mirrored being in the womb and conjoined with his brother. The harsh white of streetlights flashed past as the coroners' van swerved through the city, taking seemingly random turns. The road narrowed from the major thoroughfares to the narrow neighborhood streets; the well-lit sidewalks gave way to darkened yards and driveways. Andrew concentrated and managed to turn the eyes he was seeing through to the entrance of a neighborhood with a manicured front entrance and subdued illumination. *Oxford Commons.* They were closing in on the soccer complex. His eyes snapped back to the road and the van lurched left, then back to the right. The vehicle's headlights were cut and they rolled slowly along the side of the street.

Brother, you will never be able to throw me off your trail. Andrew smiled. At the same moment, the corners of his brother's lips curled subtly up.

The eyes through which he watched the dark streets closed momentarily, then shot up. He felt the lungs take a deep breath and the shoulders arch against the back of the seat and shake subtly.

Tired? Andrew sent.

The van swerved off the edge of the road, then back into the center. A shot of fear crashed through Andrew's brother, then a flash of anger that turned his lips into a snarl. The emotion was swallowed up almost instantly.

Dear brother, welcome back! I was afraid I had run you off.

Far from it, brother, Andrew sent. *I'm here to watch your run come to an end.*

And you think you can stop me?

Oh, there's no thinking to it. I'm certain I can. I just wish I had a box of popcorn to watch events unfold, Andrew sent.

Andrew felt his brothers eyes close, then snap back wide. His brother's lungs took on another full gasp of air. *That, my brother, is an overdose of Benadryl. We are extremely sensitive to antihistamines, which I'm sure you know. I took four. Either head for a hospital or die here in this death van.*

But you will die too!

I have someone waiting to drive me to the hospital if I need to go. A hard shudder rocked Andrew; his thoughts floundered as he fought to drag in a heavy breath. *But you have no one.*

You'll never write another book, his brother responded slowly, the words dropping in mental volume. *If not for me, you'd be a nobody. A joke.*

242

Next, you'll tell me "you created me." Andrew sent with a gasping laugh. *I could care less.* Fear spiked inside him when his lungs failed to draw in air. *I'm over . . . you.*

Chapter Forty-Seven

There was no reply, but Andrew knew the car had stopped moving. The eyes he was seeing through lost focus, the world outside the windshield now a mottled scene of bright yellow and white lights. The gaze slowly slanted left and stopped at about a thirty-degree angle. The image dimmed and the breathing sensation became labored.

It doesn't have to be this way, Andrew sent, the effort nearly depleting his mind's reserves.

What other way would you have it?

Andrew struggled to form thoughts, the words becoming a fog-shrouded plain. *Surrender. Seek professional help.*

Another long pause followed. His twin worked at building effort—and he had deeper reservoirs than Andrew. The view changed to world beyond the windshield, the cloudiness parting. A hand wiped the eyes he saw through and the vision sharpened. In the distance, muted blue lights illuminated the night sky.

Not going to happen, Andrew thought, keeping the comment to himself.

The van lurched forward and swayed. The flashing lights increased in brilliance; the yellow house lights passed by faster. Andrew wanted to withdraw from his brother's mind, but was now too paralyzed to do so.

It will be over soon, dear brother. Anything you want to talk about before we go out like Butch Cassidy and the Sundance Kid?

Why? Andrew could no longer concentrate.

Why did I kill? Why did I torture the dogs?

Andrew felt the face smile as he drifted further out and away.

Why does someone knit potholders or spend hours gazing at artwork?

Why . . . do you . . . . Andrew couldn't finish. The colors outside the windshield dropped to a pinprick. His brother's thoughts faded with them.

Because I enjoy it.

That's not a reason, Andrew sent as the strobing light pushed him further away.

As Andrew faded, the streaking blue flashes drew closer, filling the van with shards of icy light. His brother fought through the Benadryl and attempted to exact control. The more he did, the further Andrew's presence diminished.

The van swerved around a corner. Distantly, tires whined and an engine revved.

That's all the answer you're going to get. The words were terse when they reached Andrew.

Breathing was almost non-existent; the noise of the van pulsed wildly. *Don't be such a wuss and tell me*

With exaggerated slowness, the spot of vision turned to the rearview mirror. His brother was smiling. *Write a book and explain it yourself!*

Andrew flailed in the blackness of an oxygen-starved brain as the windshield exploded inward, the glass following him as he fell from his brother's mind. "*No!*" In the far edges of his consciousness, he felt the heat as bullets ripped through his brother and the burning pain that followed.

A searing white discharge erased his brother's essence. Andrew was back in the Taurus, screaming and tearing at his shirt.

The shock of ice-cold fluid hitting his face severed the telepathic trauma. With coldness dripping down his face and his shirt soaked, Andrew uncurled his fist and forced himself into the upright position. The sound of traffic and the overwhelming glare from streetlights pushed his brother's touch further away.

He glanced at Vanessa.

She stared back, trembling, her face white, her eyes larger than he'd ever seen them. She held a quart-size Styrofoam cup, dribbles of soda still clinging to the rim.

Andrew licked his lips and shuddered. "You know I hate diet soda, don't you?" He wiped his face on his shoulder.

Vanessa blinked twice at him. "What?"

"I can't stand diet soda. Never understood how you could drink it."

"I'm sorry," she said slowly. "It was the only thing I had to snap you out of—whatever was going on with you!"

Andrew took the cup out of her hand and rotated it slowly. "McDonald's? You went to McDonald's while I was in a life or death battle with my brother? I thought you were going to head toward the hospital?"

Vanessa shrugged, the color returning to her cheeks. "You said to only head that way if you looked to be in destress. But you looked like you were having a nice nap, and I was thirsty."

"A *nice nap*? Are you serious? I was in an all-out battle with my brother, in *his head!* I didn't know if I was going to live or witness Armageddon!" Andrew crushed the cup, ripped it into pieces, and showered the inside of the car with the remains.

"And did you?" Vanessa asked with an air of calm.

"Did I what?" Andrew snapped.

"Live or witness Armageddon?"

"No, of course not! I mean, I lived, but . . . ."

"The Benadryl!" Vanessa suddenly gasped. "Are you okay? You took four of them!"

Andrew sat back hard in the seat, his eyes wide, breath coming rapid. He was silent for a moment. "I'm...okay. I think. Maybe sharing the connection with my brother helped. Or maybe the adrenaline rush held the medicine at bay. But I'm really, really tired, but I think I'm..."

Vanessa grabbed Andrew by the shirt and pulled him in tight. She kissed him hard, fast, then buried her head against his shoulder. "Is it over?"

Andrew hugged Vanessa back, tears starting to fill his eyes. "Yeah, I think so." Tears ran down his cheeks. "Dear God, I hope it is." They clung to each other for a few minutes more.

Andrew glanced up and shielded his eyes. A pair of raised, bright headlights bore down on them. A large truck grill stopped just short of his car, right beside the driver's window. A dark, trim man jumped from the cab of the truck and stumbled over.

The first thing Andrew noticed was the gleaming white teeth. "Caleb, why aren't you in the hospital?" he asked, his voice rough from crying.

"You know me, man. No hospital can keep me contained for long."

"But you looked like shit when I left."

"Still feel like shit. But when no one could get ahold of you, I told the doc that if I wasn't dying, I was outta there. They protested like hell and back, but there's no way I was staying."

Vanessa squinted at Caleb. "My phone never rang, and neither did Andrew's." She pulled her phone off the dash and showed it to both men. "See? No missed calls."

Andrew picked his phone off the floor, examined it, and shook his head. "Me, neither."

Glancing at the chrome grill that towered over his car and looked like it was about to take a bite out of his roof, Andrew nodded with his chin. "Who's truck?"

"Deputy Mosh's. New kid. I think you'll like him. Met the ambulance at the hospital, said he wanted to see how I was, and that he had some business to take care of. I told him I had a quick errand to run and asked if I could borrow it."

"How long ago was that?" Vanessa asked.

"Oh, about an twenty minutes ago." Caleb grinned large enough to wrinkle his entire face. He relaxed and his eyes turned worried. "How about you, Copper-Top. You okay?"

Andrew held up a hand and rocked it back and forth. "Not sure, Kemosabe. I've laughed and I've bawled and now I'm numb. Any word on my brother?"

Caleb nodded. "We got him, stopped him near the park. He tried to run a roadblock, and we had a little shoot-'em-up with him. He's critical, not expected to live. They called in a chopper to fly him out."

Andrew sagged back in the passenger seat and stared straight ahead, not speaking.

Caleb stooped to look inside the car, elbows on the window molding. "You don't look happy with that answer."

"To be honest, I'm not sure how I feel," Andrew said quietly. He took a deep breath and stared at the car's ceiling. "I want this to be over, and I mean *over*. If he survives, I don't think I'll ever be done with him."

Caleb shrugged. "Sorry, man, can't help you there. If it makes you feel better, they managed to save the boy and the woman. Both are in bad shape and on in the ICU." Caleb stood and put his head on the roof. "And I think I better head back to the hospital. It feels like all the air has been sucked out of me."

"Do you need me to drive you?" Vanessa asked.

Offering a weak smile, the wattage only a third of its normal brilliance, Caleb nodded. "Let me park this beast and lock it up."

"I can drive it," Andrew said, perking up.

"You're still drugged from the Benadryl!" Vanessa eyed him with disapproval.

"Oh, yeah, still blurry as hell." He grinned. "Doesn't mean I can't drive."

"Dream on, silly man," Vanessa replied and tasseled his hair. "I think it's time you started sleeping this one off."

Andrew nodded and reclined the seat.

The rear driver's door opened, and Caleb got in, then toppled over. "Hospital, please."

"On our way," Vanessa answered and put the car in gear.

"Caleb, how did you know where we were?" Andrew asked, his voice dropping off as the Benadryl weighed down heavy on him.

Caleb pointed at Vanessa and made phone texting gestures.

"You've been texting my best friend while I was in a fight for humanity?" Andrew's eyes closed and weakly opened again.

"Of course. I was bored, and you were sleeping. Had to find a way to entertain myself." Vanessa pulled out on the highway and accelerated.

"That's good." Andrew sighed. "Did you give away all my secrets?"

"Only the embarrassing ones." She took his hand and squeezed it.

"Thanks. Knew I could count on you." Andrew's eyes closed.

Chapter Forty-Eight

Andrew and Vanessa stood hand-in-hand under the shadow of a large water oak, the hot South Carolina coastal sun held at bay by the sprawling limbs, and stared down at Joseph's gravesite. The minister and hundreds of Joseph's friends slowly winded their way back to the nearly mile of cars lining the cemetery. The ground's crew stood a respectful distance away, giving the last of the old man's friends a chance to say their final goodbyes. Caleb waved from across the field and made his way through the sea of departing mourners, shaking hands and giving out warm embraces. He wiped his brow to remove the beads of sweat courtesy of the oppressive humidity.

Vanessa reached out and hugged him. "It was an amazing ceremony!" She released Caleb and wiped her eyes. "I had no idea how many friends he had. I always thought he was a nutty old coot."

"He was." Caleb laughed. "It's why folks liked him. He was unique, crazy, strange, and completely harmless."

"Barnes looks good driving Lucille," Andrew said. "Having him drive Lucille *ahead* of the hearse was different. Is he going to keep her?"

"It's what Joseph always wanted. Lucille was his baby since he drove her off the lot back in seventy-three. He wanted to be carried in her, but the casket wouldn't fit." They all laughed. "Initially, he was pretty adamant about being buried with her."

"Really?" Vanessa asked. "What changed his mind?"

Caleb smiled and shook his head. "The thought of his beloved car rotting and rusting in the ground was too much for him. He wanted someone in his family to have her. Barnes was his closest living relative."

"Well, Barnes will ride in style patrolling in that old Buick Two-Twenty-Five." Andrew cupped his eyes to watch the last of the guests drive away.

"He's going to have to wait a while on that," Caleb replied. "When the hearse pulled up behind him at the edge of the gravesite, the engine threw a rod out the bottom of the engine, pretty much killing the motor."

"Are you serious?" Andrew shook his head. "It's like the car knew its master had died."

"That's chilling." Vanessa wrapped her arms around her chest despite the upper eighty-degree temperature.

"Just more lore to surround Joseph with," Caleb said and walked over to the edge of the grave. "Rest well, my friend." He scooped up a handful of dirt and let the grains fall softly on the darkly polished casket. Vanessa and Andrew followed suit. They then walked to Andrew's car as a wrecker wound its way through the exiting sedans.

Andrew leaned against the Ford as Barnes walked his way.

"Mr. Alewine," Barnes said and held out his hand.

"Sheriff," Andrew replied shaking the offered hand

Barnes took a deep breath and turned his face to the breeze, removed his ever-present mirror shades, and took a moment to compose himself. His heavy brown eyes were red-rimmed and tear-stained. "I just wanted to thank you for all your help in this case. I truly do apologize for the heavy-handed—"

"Sir, it's okay. Water under the bridge and all that. You did what you had to do, and I get that, I do. No hard feelings, sir."

Barnes nodded, smiled briefly, and glanced at Vanessa. "Counselor, I hope the next time we meet it's for a cup of coffee at the courthouse."

Vanessa smiled. "I'd like that, sir. Anytime."

Barnes put his shades on, adjusted them to his face, and started to leave. He glanced back at Andrew. "Your—gift," he said haltingly, "might help us in the future. If you're willing, that is."

"Sir, I would be more than happy, anytime. Except," Andrew paused and shrugged. "It might have left. I don't sense it inside me. Might be due to my brother being on life-support. Or maybe it was just time for it to go. But if it ever returns, I'll let you know."

The sheriff nodded. "Very well, Mr. Alewine. And take care. You too, Counselor."

"Sheriff," Vanessa asked quickly. "Did anyone figure out who pulled the guys out of the house?"

"Yeah, I've been wondering about that too," Andrew added.

Barnes shook his head. "No, counselor, we have no idea, and no one has come forward."

"Thanks. Just curious."

Barnes nodded briefly then turned and walked away, the sun shining down on the large man, his shadow spreading out wider and wider.

The wrecker pulled Lucille onto its flatbed, oil running down behind the car like black blood. Caleb rejoined them.

"Where have you been?" Andrew asked. "I didn't see you leave."

"Well, the cute as a button writer for the *Sun Beacon Times* had a few more questions."

"And you asked her out, didn't you?" Vanessa laughed, shook her head and crossed her arms over her chest. "At a funeral!"

Caleb grinned and held up a slip of paper. "Got her number, too! By the way, Copper-top, she's a big fan of yours—actually, a huge fan. It's what got me the date."

"Yeah, well, the Amazing Andrew might be retiring. I might be needing another career." He shrugged. "This deputy thing looks easy. Maybe I'll apply."

"Easy, my ass!" Caleb laughed and took a fake swing at Andrew, who ducked and took off running. Caleb chased close behind as Andrew zigzagged around trees and monuments, leaping, squawking, and flapping his arms as if he were trying to fly.

"Boys!" Vanessa shook her head and sat on the hood of Andrew's Taurus, waiting for the two adult juveniles to tire.

Epilogue: Six months later

Andrew sat at his computer typing, fingers pounding on the keyboard in a manic blur. His hair was over collar-length and in disarray. His desk was marked with condensation rings of forgotten drinks; dark circles lined his eyes. He had pushed day and night to finish his newest novel, *Dear Brother*. Standing, he dropped a white Minnesota Twins button on his desk. It bounced twice, stayed upright, and rolled to the edge keyboard. A new, blank word document formed on the screen. The cursor started moving across the page followed by brotherbrotherbrotherbrotherbrother...

251

About the Author:

Jay is a proud resident of the Chapin, South Carolina (Go Gamecocks!) and is the author of six novels ranging from Mystery/Detective, to Sci-Fi, to NASCAR-based racing to Thrillers. He's been married to his beautiful wife Sherry since 1986 and is the proud father of two amazing kids, Dakota and JJ. Completing the family members is Walter, a 13 year old cocker spaniel, and Pip and Patches, two overly spoiled and highly-opinionated guinea pigs.

When not writing Jay can be found driving his beloved Pontiac Aztek, riding his Suzuki Bandit 'Sir Blurr' or sailing on Lake Murray.